WHATEVER YOU CALL ME

BY
LEIGH FLEMING

Published by Envisage Press, LLC

Copyright © 2016 Envisage Press, LLC

Cover by www.spikyshooz.com

ISBN: 978-0-9977351-0-9

This is a work of fiction. All of the characters, names, incidents, organizations, and dialogue in this novel are either the products of the author's imagination or are used fictitiously.

For Pat...

Also by Leigh Fleming

Precious Words

ACKNOWLEDGMENTS

This book wouldn't be possible without the help and support of so many people.

My amazingly talented editor, Rebecca Heyman, has been with me from the start. Her brilliant insight and keen eye for detail have helped me beyond measure. Thank you, Becca!

Thank you to former congressman and governor of West Virginia, Bob Wise, for chatting with me about Washington politics.

Thank you to Rick Patchell for sharing the story of his bootlegging grandfather.

A special thank you to friend and fellow author, Jessica Peterson, for her advice and guidance.

Thank you to friends and fans that have patiently waited for the release of this book. On days when I thought it would never make it to print, it was encouraging to know there were people anxiously awaiting its release.

I based the fictional town of Shady Beach on my hometown of North East, Maryland. I hope the folks who I've known since childhood will recognize the similarities. Thank you for the memories.

Finally, I thank my husband, Pat, and my children, Tom and Liza. I'll never be able to express my appreciation of your support through this crazy process.

ONE

Annie shimmied onto the hip-high barstool and flagged the waiter. "Strawberry mojito, please." She shrugged out of her business suit jacket, shedding the smell of metro grate steam, sticky humidity, and the political stink that permeated this city. Tears threatened as Annie secured the cardboard box on the seat beside her—a box which contained personal items that had adorned her office until about thirty minutes ago. Still fighting back tears, she glanced around the bar, hoping to see a familiar face, but only noticed a businessman sitting two seats down. She didn't recognize him, and was relieved he was too absorbed in his phone to notice her disheveled arrival. When the bartender placed the sparkly pink cocktail in front of her she slid her platinum credit card across the bar. "Keep them coming."

A quick glance at the clock overhead showed it was eleven forty-five in the morning. "It's five o'clock somewhere," she muttered to herself. The clock was an antique replica not unlike those she'd seen in pubs in England during her trip last year with her best friends Kate and Emberly. So little had changed for her in the past year, until this morning.

She drank the sweet concoction in two long gulps. A strangled sob followed, breaking the silence around her. She searched through her purse for a tissue and jumped when a handful of cocktail napkins magically appeared in front of her.

"Having a rough day?"

The businessman from two seats down smiled warmly and lifted his hand from the pile of napkins. His eyes were soft and caring, and intensely focused on her. The kindness she saw there, combined with a rather alarming dose of liquid courage so early in the day, prompted her to tell all.

"The worst." Sensing her need, the bartender set another cocktail in front of her.

"Uh oh."

"I mean, it started out fine. I went to work like any other Monday, but was called into my boss's office and…I…well, I still can't believe what happened." She picked up the wad of napkins and blew her nose enthusiastically.

"Want to tell me about it?"

With a heavy sigh and another fortifying gulp of mojito, Annie recalled her awful morning.

Three hours earlier, Annie had been sitting in her office, brushing off a light coating of dust from her computer screen, when she'd received a call from John Wolfe's assistant. She had felt the blood drain from her face. The managing partner in Howard, Wolfe, and Richards, the big-five accounting firm where she had been working the past four years, wanted to see her.

"Sure," she said, trying to sound nonplussed. "I'm available any time this morning."

After confirming a time, Annie had slowly returned the receiver to its cradle and leaned back in her chair, swiveling to look out the narrow window toward the building next door. Why would John Wolfe want to see her? She had always received excellent performance reviews and had even received a promotion last year. Before today, she had never had a one-on-one meeting with any of the senior partners. The only time she had interacted with them was at company-wide meetings or parties. Their offices were three floors above hers and she rarely saw them in the building.

While taking a sip of tea from the floral china cup she drank from each morning, she glanced around the pretty office she'd decorated with framed photos, college memorabilia, and the fresh flower arrangement she purchased every Monday morning. The pictures showed her with her two best friends, Emberly and Kate, outside Buckingham Palace, and again in a London pub. It was hard to believe their dream vacation to England had only been a year ago. So much had happened since then for her friends: Emberly had met the love of her life and moved to Rome six months ago with her pro tennis player fiancé, while Kate had been asked to be the lead associate in a complex law suit at the prestigious law firm where she worked.

As for Annie, she had returned from England to the same old job and same old routine. At least once a month for the past twelve, she'd asked herself if public accounting was what she really wanted to do. Did she want to go through another tax season working endless hours plugging numbers into a computer program? As for her social life, did she really want to go out to the same old bars every Saturday night with the same group of friends with the same result: a massive hangover on Sunday morning while she suffered through brunch with her parents? Sadly, she realized the highlight of her week—the only thing she didn't want to change—was trivia at the Olde Towne Tavern on Thursday nights. Was she growing old before her time?

Annie dropped her head in her hands as she considered how pathetically boring her life had become. Whatever was about to happen in Mr. Wolfe's office might just be the ticket to enlivening her dull, same-old existence. She stood and brushed imaginary wrinkles from her skirt, pulled back her shoulders, and marched out of the office, chin held high, as she went to seek her fate three floors up.

She noticed John Wolfe's commanding presence filling the doorway as she rounded the corner to his office. He was tall, dressed in a tailored gray suit, and his bald head glowed in the reflection of overhead lights. He welcomed Annie to his office with a large outstretched hand and a warm smile.

"Would you like some coffee, Annie?" Mr. Wolfe asked, as he gestured for her to sit in an upholstered armchair situated in the sitting area of his office. She did her best to appear relaxed while her stomach roiled with fear.

"I'm glad we could get together this morning. I've been meaning to get to know you better."

"Thank you, Mr. Wolfe." Annie cleared her throat, forcing air through her tight vocal chords.

"Please, call me John." Mr. Wolfe smiled as he placed a company logo mug on the coffee table in front of her.

Annie's upper lip quivered as she smiled, bewildered as to where this conversation was headed. She crossed her right leg over her knee and covered her thigh with a tug of her black skirt. Still uncomfortable, she dropped her right leg and draped her left leg over top. No position alleviated the jitters she felt.

"You know, I've heard a lot of great things about your work here. Many of the clients you've worked with over the past four years have expressed high praise for your attention to detail and your genuine concern for the success of their businesses. I'm really impressed."

"Thank you."

"I'd like to make sure that you continue to be a part of the future of HWR. We wouldn't want to lose you to another firm."

"Thank you, sir." Annie lifted the mug and took a sip of rich coffee, feeling a bit more confident.

"Annie, we're bidding on a government contract we think will be very beneficial to this firm. I have a good feeling we'll receive the bid if we have the right team in place."

"Oh? What's the project?"

Mr. Wolfe placed his elbows on his knees and studied his cuticles. "Several government agencies are going to start sub-contracting their auditing. If we win the contract, it will mean adding about twenty people to a newly formed department here. I'd like to offer you the position of director for that team." His head remained tilted downward while his eyes lifted, seeking a response.

Annie's mouth flew open but no sound came out. Director of a new government auditing department? She hadn't done auditing since her first year at the firm. "Well, Mr. Wolfe, I don't know wh-what to say?" Annie fought to control her nerves. "Don't get me wrong, I'm very flattered, but you do realize I haven't done auditing in a while. Surely, there must be someone else more qualified than me."

"Now, don't be so modest. I know the fine work you've been doing with our clients and you have all the qualifications necessary to run this department. Let me see…" He opened a file that had been lying on the coffee table between them and began rifling through the papers. "You have your bachelor's degree in accounting, your master's degree in leadership development, you're a CPA, and you have all your auditing certifications. You've worked hard and deserve this promotion. I don't have to tell you that you will, of course, receive a substantial raise and a bigger office." Mr. Wolfe chuckled as he picked up his coffee cup, taking a long sip while watching Annie over the rim.

Annie's mind was swirling. This was a big opportunity. A raise would certainly help her shopping habit. But auditing? The year she had worked as an auditor nearly drove her crazy. Some accountants might like that sort of thing, but not her. Why wasn't she being offered a promotion within her own department?

"Besides," Mr. Wolfe continued, setting his mug gingerly on the table, "seeing as you're the daughter of one of our most powerful senators, you should have a firm grasp on government affairs. You've probably met some of the heads of the departments we'll be working with."

Annie shivered. She could feel her blood pressure rising at the mention of her father's position as chairman of the appropriations committee. She hated when people made comments about her connection to him, or when they implied she could help them out in some way. Did Mr. Wolfe think that by listing her name as director on the bid they'd have a better chance of winning the contract? Was that the only reason she was being offered the job?

"Actually, Mr. Wolfe, I prefer to keep my personal and professional life separate. I won't allow my father's connections to affect my career path here or give me some sort of upper hand. Whether or not I've met any of the agency directors shouldn't be a reason to put me in this new role."

Mr. Wolfe's mouth broke into a wide grin, but his eyes remained hard as he nodded his head. He pointed a finger at Annie and said, "I knew I picked the right person for this job. You're assertive, won't take any crap from anyone. I like it. Working with government agencies can be challenging and I think you'll do a great job. That's why we chose you. It has nothing to do with your father. I'd never insult your integrity that way."

"Thank you. I appreciate that."

"In fact, you've been on our radar for some time now. When this position came along, I felt you would be perfect for it."

Annie glanced down at her lap, her mind spinning like a top as she twisted her fingers together. From the corner of her eye, she watched Mr. Wolfe surreptitiously check the time. He looked bored—almost as bored as she would feel as the director of an auditing team.

"Would you give me a few days to think about it?" she asked.

"Now you're coming around. But I was hoping to wrap this up today. The bid is due tomorrow morning and I'd really like to see your name listed as the director of this new division. I'll never be able to find someone else as qualified as you."

"That's very kind." She continued twisting and tangling her fingers together. Was it just her or was Mr. Wolfe beginning to sound an awful lot like a salesman?

"Kind? Hell, it's the truth. You're just what we need in this position. I'm sure if you do the kind of job I think you will—you know, be a team player—there will a partnership opportunity in the near future." Mr. Wolfe walked behind his desk to retrieve a piece of paper, which he then slid across the coffee table to Annie. "This is the agreement showing your new job title, salary increase, and additional week's vacation. Just sign at the bottom and we can get this thing started."

Annie stared down at the letters and numbers blurring in front of her, unable to focus on any of the details. This just didn't feel right. Why couldn't she have a few days to think about it? She picked up the pen, rolling it between her manicured fingers. Would she have received this offer if it hadn't been for her father's influence in the Senate? Since college she'd worked hard to achieve her successes *without* the help of the great Senator George Cooper.

"I will say," Mr. Wolfe said, "I'm sure your father will be very pleased with your promotion."

Annie looked up at her boss and once more felt a spotlight shining on the situation. Daddy dearest had apparently made a call to John Wolfe asking for a promotion for his youngest daughter. Couldn't he simply stay out of her life? He'd certainly been scarce for the first twenty years. A wry grin formed on her lips. She leaned over the paper, her mind made up, and with a flourish wrote, "I QUIT" on the signature line. They rose from their seats as Annie handed the paper to Mr. Wolfe.

He took it and started to speak even before his glance reached the bottom of the page. "This is great. I'll ask my assistant to get right on that new office for—"

Annie watched as Mr. Wolfe finally registered what she'd scrawled in lieu of her name. His eyes bulged slightly and his cheeks flushed red.

"What the hell?"

"Mr. Wolfe, I won't be manipulated into accepting a promotion, no matter what my father promised you." She formed a fist and lowered it like a banging gavel. "This offer is unethical—a backroom deal that gives government and this firm a bad name."

Mr. Wolfe's mouth was pursed tight, his brows furrowed. "I don't appreciate the accusation. You're passing up an incredible opportunity. Regardless, you must realize in order to get ahead in this world you need to use your connections. That's what networking is all about."

"This feels like more than networking to me."

Annie watched Mr. Wolfe's charming façade fall away like a curtain being pulled off a cold marble statue. "Get real. Are you that naïve? People use other people to get what they need. It's that simple. And for the record, I don't appreciate being accused of shady dealings. There's nothing untoward here. I was simply offering a loyal employee an opportunity, but clearly I was wrong about your…ability."

"Well," Annie again cleared her throat and gathered the courage to look Mr. Wolfe directly in the eyes. "I'm sorry if we don't see eye to eye on this. I don't think I can work for a firm that would condone such actions. I'll send an official two-week notice to HR as soon as I return to my office." Annie reached out for the doorknob and pulled it open.

She was about to step across the threshold when Mr. Wolfe said, "No need to write a two-week notice. Report to HR and let them know you're leaving today. They'll send you a severance check for the two weeks and any unused vacation time. Collect your things and go, Ms. Cooper. You're done here."

A half hour later, Annie was tilting her face to the hazy sun and wondering if she had made a mistake. Who passes up a promotion like that? Moreover, who passes over a huge raise like that? She plopped on a bench outside the metro entrance, running her fingers through her hair as she pulled out the band gathering her thick curls at the base of her neck.

Her cell phone vibrated in her hand and she saw "Dad" emblazoned on the screen.

Hi honey. How about lunch? his message read.

She dropped her phone face-down on her lap. Lunch with "the good senator" was the last thing she needed today. She stowed her phone in her purse and released a pent-up breath.

Annie rehashed the scene in Mr. Wolfe's office, wondering if she'd done the right thing. Nope, damn it. She had done the right thing. She was sick to death of the special treatment she'd always received because of her father's powerful position in the senate. This promotion wasn't the first time.

She had a professor in college who always mentioned something her father had done or an article he'd read about him. It was because of his infatuation with her father that she had received hateful glances from her fellow classmates and an A in the class—not the grade she deserved.

The *perks* of being George Cooper's daughter didn't stop with special favors. When she was a child she'd get invited to parties and sleepovers, feeling accepted as part of the popular group. In reality her schoolmates' parents encouraged the invitations because they liked the idea of their child associating with a senator's daughter. Those invitations quickly dried up when her father's indiscretions hit the newspapers. Annie then became the brunt of all their jokes. The ebb and flow of friendships because of her father had carried into adulthood, leaving her suspicious of every new person who came into her life.

It was during Annie's college years her father had been caught up in a huge sex scandal involving prostitutes and lobbyists. His powerful political machine was able to spin it, leaving his career intact. Thankfully, for the first time in her life, her friends had stood by her. Emberly and Kate had bolstered her through the humiliation. She would never understand why her mother stayed with him and had said as much to her mom. But she always replied with a line like, "Someday you'll understand…once you're married, dear."

Annie shook away the memories and took in the scenery around her. She decided she refused to be sucked into the depraved behavior that permeated this town. And to that end, she no longer wanted to carry the name "Cooper." How liberating would it feel to be anyone else but Senator Cooper's daughter? She'd often toyed with the idea of going by her middle name, which was her mother's maiden name. If she was going to make a fresh start in her career, she might as well make a fresh start with her life and become Annie Merriman. Now seemed like the perfect time to celebrate her new identity. Annie pulled out her phone and dialed Kate's number.

"What are you doing right now?" she asked as soon as the call connected.

"Working, what else?" Kate sounded harried as always. "What's up?"

"You need to come celebrate with me," she said, fighting back a surprisingly strong surge of tears. "I quit my job."

"What? You quit?"

"Yep and I need you to come celebrate with me…or commiserate with me. Either one. Can you meet me right now?"

Kate released an audible sigh. "I can't. I'm so sorry. Where are you?"

"I'm standing outside the Independent on 12th Street."

"Okay, wait…let me think," Kate muttered. "I can be there in about forty-five minutes. Can you wait?"

"Can I wait? I have nothing but time."

TWO

Annie raised her glass in salute and drained the pink liquid in one swallow as she nibbled on a plump strawberry while telling an abbreviated version of the tale to the attentive businessman. Several drinks in, she was committed enough to her new identity to alter certain key details—or at the very least, just leave them out altogether. "When I first walked in my boss's office he was all friendly like, oh, Annie, we wouldn't want to lose you... you're an asset to the company...blah, blah, blah. He offered me this bogus promotion, practically forced it on me, and I was like, no way, this is a shady deal and very underhanded. I told him he could take his job and shove it."

"You didn't?"

"You bet I did...but not in those exact words. Can I buy you a drink?"

"I'm good." He gestured toward his beer and burger.

Annie checked her phone and stood on the barstool rungs to see if Kate was coming through the door. Her left heel slipped off the metal bar and she knocked over her empty cocktail glass. "Oops," she giggled, as she picked up the glass and signaled to the bartender.

"Really hitting the hard stuff today. Better slow down a little," the businessman said.

"Hell no, I'm not slowing down! I'm just getting started. Today is the first day of the rest of my week." Annie slammed her hand on the bar with each successive word.

"You mean the rest of your life."

"Oh. You're right. That's what I meant. I'm leaving my old self behind and venturing out into a big new world." She dangled a wet, red maraschino cherry above her mouth and dropped it in like a mother bird feeding its baby. "I love these damn things. They can't possibly be real cherries, can they? I mean, have you ever seen a cherry this color? Probably full of all kinds of chemicals, sugar, red dye number ten…all the things that will kill us."

"You're living dangerously today, aren't you?" He moved her box to another barstool and sat in the now empty seat beside her. He reached out his hand. "Hi, I'm Tom. I feel like we've met."

"Nope, I'd remember you. I have a photographic memory. You have kind eyes and your hair is very distinctive. I'm Annie Coo—Merriman." She reciprocated his handshake and fell to the task of stirring her fresh drink.

"Hello Annie Coomerriman, it's nice to meet you. So tell me why you turned down this promotion?"

"Merriman," she said with a lopsided grin on her face. "Just Merriman. And because I have principles, damn it. Everyone in this town is so sleazy, doing favors to get ahead, working their backroom deals. He called it 'networking'." With a flick of air quotes, she continued her rant. "I won't be a part of it. I'm smart, ambitious, well-educated. Isn't that enough? Does everything have to be you scratch my back and I'll scratch yours? I'm fed up with this town. I'm getting out." Others in the bar were now staring at the slightly disheveled woman with the bright pink cocktail whose voice carried easily through the half-empty establishment.

"It can't be that bad. What do you do…or did you do?"

"I'm an accountant—a CPA and a damn good one. But I can do so much more, Tom, y'know? Quitting was the best thing, really. Really, really. I've wanted to leave for a while…do something more interesting. You know, like work for a non-profit…something that matters. It was a blessing in disguise." She waved over the bartender and said, "Could you just give me a little bowl of those cherries? They're wonderful." The bartender placed the container of cherries in front of Annie and she dove right in.

"How about you order something more substantial than cherries for lunch?" Tom asked.

"Not hungry. I just want to eat these cherries. Since I'm starting a new life, I'm doing whatever the hell I want. No more being manipulated, controlled or bribed. It won't happen again."

"I'm not exactly sure what you're talking about, but I admire your determination. From what you've told me, it sounds like you're going to be okay. Where are you going to apply? Do you have a plan?"

Annie leaned her elbows on the bar and dropped her head in her hands. "No," she moaned, "I don't have a plan. This all happened so suddenly."

"Well, maybe I can help. I'm actually looking for someone to add to our staff."

She popped her head up, a wide smile stretched across her face. "You are? What do you do? What kind of job is it?" She placed her hands on his shoulders and gave him an enthusiastic shake.

"I'm a…a political consultant."

"Oh, God no." Annie released her grip on his shoulders and took another long drink. No way would she go anywhere near politics. Politics was what made her lose her job today. She wanted to get out of DC, some place where no one knew who she was, and get as far away from politics as possible.

"Is there a problem?"

"Look, Tom, I appreciate your offer, but I have no desire to work in politics. I've had enough of politicians to last a lifetime."

"But—"

"But nothing. Please don't make a scene and beg. It would be very unbecoming of you to grovel. You're too dignified for that."

Tom's lips curled into a small smile. "Thank you. I appreciate that."

Annie noticed he had stopped eating his hamburger and reached over to pull the basket her way. "Mind if I finish this for you?" She didn't wait for a reply before ripping off a hunk of burger and shoving it in her mouth.

"Umm...no. I was finished. I thought you weren't hungry."

"I wasn't." She muffled her reply with a mouthful of French fries and patted Tom on the shoulder. "Hate to see good food go to waste."

With his beer glass empty and his burger commandeered, Tom pulled up his sleeve and glanced at his watch. "Listen, I'd seriously like to talk to you about this position, you know, when you're having a better day." He pulled a cocktail napkin from the dispenser and wrote his name and number below the logo. He slid the napkin across the gleaming wood and winced a bit as Annie's greasy fingerprints left their mark on the edge. "If for any reason you change your mind, call me. I think you'd be perfect for the job."

THREE

The shiny black Escalade flanked by two county sheriff's deputies swept through the fairground gate, passed a small group of people holding signs and marching in a circle, and then pulled behind the grandstand. A fine mist was rising off the warm gravel after an early morning shower and the sun was beginning to peek through the haze. A half-dozen members of the local press surrounded the rear doors, waiting to get the first shot of the United States Congressman from the state's 9th District. Kip Porter slowly climbed out of the back seat, buttoning his black blazer while tucking his red, black, and gold tie inside his jacket. He flashed a gleaming smile at the crowd beginning to form around the press corps and waved appreciatively at their thunderous applause. He chose to ignore the angry shouts coming from the protesters along the road.

Kip was escorted inside the steel building where the annual Four-H county steer competition was taking place. The pungent smell of bovine dung and straw was overpowering inside the warm building. As soon as the blue ribbon was pinned on the fifteen hundred-pound Black Angus, Kip walked toward the animal and stood beside its handler for a photograph. Then he made his way to the strawberry pie baking contest going on in Pavilion Three. Strolling through the throng, shaking hands as he went, Kip's perpetual smile never wavered. He was in his element—center stage to his adoring constituents. Someone handed him a nine-month-old baby wearing a puffy pink dress. He enthusiastically kissed her on the cheek, swearing to her mother she was the most adorable baby he'd ever seen.

He took his time circling the pavilion, admiring every pie as if it were a masterpiece. Photographs of him alongside the winner showed beaming smiles all around.

The last part of Kip's appearance involved a brief question-and-answer session with the press beside the FFA booth, where the strong smell of crab meat and frying oil wafted through the air as the club created their famous quarter-pound crab cakes. Before answering questions, he took a bite of a crab cake sandwich, which he then washed down with a gulp of sweet tea.

"Mm-mm. There's nothing like an Eastern Shore crab cake. I dare you to find a place that makes them better."

An explosion of cheers, whoops, and hollers erupted as Kip wiped the tartar sauce dripping from his chin. "Okay, so I hear you want to ask me a few questions. Who wants to go first?"

"Don Smith, *Baltimore Sun*. How do you plan to vote on the Bradley transportation bill?"

"I plan to vote in favor of the bill, Don. Bradley will support the trucking industry so vital to our state by keeping goods moving and our economy growing."

"You're eligible for re-election next year for your third term. We haven't heard whether you plan to run. Would you care to tell us your plans?"

"Sure. I was planning to make a formal announcement next week, but there's no reason not to say it now." Kip chuckled. "Yes, I plan to run for Congress again. I feel like there's so much more to do and I wouldn't want to abruptly stop the momentum. As you know, I'm sponsoring a bill to bring the expanded east coast oil pipeline through this district, which will bring long-term economic benefits to our region."

"Are you concerned at all by the group of protestors outside the gates?"

"Well, Don, as you can see, that's a small group and our research shows the majority of folks in this area are excited about the future prospects of the pipeline. The economic benefits certainly outweigh whatever it is that group is protesting. Next?" Kip looked around at the small press contingent and locked eyes on a reporter whose hand was raised.

"Jerry Mathias, *Capital Gazette*. A recent poll has you dropping in popularity among thirty-to fifty-year-olds in your district. Some suggest the stat is due in part to the fact that you're not married. Would you care to comment?"

Kip shook his dark head and placed his hands on his hips, as his handsome face grew red and his smile wide. "I thought you all just wanted to talk about the issues. Hm, wow, okay. You want to talk about my personal life, huh?"

"Well?"

"Okay, Jerry, all I'm going to say is when the right woman comes along, I'm sure I'll be ready to settle down. That's it. Now, I've got to meet up with the folks down in Sanford Island. Thank you for having me and best of luck with the rest of your fair."

The sea of bodies parted and Kip walked back toward his waiting SUV, shaking hands, posing for photos, and eagerly greeting everyone along his path. He climbed into the back seat and immediately removed his blazer, loosened his tie, and opened the top button of his shirt.

"Damn it. I smell like shit. I can't go to this Chamber of Commerce mixer smelling like I've been riding a bull," Kip mumbled to himself. He released a pent-up sigh and reached into the black duffle bag in the cargo area behind him. He pulled out a pair of wing tips, a fresh button-down, and another jacket.

His cell phone began vibrating in his pants pocket and he saw Tom Garrett's name on his screen, his college best friend-turned-campaign manager and chief of staff. Tom had been with Kip since he first ran for office, and had been by his side ever since.

"Tom, where the hell are you? It couldn't possibly be as exciting as where I've been."

"Wanna bet? How are things down on the farm?" Tom laughed.

"Smelly, but hey, if it gets me re-elected, I'll kiss every steer in the state."

"I hear ya. So you'll never guess who I had lunch with today."

"Who?"

"Actually, I ate lunch and she drank hers."

Kip chuckled as he re-tied his University of Maryland necktie. "I'll ask again…who?"

"Annie Cooper, Senator Cooper's daughter. She goes by Merriman now."

"Oh, is she married?"

"Not as far as I could tell."

"Interesting. How did you end up having lunch with her?"

Tom's smugness traveled through the phone. "I'm just one lucky son of a bitch. I was at the Independent eating lunch at the bar. That asshole Connors didn't show up and I noticed this hot chick sitting two seats over, drinking some tooty-fruity drink, tears streaming down her face. I asked her if she was having a bad day and she just started venting. Turns out she quit her job this morning and is now seeking employment."

"Is that so? George Cooper has a daughter who happens to need a job. And did I hear you say she's hot?"

"Yeah, bro, smokin'."

"Must take after her mother."

"True. But wait—it gets better. She didn't seem to remember that we met a couple of years ago at a golf tournament in Bethesda. She and her friends were playing ahead of us and her friend, damn if I can remember her name, just busted my balls all day long. Nothing but a tease. I asked Annie if we'd met before and she said no."

Kip slipped into his blazer and finger-combed his thick dark hair back in place. "Okay. Senator Cooper's daughter is unemployed and hiding her identity for some reason. Duly noted."

"You're not getting this, man."

"Getting what?"

"We need her father to back the pipeline bill—usher it through the Senate Appropriations Committee."

Kip heard Tom's enthusiasm but didn't know what any of this had to do with Annie Merriman Cooper. "And?"

"And…let's hire her. Give her some bogus job so you can get close to her." Tom sighed heavily when Kip didn't respond. "Let's bring her on board as your campaign manager. Keep her busy folding newsletters and sending out mailers. While she does that, you lean in with your famous Kipster charm and woo an introduction to dear old dad out of her."

"I get it." Kip chuckled, continuously amazed at Tom's cunning mind. "Even though you're running the campaign, we'll let her think she's in charge. Another masterful plan, my friend."

When Kip clicked off the call, he watched out the tinted window as small, one-story clapboard houses flashed by, dotting the rural countryside. They reminded him of the home he'd grown up in. His father had been an electrician and his mother a homemaker—a hardworking couple who devoted all their time and energy to creating a better life than they'd had for their three sons. His two younger brothers had joined the military after high school graduation, but Kip received an offer from the University of Maryland to play tight end. That's where he met Tom, the quarterback. At college, Kip had discovered his leadership abilities and began thinking about a career in politics. Growing up in a ranch-style home in a farming community, and sharing clothes with his brothers, he never would have believed he'd be sitting where he was today: a two-term congressman and chairman of the energy committee. His career was fully on track and a bright political future appeared to be his for the taking.

And that's exactly what he planned to do.

FOUR

Annie walked into her apartment, dropping her purse on the floral armchair. She pulled the blinds on the living room windows and flopped face down on the couch. This was the position Kate found her in when she walked through the door an hour later.

"What are you doing? Why are you laying here in the dark?" Kate placed her briefcase beside the door and walked toward Annie, who was burrowing her head under a pillow.

"Ugh, what a day! I was thinking I'd just lay here in the dark for the next century. It would make my life so much easier."

"No luck today? Do you mind if I turn on a lamp?"

Annie's face was still planted into the sofa cushion, so Kate could barely hear her muffled reply. "If you must."

Kate turned on a lamp and then walked into the kitchen. "Would you like a glass of wine? Sounds like we could both use one."

Annie lifted her head but remained planked on the couch. "I better pass."

Kate pulled a bottle of pinot out of the refrigerator. She poured herself a generous glass, grabbed a bag of pretzels, and rejoined Annie on the couch where she was now sitting up, staring into space. Kate settled herself beside her friend, wrapping her arm around Annie's shoulder.

"Okay, start from the beginning. Why are we going full hermit for the next century?"

Annie sat silently for several minutes, but when she felt some of the day's tension start to dissolve, she filled Kate in on yet another unsuccessful job interview. "They told me I was over-qualified. I even told them I'm willing to start at the bottom."

"Did it make a difference?"

"Nope. They just wished me luck and showed me the door. What am I going to do? I've interviewed with four non-profits here in the district and sent resumes to dozens of companies up and down the east coast. The only promising leads I've had were from two head hunters who called me about accounting positions, but I told them I wasn't interested. Maybe I should call them back. My funds are getting dangerously low."

"How dangerously low?"

"I can just make rent and pay utilities this month and then I'm officially broke."

"What about a loan from your mom?"

"I can't continue to go back to that well. It's time I stood on my own two feet."

"You can always go back to accounting while you look for something else," Kate said.

"No, I wouldn't do that. If I go back to accounting, I'll just stick with it. Ugh! Why can't something exciting happen for me?" Annie stood, stretched toward the armchair for her purse, and began digging around for her cell phone. "I should have one of the head hunter's numbers still in my phone." Her fingertips grazed something soft and she pulled out the napkin she'd been carrying since her boozy lunch three weeks before. "Tom Garrett," Annie murmured.

"Who's Tom Garrett?"

Annie dropped down beside Kate while still studying the napkin. "He was that political consultant I met at the Independent the day I quit. If you had been on time, you would have met him."

Kate ignored the gentle barb about her chronic lateness these days. "I thought you didn't want anything to do with politics."

"Yeah, but I also don't want anything to do with accounting. Looks like I don't have much of a choice. If I don't want to starve, I need to find a job and fast. I think I'll call him tomorrow to see what it's all about. Can't hurt, right?"

Later that day, Annie sat in the Olde Towne Tavern, alone. For a moment, she had a slightly panicky thought that she'd found herself sitting solitary at a bar too often in the past month. The smell of beer-soaked wood permeated the air and country music blared through the speakers. It was Thursday night trivia and she was in her team's usual booth, waiting for everyone else to arrive. She'd come directly from Starbucks, where she had met with Tom Garrett to talk about the "amazing opportunity" he had for her. Kate, Derek, their old friend from college, and Gail, a former co-worker, strolled through the door.

"It's not healthy to drink alone." Derek gave her a shove, pushing her deeper into the wooden booth.

"Well you better catch up, then." Annie shoved back.

"Annie, I can't stand you not being at work. I've had to eat lunch with Mallory every day since you've been gone and all she talks about is how wonderful her new boyfriend is," Gail said, as she wrapped her hands in a choke hold around her own neck.

"At least she's got one," Annie replied.

"But, God, does he have to be so perfect? He can't possibly be that perfect, can he?" Gail asked as she flagged down a passing waiter.

"Nope, definitely not…no such thing as a perfect guy," Kate chimed in as she picked up a menu.

"Whoa, what about me? I'm pretty damn perfect."

Annie laughed and wrapped an arm around Derek's broad shoulders. "You're hot, not perfect. And that's a good thing. Perfect is boring."

After placing their drink orders, Kate lowered her menu and leaned toward Annie. "Well, how did the interview go?"

"Oh, yeah…wasn't this an interview with the guy you met when you went on a drinking spree in the middle of the afternoon?"

Derek's question made Annie's face grow red as she gave a sheepish grin. That afternoon had definitely *not* been one of her finer moments. She cringed just thinking about it. "Don't remind me. Apparently he forgot about it because it never came up and the interview went surprisingly well. I'm now officially employed."

"Drinks are on Annie," Derek said.

"Maybe after my first paycheck."

"So tell us everything," Gail said. "What's the position? What will you be doing?"

"Apparently, Tom isn't exactly a political consultant. He's the chief of staff to Congressman Kip Porter from Maryland. Ever heard of him?" Annie glanced around at three blank faces all shaking their heads. Well, that would have to be one of her first agenda items: get Kip Porter some more press time.

"Anyway, he's running for re-election in November...he's unopposed in the primary and they need a campaign treasurer. That's where my accounting skills come in. Along with that, Tom said he's too busy to run the campaign because being chief of staff takes up all his time. He's essentially turning the whole campaign leadership over to me. In the beginning, he'll guide me through until I get the hang of it and then he's going to 'turn me loose.' Those were his exact words."

"Amazing. That sounds really exciting." Kate gave Annie's arm a squeeze and lifted her glass in a toast. "To Annie—once again gainfully employed."

"Wait," Derek said, "I thought you didn't like politics. How did you end up taking this job?"

At that moment, Annie's cell phone rang and she saw it was a call coming in from her father. "Speaking of politics..." she said, turning the phone to let everyone see "Dad" and her father's familiar campaign photo flash on the screen. She clicked the ignore button and laid the phone face down on the table. "So...what were we talking about?"

Kate—jokingly known as "Annie's sometimes legal representation"— brought them back to the subject. "How you decided to take the job. Let's review the evidence: She's been out of work for over a month, she barely has enough savings to pay rent, and there's a pair of wedges she's been eyeing at Nordstrom ever since she quit her job. I'd say she has no choice."

"Exactly right. And the great thing about this job," Annie continued, "is it's only temporary and I won't really be involved in politics. It's more like a marketing job. I have to find ways to sell the candidate to the people. I'll be managing the volunteers and interns at the campaign office, which is located outside DC. It won't be that bad."

"I'm convinced. Let's drink to Annie." The three friends joined Gail as the first trivia question popped on the screen.

As soon as Annie got home that night, she climbed on top of her bed, flipped open her laptop, and searched Kip Porter, trying to imagine what a guy named "Kip" would look like. She pictured an overweight, gray-haired man in faded overalls and a blade of wheat sticking out of his mouth. Or maybe he was a short, thin, nerdy professor-type with dark plastic glasses. Then again, Kip sounded like he could be a blond surfer-dude smiling blankly while his hand flashed a "hang-ten" sign. She tapped on the first link to the congressional website and fell with a thump against her headboard. Kip Porter certainly didn't have gray hair or dark glasses. And there was nothing vacant about his smile. The man smiling back at her was handsome—breathtakingly handsome—with dark hair groomed short, pale blue eyes, and a mouthful of gleaming white teeth. Pictured standing outside a doorway talking to constituents, it was obvious he was tall. In another picture he was holding a football on the turf at the University of Maryland. And in another picture, he was talking to some fishermen along a shoreline. She clicked on the bio tab and learned the history of Kennard Irwin Porter, III—no wonder they called him Kip, she thought. Born and raised in the small Eastern shore town of Shady Beach, Maryland, where he grew up playing football and baseball, Kip landed a full scholarship to play tight end for the Terrapins. He began his political career as a state delegate right after graduation and quickly gained popularity within his party. Now thirty-four years old, he was unmarried, a member of Rotary International and the Shady Beach United Methodist Church, and had been an Eagle Scout.

"Sounds damn near perfect."

FIVE

For a quiet riverside haven, it sure was noisy at six o'clock in the morning. Robins and cardinals were singing merrily outside the screened window to Kip's bedroom and the buzz of the occasional outboard engine could be heard a hundred yards away along the river. He tucked his head under his pillow and groaned. Unable to return to sleep, he threw his legs over the side of the bed. "Noisier than the damn city," he grumbled.

Kip shuffled across the avocado green linoleum in the small kitchen and started a pot of coffee. After filling a mug—two sugars and a splash of cream—he wandered onto the screened porch and dropped onto the Adirondack chair's faded striped cushion. Looking across the grassy knoll toward the river where the water was like glass at this time of day, he watched a mother mallard and her eight ducklings skim along the shore. A contented sigh escaped his lips and the earlier sleep disruption was forgotten. He was home in his eight hundred-square-foot cabin along a quiet tributary of the Chesapeake Bay. The place had been used by his grandfather and great-uncle for weekend fishing and crabbing. The dock they'd built fifty years ago was still standing strong at the edge of his property, but no longer had a boat tethered to it.

When Kip and his brothers and male cousins were kids, they'd come to the cabin in the summertime to swim, fish, and camp. With only two bedrooms among them, their fathers and grandfathers would sleep inside in beds while the boys slept outside in tents, waking in the morning with hundreds of mosquito bites dotting their skin. Back then, several similar shingled cottages lined the shore, creating a campground of families where lasting friendships formed over a blazing fire or a steaming bushel of crabs. The summer families and their tiny cabins were all gone now, replaced by million-dollar waterfront homes from which Annapolis executives commuted each day. Kip had purchased the cabin from his grandfather's estate after graduating college and had left it just as it had been when it was built. The only upgrade was a fresh coat of paint throughout and new kitchen appliances. The cabin was where Kip came on weekends when he needed a break from political life in the city, though he never seemed to get there as often as he would have liked.

His hometown of Shady Beach was only ten miles inland and his mother still lived in the three-bedroom house where he'd been raised. Currently, she was vacationing in Ocean City with a group of ladies from her church and wasn't expected home for another few days. His brother, Rob, lived a mile from the old homestead and looked in on their mother frequently since their dad had passed. David, the youngest of the boys, was stationed at the Marine Corps Air Station at Cherry Point, North Carolina.

Kip stood and stretched his long arms over his head. He needed a run and a hot shower before he met Tom at the new campaign headquarters at nine. His few minutes of tranquility were over.

Two hours later Kip was driving down a two-lane road towards downtown Shady Beach, scrolling through his texts while taking quick peeks at the long line of trucks pulling skiing and fishing boats on their way to the river. Taking a sip from the coffee he'd picked up at a convenience store, he lowered the visor to block the morning sun and turned up the volume on his radio. He pulled in front of the new campaign headquarters on Main Street and slammed the door on his Lexus GS350. He dropped a quarter into the parking meter and took a quick look around the quaint town while tapping his cell phone to connect with Tom.

"Hey, where are you?" he asked.

"Stuck in traffic on the bridge. Damn beach traffic has everything backed up. What about you?"

"I'm outside the campaign office. Where'd you say you put the key?"

"Under the flower box," Tom said.

Sliding his hand along the window sill below the wooden box full of last year's dead, dried-up blooms, Kip discovered the brass key and inserted it into the lock.

"Damn, Tom, you outdid yourself. This place is a real palace." Kip laughed as he looked around the empty, dusty rooms, which had recently been home to a second-hand store. Clothing racks and boxes were still scattered throughout the space.

"Okay, smartass, it doesn't look like much now. We just need to get the crap out of there and clean it up. I'll rent furniture next week. It'll be fine," Tom replied.

Kip wandered around his new headquarters, leaning his head inside a back room he imagined could be used for conferences, then stepped into a small galley kitchen centered by the back door. He noticed a small woman in a baseball cap coming toward the building.

"Here comes the answer to our prayers. The cleaning lady's here," Kip said, as he reached for the door knob.

"Cleaning lady? I didn't know we had one. Maybe Annie hired her. God knows we need one."

"When do I get to meet the infamous *Ms. Merriman?*"

"On Monday at the staff meeting. I asked her to join us."

Kip reached for the door knob. The diminutive woman's hands were full with a mop, broom, and bucket filled with bottles of cleaning supplies. Once she deposited the items inside the kitchen, she went back out to her car and brought in a vacuum cleaner, then made a final trip to carry in four grocery bags. All the while, Kip ambled around the main room, moving old boxes with the edge of his toe and listening to Tom curse a sea of bad drivers on the other end of the line.

"So what kind of a lease did you get on this place?" Kip asked, as he tipped back his cup for the last drop of coffee. He glanced around the room for a trash can but didn't see one. The cleaning lady walked in carrying a large plastic bin and he handed her the empty cup.

"Gracias," he said.

He found a stack of boxes to lean against and watched as the cleaning lady bent over to pick up a pile of hangers off the floor. His eyes trailed from her tight little ass down to her red painted toenails. She was wearing cut-off denims, a baggy shirt, and flip flops, and her dark curly hair was pulled through the back of a baseball cap. The baggy shirt did little to hide her ample breasts. Tom put him on hold to answer another call and Kip decided to make conversation with the busy little woman.

"Habla Ingles?"

Still with her back to him, she put her hands on her hips and answered, "Yup."

Kip shrugged and went back to exploring the space, while occasionally casting a glance at the maid's shapely bottom.

"Who was that?" Kip said when Tom came back on the line, tearing his eyes away from a pair of tan legs.

"The speaker's assistant. He had some questions about the pipeline bill. I'm a block away. Be there in a minute."

Kip clicked off and watched as the cleaning lady pushed a wide broom across the floor. "Honey, you missed a spot." He pointed at the corner and flashed his pearly white smile as he stepped outside to meet Tom.

Tom climbed out of his SUV and shook Kip's outstretched hand.

"So, what do you think? Nice location, huh?"

"Yeah, great location. It's big enough. Maybe once that cleaning lady's done and all the stuff is out of there, I'll be able to envision what it could look like."

As the two men stood on the sidewalk, watching a few passing cars, the loud squeal of burning rubber split the quiet. A silver convertible fishtailed around the corner, whizzing by at breakneck speed.

Tom said, "Hey, that was—"

"The cleaning lady. She looked pissed."

Tom let his sunglasses slide down the bridge of his nose as he looked at his friend over their rim. "Bro, that was no cleaning lady. That was Annie Cooper."

Monday morning, after continuous tongue-lashings from Tom about the importance of getting in Annie's good graces, Kip plastered on his most sincere smile and welcomed his staff to their weekly meeting. He paced back and forth at the head of the conference table, jiggling his keys in anticipation of their introduction. A moment later he spotted her speaking with Tom outside the conference room door, affording Kip a moment to study her dignified, professional attire. The high-necked white blouse and navy suit did nothing to hide her incredible figure. She had dark, curly hair, the kind he'd always found so sexy, and this morning she had it piled high on her head. He envisioned pulling out the pins and letting it tumble down her back. His eyes trailed down the tan legs he had admired on Saturday to a pair of four-inch pumps that only enhanced her shapely calves. He had toyed with the idea of feigning ignorance of their encounter, but decided it might be to his advantage to admit his faux pas in an attempt to show her a more contrite side. Feeling it might be best to have a private word with her before the meeting began, Kip walked out of the conference room, hand extended, and greeted Annie with a smile.

"Good morning. You must be Annie Merriman. Kip Porter. Welcome."

Annie extended her hand. "Thank you, but I believe we've met."

Kip noticed the disdain on her face and chuckled, hoping to ease the tension. "Yes, I realize that now. I'm very sorry for the mix-up. Please, forgive me." He placed his other hand over their clasped palms, refusing to let her go until he saw some kind of absolution. "If I'd had some warning you would be there I never would have made that mistake. Can we just forget about it and start again?"

He watched Annie's eyes trail down to her imprisoned hand and then glance back up. "Perhaps that's best." Her face remained implacable and Kip knew he had his work cut out for him if he was going to work his magic on this much-needed ally.

"Well then," he said as he released her hand, "please come in and meet the rest of the team. I, for one, am very excited to have you on board. I'd like to talk about the campaign and your ideas. Perhaps we could get a cup of coffee after the meeting?"

"Coffee won't be necessary, but I do have several ideas I'd like to run past you." Annie brushed past him and entered the conference room, where Tom made introductions. Kip raked his hand through his thick hair and laughed. Damned if this little charade of theirs wouldn't be interesting, he thought, as a huge smile spread across his face.

Twenty minutes into the meeting, Kip couldn't resist casting glances at Annie, whose leg crossed over her knee gave him a small glimpse at her lower thigh. He was having difficulty concentrating on his staff assistant's list of phone calls and letters that needed his attention, until Annie spoke up.

"Is there a reason why this woman continues to call and send letters?" she asked.

Kip cleared his throat and joined the discussion. "I'm sorry, who did you say called on Friday?"

"Martha Mahan. She called again to complain about the smell coming from the chicken farm next door," said his assistant.

While the entire table, including Kip, chuckled and mumbled disparaging comments, Annie murmured to herself, "Well, I guess some constituents just aren't to be taken seriously." She pointedly stacked and restacked the collection of papers in front of her.

"Annie, did you have a question?" Tom asked.

Annie shifted in her chair, glancing at the twenty blank faces surrounding the table. The silence in the room seemed to echo around her. She cleared her throat and looked at Tom then Kip. "I'm sorry, it's just that maybe someone on your staff should call her back. I mean… maybe she has a legitimate gripe."

Kip leaned forward, resting his elbows on the table and looked at Annie's big brown eyes. How could he deny her earnest suggestion? "Well, okay. Maybe you're right. I'll put a call into Martha Mahan as soon as we're finished here."

The staff meeting ended ninety minutes later and Kip caught up to Annie as she walked out. "Annie, would you join me in my office, please?"

"Of course."

Kip led the way into his office and offered Annie a seat in front of his desk. "I thought you might like to be here when I call Martha Mahan." He flashed his most charming grin and noticed her brushing her hands across her skirt.

"It's really not necessary, but if you'd like me to be here, that's fine."

Kip tapped in Martha Mahan's number and put the call on speaker phone, continuing to smile at Annie across the desk.

"Hello?"

"Ms. Mahan, this is Kip Porter, your congressman," he said in a cheery voice.

"Finally. I was starting to wonder if you'd ever call me back."

"I apologize, Ms. Mahan. You can imagine how busy my job is representing the fine folks of the 9th District."

Martha Mahan snickered. "Okay, sure. Well, the reason for my numerous calls and letters is because the chicken farm a half mile down the road from my house is polluting the air around here. Everyone within a three-mile radius can smell it. There's something not right about that place. I've lived here my whole life and…"

While Martha continued to vent her frustrations over the chicken farm and the county's lack of response, Kip kept his eyes trained on Annie, who was looking intently at the phone. Surely Annie could tell this woman was crazy. She had a screeching voice and Kip could hear cats meowing in the background. Annie looked at Kip suddenly; he gave her a shrug and a playful smile. He watched Annie reach across his desk, pick up a Post-It note and pen, and write the words you need to go see her and the farm. Kip knew this was a wild goose chase, but he would do anything to be in Annie's good graces.

He interrupted Martha's rant. "Ex—excus-excuse me, Ms. Mahan? Sorry to interrupt. I think your problem is worth investigating. How about I contact the department of agriculture and come out there with one of their inspectors? Oh, and do you mind if I bring along one of my staff members? She would be very interested in this." He winked at Annie and watched as her face turned to stone.

After a few more minutes of Martha Mahan reiterating the problem, Kip was able to hang up, feeling very satisfied with his plan.

"I hope you don't mind me including you on this little jaunt, since you seem so concerned with Ms. Mahan's dilemma," Kip said as he came around the desk, extending his hand to help Annie out of her chair.

Annie's expression was inscrutable. "Not at all. I think it would be helpful for me to see you in action."

She picked up her leather bag and as she traversed the office, he couldn't help but whisper to himself, "This is going to be fun."

A few minutes later Tom burst through Kip's office door. "Bro, you have got to stop pissing that girl off."

Kip dropped the report he had been reading and tilted back in his leather chair. "What are you talking about?"

"I just passed Annie in the hall and could practically see steam coming out of her ears. What happened?"

"I called her bluff," he said with a slightly sinister chuckle. "She wanted me to deal with the Martha Mahan situation and I did, but I told Ms. Mahan one of my staff was coming along to check out the chicken stink. I'm not sure our dear Ms. Cooper appreciated that."

"Shit, man, you're supposed to be ingratiating yourself, not starting World War III. We need to get Senator Cooper on our side with this pipeline bill. And it's Ms. Merriman these days—she doesn't know we know who she is, and for now I think it should stay that way."

"Okay, okay." Kip began rocking in his chair, drumming his fingers on the desk. "What do you want me to do?"

"Tomorrow is the Women's Club luncheon at the Hay Adams. I'll tell Annie I can't go, and that she has to be there instead. And you, my friend, turn on the charm and get this girl to ask you to Sunday dinner with the family. Don't blow it this time."

SIX

Annie stood beside Kip at the entrance to the ballroom, where a monthly luncheon hosted by the Greater Washington Women's Club was being held. The cream colored walls, yellow tablecloths, and soft chandelier lighting gave a golden glow to the room. Dozens of well-groomed women mingled among their important guests. Mainly politicians, diplomats, and heads of departments were gathered in twos and threes, engrossed in conversation with these ladies whose husbands were some of the most powerful in the country. Today's luncheon agenda focused on music education in public schools and the guest speaker was a world renowned violinist.

"Congressman Porter, so delighted to have you here." An attractive older woman rushed toward Kip, her manicured fingertips wiggling at the end of her outstretched arms, causing her collection of gold bangles to clatter on her wrist. "So happy you could come and how disappointing that Tom got tied up in all those meetings." She air-kissed Kip on each cheek and then turned her nipped-and-tucked face toward Annie. "Who do we have here?"

"This is my new campaign manager, Annie Merriman. Annie, I'd like to introduce you to Amelia Wentworth."

The two women shook hands as Kip continued. "Mrs. Wentworth is very interested in improving our public education system and is a big supporter of the arts."

Feigning embarrassment, Amelia chortled, "Oh, I just try to do my small part. Annie, it is so nice to meet you. Kip is such a darling—he'll make your job so easy. Who wouldn't want to vote for that handsome face?"

That same handsome face had turned red. "Thank you so much, Amelia. That's very kind of you."

While Amelia and Kip continued to laud one another, Annie kept a broad smile plastered on her face. Really? She thinks my job is going to be easy? If the first three days were any indication, she was going to have her work cut out for her. To put up with Kip's smug, annoying "perfection" for the next five months was going to be torture. Thank God there was a light at the end of the tunnel: Election Day.

"Do you mind if I steal your handsome boss away for a few minutes? I have someone he must meet," Amelia said.

"Oh, be my guest, please," Annie answered with a gracious smile.

She watched them walk away, Amelia's arm tucked tightly inside Kip's, their heads pressed together in quiet conversation. They stopped only a few feet away near the bar and Annie watched Amelia's face grow red with each word Kip murmured. She was fairly blushing and Annie wondered what he could possibly be saying to her to make her act like a school girl.

Such is the behavior of every politician, she guessed. Annie picked up a glass of iced tea from a passing waiter and leaned against a marbled column. Charm the wealthy and you can rest assured re-election is in your future. It appeared Kip Porter had learned that lesson as he continued flattering Mrs. Wentworth. She wondered how far that Hollywood smile would get him.

"Annie, sweetheart, what are you doing here?" Annie jumped, disrupting her observations. She turned and found her mother coming toward her with outstretched arms.

"Hey, Mom," Annie said as she hugged her mother.

"I'm surprised to see you here," Marjorie Cooper said, brushing Annie's curls away from her face.

"I'm here with my new boss." Annie froze as she realized her mother was standing beside her...and Kip didn't know Cooper was her last name.

She turned and pulled her mother through the doorway into the foyer. "Mom, listen, you can't let on to my boss that I'm your daughter."

"Why? What are you up to?"

"Look, when I met his chief of staff I told him my name was Annie Merriman. They don't know I'm a senator's daughter."

"Why did you do that?"

"I can't talk about this now."

"Does your father know? What's this all about?"

"Mom, please…no, he doesn't know. For once I just want to be my own person."

"I don't understand." Her mother took a quick sip of her cocktail. "You're not making sense."

"I'm tired of the expectations—the assumptions—that go along with being Senator George Cooper's daughter from the great state of North Carolina." Annie whispered his name, making sure no one around them heard. "And, I'm tired of his meddling."

"Well, you don't have to act like it's a curse or something."

"It is a curse."

"That's not very nice, Ann. Your father is a wonderful man and cares deeply for your happiness and success."

Annie cocked her head and put a hand on her hip. "Really? Seriously? Mom, please, do you hear yourself?"

"Things have been wonderful between your father and me for several months. If you'd come to brunch once in a while you'd see that."

"I've been…busy." Annie glanced over her shoulder at a group of people coming into the foyer. She hadn't been to her mother's weekly Sunday brunch in over a month, preferring to avoid her father altogether. The last time she'd been there, he was so ingratiating to her mother, so affectionate…it was infuriating. He'd probably gotten caught red-handed again and was trying to make amends. And worse, Marjorie Cooper was letting him get away with it. Again.

"So, if you're impersonating someone named Annie Merriman, what will you tell your boss when you introduce us?"

"Technically, I'm not impersonating anyone. Though I can't introduce you." Annie tipped her head toward the door, making sure Kip hadn't seen them talking. She needn't have worried; Kip was surrounded by Women's Club members, giving them his undivided attention.

Marjorie craned her neck to get a better view of Kip. "He's quite handsome, isn't he?" "Oh, my God, please, Mom. Let me get back to work."

After the luncheon, Kip drove Annie to her apartment, since she had taken the metro to the hotel. They were silent for several blocks, both seeming deep in thought. Annie couldn't stop reliving the luncheon, picturing Kip fawning over the club's members and graciously chatting with various government officials. He could work a room better than the best of them, shaking hands, smiling warmly, doling out compliments. He had regaled them with stories of his football career and years of piano lessons in an attempt to show his interest in music education. If she heard one more middle-aged, strongly-perfumed lady tell her what a marvelous person Kip was, she thought she'd gag. His charming, downright flirtatious demeanor around these women was quite annoying and yet...rather telling.

During the official entertainment portion of the afternoon, Kip had seemed mesmerized by the melodic sound of the violin, his head tilted back and his eyes closed. Annie swallowed a laugh, wondering if he had actually been sleeping. Of course, she knew he hadn't been, since she caught him covertly looking at her several times.

Mere blocks from her apartment, Kip finally broke the stillness. "Why didn't you drive to the luncheon?"

"It's a waste of energy. When I'm in the city, I try to use mass transit."

Kip nodded once. "But, you've got a car."

"Which I drive when necessary. Besides, it has great gas mileage. Why do you drive a Lexus?"

"It's a great car, very comfortable."

"Very expensive."

"That's true, but—"

"But what? Tom had me review the office books and I noticed you pay quite a hefty lease payment for this car. Is that the best use of taxpayer funds?" Annie had turned in her seat and drilled Kip with a large-eyed stare.

"It's a legitimate expense. I'm not breaking any rules. I travel quite a bit for my job and need a comfortable car. I won't apologize for it." Kip glared back at her.

"It just doesn't seem like the right image to portray to your constituents, who are primarily blue collar. I mean, yes, some of the folks in your district are higher income Annapolis and DC commuters, but for the most part your people are living paycheck to paycheck. Shouldn't you have more of a 'man of the people' image?"

Kip didn't respond, which gave Annie time to notice his shallow breathing and flaring nostrils. Was he bothered by the district from which he came? Meager beginnings were nothing to be ashamed of. She could see that she'd struck a nerve and he was doing his best to control his anger.

"I'll discuss it with Tom," he murmured.

"Do you make any decisions without Tom? How does this whole thing work? Who's the boss?"

"Tom is my chief of staff and closest advisor," he said, barely containing his rising annoyance. "Of course I'm the boss, but we work more like a team. For example, Tom hired you and you may report directly to him, but ultimately, I'm your boss."

Annie smiled sweetly. "Point taken. I'll remember that."

Again, for several blocks the car was silent but for the steady purr of the engine and Kip's heavy breathing. A moment later, he pulled his sedan to the curb outside Annie's building and tapped the console between them.

"Sit right there," he said before climbing out of the car. He walked around the front fender, buttoning his jacket, then opened Annie's door while extending his hand. She placed her hand in his and he tightened his grip, throwing Annie for an unexpected loop when she looked into his crystal blue eyes.

"Thank you," she said sheepishly. The irritation that seemed to have been seething just beneath the surface during the car ride had completely dissolved, leaving Kip's face relaxed and…was that a smile?

"It's been an interesting afternoon. I'd still like to get to know you better and wish you'd reconsider that coffee…or even dinner."

Kip kept a firm grip on her hand and for some strange reason she couldn't tear her eyes away. "I'm sure we'll get to know one another at the office," she murmured. "You know, as we discuss your campaign strategies."

"True, but I'd like to get to know you on a more personal level."

With sheer force of will, Annie drew her hand and eyes away. She ducked around him and stepped deliberately to the sidewalk. "I'm not sure that would be appropriate. I've got to go. Thank you."

As she opened the entry door, she cast a glance over her shoulder and saw Kip leaning against the car, arms crossed over his chest, a smug grin on his face.

When Kip arrived back at the congressional office, Tom was sitting at his desk, staring at the computer screen. He didn't seem to notice Kip's return.

"Hey," Kip shouted, making Tom jump in his seat.

"Damn it, bro, are you trying to give me a heart attack? What the hell's the matter with you?"

Kip chuckled and dropped into the chair adjacent to Tom's desk. "Just making sure you're awake."

"How did the luncheon go? Make any headway with Princess Annie?" Tom turned in his seat, giving all his attention to Kip.

"It depends on what you call headway. Did I get invited to Sunday dinner? No."

"Okay, then what kind of progress did you make?"

Kip propped his ankle over his left knee and leaned his elbow on the desk. "I'd say…very little. But—and this could just have been my imagination—I think we had a moment when she climbed out of the car. I think I flustered her a bit. Damn it, she's a tough one. I usually have no problem warming up women."

Tom rubbed his hands up and down his face and the effect made a sound like sandpaper on wood. "Uh...man...what can we do to get on her good side?"

Only the tick-tock of the pendulum clock on Tom's desk could be heard in the small office where both men thought about a change in strategy.

"The problem is," Kip said, "we've only been in the office or on official business when I've talked to her. Maybe if we were in a social setting I could thaw her out. I wonder what she does for fun."

"Let me do some research," Tom said as he picked up the phone. "I'll get back to you."

"Though, I'll tell you man, it might not be worth it. Maybe we can think of another way to get close to her dad."

"Don't give up yet. We're only in the first quarter."

SEVEN

"You should've seen him. He was practically dripping with women. My God, I wish I could've put a bug in that little flag lapel pin of his and heard what bullshit he was feeding them. They were totally enraptured." Annie took a long draw on her beer and then continued. "Oh, oh and then? When we were talking to this woman, Amelia Wentworth," Annie crooned in a sweet southern drawl, "I swear his hand slipped onto her lower hemisphere. Mark my words: these politicians are all alike." Annie dove into her salad, stabbing madly at the greens.

"You would know," Derek mumbled, and Kate affirmed with a knowing eye-roll. When the photograph had surfaced during their junior year of the senator on the yacht of a wealthy lobbyist with an eighteen-year-old prostitute on his lap, Kate had supported Annie through the embarrassing situation. With the love and support of his family by his side and a considerable dose of creative spin from his camp, Cooper had been able to brush this sordid tale under the rug and get re-elected once again. Gail and Derek had heard the story and even witnessed themselves how Senator Cooper's political posturing had affected Annie.

"Seriously. You know I've seen this fake, overly-friendly, touchy-feely stuff too many times. Believe me—I know what I'm talking about."

"Okay, so he loves the ladies. What else can you tell us about him? What's his platform or main cause or whatever?" Gail asked, shoving her empty mug toward the edge of the table.

"So, he's sponsoring this oil pipeline expansion bill that seems to be his highest priority right now. It came up several times at the luncheon today."

Kate drained the last of her beer. "Where is this oil pipeline?"

"Apparently along the east coast?"

"I didn't even know there was a pipeline there to expand," Derek said.

"Neither did I, but this expansion is supposed to go through the eastern shore in his district. Ugh…let's stop talking about this. I need another beer."

"Wait, here's our next trivia question." They all turned and looked at the overhead screen as Kate read to them. "Who was the first United States president to be impeached?"

"I have no idea. Anyone know it?" Annie glanced at Kate, who was sinking her teeth into a veggie burger while shaking her head. "Derek? Any idea?"

"Nope. Good ol' Bill is the only one I know of, and I'm sure he wasn't the first."

"I think I might know." Gail shoved her plate aside and leaned toward the center of the table. In a hushed voice she said, "Wasn't it Andrew Johnson?"

Three blank faces stared back at her.

"That's right, isn't it?" Gail urged the group to respond.

"I have no idea. Sounds good to me though. I'll just put that down." Kate filled in the blank space on the trivia game form and went back to eating her burger.

Annie looked over her shoulder. "Where is our waiter?" As if by magic, he appeared with a tray full of fresh beer mugs, foam spilling over the sides.

"Perfect timing," Derek said as he reached for a cold mug.

The waiter handed the remaining frosted glasses to Kate, Gail, and Annie.

"You must have read my mind," Annie said.

"Actually, these are compliments of the gentleman in the booth behind you."

All four stood up and looked behind them over the tops of the booth. The table backing Annie and Derek was empty, but when she sat back down Annie saw Kip rising out of the booth behind Kate, buttoning his jacket as he turned toward them. Her heart started pounding, fairly jumping out of her chest.

"Good evening, everyone. I'm Kip Porter."

No one responded. No one moved. All eight eyes stared in disbelief as Kip pulled up a chair, setting his own beer on the table.

"How's trivia going?" He glanced around the table at four wide-eyed faces before his eyes came to rest on Annie. She was speechless, paralyzed.

Kate finally broke the silence. "Oh, um, it's going well. Hi. I'm Kate and this is Gail and Derek. And...of course you know Annie."

His warm, sincere smile made Annie that much more nervous as she tried to stop her hands from wringing in her lap.

"Of course, I know Annie Merriman," he said with a broad, playful grin.

"What are you doing here?" Annie croaked, reaching for her beer.

Kip directed his answer to Kate, Gail and Derek, seeming to ignore the fact that Annie had asked the question. "I was supposed to meet a friend of mine here tonight, but it looks like he's not coming. While I was waiting I could hear someone speaking and I thought to myself, I know that voice. I glanced over the back of my booth and there you were." His smiling eyes bore into Annie's. "What're the chances?"

Annie's salad began churning in her stomach. The thought that Kip could have heard what she had been saying was making her nauseated. She was afraid to open her mouth for fear of what may come out.

"Seems like a million-to-one chance if you ask me," Kate blurted. "Here's our next question." Once more she read aloud. "What was the name of the future politician who led the AFL in passing yards in the 1960s?"

"Jack Kemp."

The table fell silent as Kip raised his glass, smiling proudly at his ability to provide a correct answer.

"How did you know that?" Gail asked.

"How does anyone gather useless trivia? I guess I read it somewhere," Kip said, pointedly focusing all his attention on Annie's friends. "I like to read political history, autobiographies, and of course I follow sports. But I have lots of other interests, too. I went into politics because I have a genuine interest in several causes and want to make this country a better place."

"Well said." Derek saluted with a tip of his mug.

"Now some people think that all politicians are just power hungry, womanizing sleaze-balls who can't keep their hands to themselves. But that isn't true." Kip took off his jacket, hung it on the chair back, and loosened his tie.

"I didn't say sleaze-balls," Annie said to her napkin, while she systemically tore it to shreds. She was doing all she could to avoid Kip's gaze.

"The thing is, most people don't understand politics and how important it is to keep the voters and donors happy. They often misunderstand what they see."

Regaining her resolve, Annie looked straight at Kip. "I understand politics." She then turned to the others, brushing aside the napkin shavings. "I saw what I saw and I don't think that's the way to get donors. Being a leader and introducing good legislation, and most importantly, listening to your constituents is the way to gain support."

Kip directed his response to Annie's friends. "Coach here was hired to handle my campaign, so you'd think she'd be encouraging me to drum up support. She's seen the books and knows how expensive a campaign is to run."

Annie's mouth dropped open and she furrowed her brows at Kip.

"That's right, I called you 'Coach'," he said. "I think it fits. You remind me of my middle school football coach back in seventh grade. He had a really low opinion of us and he was always right—even when he was wrong."

Derek barely suppressed a snicker and Kate hid her half-smile behind her beer. Annie leaned toward Kip, her elbows on the table. "Well, Porter, I don't happen to be wrong in this case." She turned to the rest of the table. "I just think there should be a better way to go about getting the issues in front of supporters as well as raise money."

"Hold on—another question," Kate interrupted. "According to the ancient Egyptians, who is the god of fertility, life, and death?"

Before anyone could even take a breath, Kip answered, "Osiris."

"Are you sure?" Gail asked.

"Absolutely," Kip answered and once more gave a sparkling smile to Annie, who couldn't seem to close her mouth. Annie began rapidly drumming her nails on the side of her mug while glaring at Kip. How did anyone know if his answers were even correct? He could be charming the team with his quick responses, but not know the first thing about either subject.

"Want me to Google it, Coach?" Kip glared back with equal intensity.

"That was the last question. I'll turn in our sheet and see how we did." Kate got up from the table to deliver the answer sheet to the hostess, while the rest of the table sat silently. Annie continued tapping her fingernails against the side of her beer mug, while she and Kip carried on their staring contest. As soon as Kate returned, Annie resumed her defensive argument to the rest of her team. For a woman who had just spent the last few minutes staring daggers into Kip, she couldn't be bothered to pay him the least mind as she spoke.

"As I was saying, I think candidates could go about fundraising with a little more integrity. Let me get some good press out there for him and donations will start flowing in. Schmooze the big guns, yes, but keep your hands to yourself."

"I'm not sure what I've done to make her so pissed at me," Kip said to Kate, "but I think she's trying to penalize me for something I didn't do." Kip shoved his beer mug an arm's length in front of him and propped his left elbow on the table, turning to face Annie. "I promise you my hand didn't go anywhere near her ass."

"It sure looked like it to me."

"You were across the room! How could you see anything?"

"I had a clear shot. I know what I saw."

"You need your eyes checked."

"Oh, really? Anything else you think I need, Congressman?"

Kip sat back and retrieved his beer, tilting it contemplatively. Annie felt the flush on her face rise. Kip's beer mug hit the table with a thump as he slid his chair even closer to Annie, so close their knees touched. "Since you asked…"

"Let's hear it." Annie scooted closer to the edge of the booth.

"Stop insisting I call back constituents who are obviously crazy."

"She may have a legitimate gripe."

"There were thousands of cats meowing in the background." Kip's voice echoed off the booth's walls.

"So maybe she rescues cats. Have a problem with that?" Annie matched his volume, rising slightly from her seat.

"Damn it." Kip took a long draw from his beer and mumbled, "I just don't like cats."

Annie burst out laughing and threw her head back gleefully, then leaned forward to bring her face within inches of Kip's. "What's the matter, Porter, are you afraid of a little furry feline?"

"Of course not."

"So, what's your problem?"

Kip's face grew red and he nearly pressed his nose to hers. "I'm deathly allergic. Satisfied?" he said through gritted teeth.

"Oh." Annie jerked to attention, noticing they were but a millimeter apart, and slowly slid back into her seat, pressing her back against the booth. Around the table, Kate, Derek, and Gail stared at the combatants, who seemed to have slipped into their neutral corners. Annie picked up her mug, taking a deliberately long drink while keeping her eyes cast downward. The threesome exchanged knowing glances while Kip spun his empty glass around and around in a circle.

Kate broke the silence. "Um…so…it looks like we won."

"Our first win. Congrats to us," Gail said.

"I have a feeling it was the congressman's help on the last two questions that put us over the top. Thanks, man," Derek added.

Kip stood, pulling his jacket from the back of his chair. "You're welcome. Glad I could help. So, what did you win?"

"We won fifty dollars toward our next bar tab," Kate said. "You should join us again."

Annie aimed a withering glare at her friend.

Kip re-buttoned his navy blazer and tossed a ten-dollar bill on the table. "That's very kind of you, Kate, but I think I'll pass. This was a lot of fun, but I'm usually still working in the evenings." Kip looked down at Annie, who was fingering her pile of shredded napkin. "Besides," he continued, "I never like being the second smartest person at the table."

Annie's head popped up and he gave her a wry grin, then slowly walked out of the bar.

EIGHT

The mid-morning sun sparkled through mullioned windows, casting white streaks across the polished wood floors and illuminating the pristine space. Kip turned slowly in the tomb-like silence, his jacket shoved back, hands on his hips, taking in the main room of the campaign headquarters that now looked like it could be featured in a design magazine. On the walls were large framed photographs of Eastern Shore life: two men crabbing off a dock, a farmer harvesting an abundant crop of corn, a white sailboat gliding along the bay, a group of locals watching a Fourth of July parade. Tea-stained Americana bunting was draped at the windows and a large bouquet of black-eyed Susans adorned a round antique table in the center of the room. A life-sized cardboard cut-out of Kip stood nearby. Another antique table sat at the back of the room, acting as a reception desk, and to its right was a large wooden cabinet holding a coffee pot and cups.

Kip let out a low whistle. "Who the hell decorated this place?" he said to himself. "Martha Stewart?"

"Actually, it was me." Annie glided into the room in her bare feet and dropped a stack of brochures on the reception desk.

Startled, Kip turned and crossed the room, reaching out to help Annie with a box she was holding. "Hey, I thought I was the only one here."

"Obviously not. So…Martha Stewart, huh?" Annie leaned her hip against the desk and crossed her arms across her ruffled, sleeveless blouse.

"That was a compliment. This place looks incredible." Kip moved forward and stood inches in front of Annie, his tall, lean body towering over her. "I'm really impressed. This sure doesn't look like my last campaign office."

"Well..." Annie cleared her throat, tucked her hair behind her ears, and retrieved a pair of tan pumps from below the desk. As she slipped them on, she said, "Thank you. I appreciate that."

"I can see how hard you've worked." Kip took another quick spin of the room. "I'm just curious how much all this cost...I mean it's great... but we're on a tight budget, remember?"

Annie quickly walked across the room, stopping at the crabbing photo, her hands moving like an orchestra conductor's. "It cost next to nothing. Two blocks over there's a photography studio and I'd noticed these beautiful photos in his window. We worked a deal and he's letting me borrow the framed photos until after the campaign in return for displaying some of his business cards and brochures." Her heels clicked on wood floor as she walked toward the center table and adjusted the vase in several directions until she gave the arrangement a satisfied nod. "It's the same deal with the silk flowers. The florist next door is lending them in return for free advertising." Without casting a glance at Kip, she continued to glide around the space. "The antique tables are from my parents' attic. My mother has a whole stash of furniture up there she just can't seem to part with. Even the wooden desk chair is an antique. I think it belonged to my great-grandfather. Let's see..."

Kip watched Annie flit around the room, noticing the way she occasionally wiped her hands across her navy blue skirt. Had her voice risen a full octave while she chattered about her decorations? She was talking at warp speed and her hands appeared to quiver.

"You okay?" Kip stepped closer to her. "I'm not making you nervous, am I?"

Annie flicked her hand as if swatting a fly. "Pfff...not at all."

He stifled a satisfied grin while her melodious voice put him in a near-trance. He began imagining what it would be like to plant a long, lingering kiss on those pouty pink lips. He wasn't supposed to have erotic daydreams about one of his employees—a pain-in-the-ass, self-righteous, goody-two-shoes employee—but he couldn't stop himself from thinking about slipping his hand into the thick curls at the nape of her neck and pulling her in close, his other hand gripping her cute little bottom. He was suddenly wrenched from his musings when he noticed Annie had stopped talking and was staring at him.

He cleared his throat. "Good...I mean you've done a great job." Kip turned his back to her and tried to get his mind back on the subject at hand when he took a longer look at the beverage station. "Are those tea cups?" He walked over to the cabinet where a coffee pot, sugar packets, a basket of tea bags, and cream pitcher were arranged. On the shelves above were a variety of floral tea cups and saucers.

"Oh...um, yeah...tea cups. Remember this was a secondhand store?" Kip nodded.

"I found this box of tea cups out by the dumpster. Can you believe it? I mean, who would throw out these beautiful old cups? I have a thing for china—always have. When I was little girl my grandmother gave me a real china tea set and I used to play tea party for hours." Annie poured boiling water from a carafe into a blue and yellow cup and dunked an Earl Grey bag while adding a packet of sugar. "When I was in England last year, I insisted on going to a tea room every day, just so I could see what kind of cup they'd serve it in. And of course, to have a scone with clotted cream. I even bought a few cups while I was there."

Annie turned and looked up at Kip, her brown eyes growing larger. "So I thought it would be a nice touch to use them for coffee and tea. You know, when someone comes in we can offer them a drink in these pretty cups and make them feel at home. Personally, I prefer drinking from a real china cup. In fact, that's the only way I drink tea or coffee."

"Fascinating."

"Porter," Annie snapped her fingers at Kip's face. "Are you even listening?"

"You prefer china over coffee mugs. Got it. Another great idea."

"Okay then. I still have brochures and information sheets to set around and then I'll go pick up the cookies from the bakery down the street. Are you ready? Did you write a speech? I was thinking about a half-hour after people arrive, you should take some time to speak about your platform, your goals, ask for their support, that kind of thing. Someone from the local paper is supposed to be here at 1:30."

Kip leaned against the round table and smiled at Annie. "Yes, Coach."

"Do you know what you're going to say?"

"Not really, but I've done this before. It's all good."

"I hope so." Annie rushed toward the conference room door then barked over her shoulder, "Don't just stand there. We've got work to do."

An hour after the open house began, the headquarters was filled with local politicians and party members, as well as interested citizens who came out to support Kip in his third run for office. Flash bulbs lit up the room as the press took photos of Kip finishing his speech to rousing applause. He had removed his jacket and loosened his tie as the room filled with more and more people; the air conditioning was not up to the task on this warm July day. Annie was leaning against the wall in the back of the room, watching Kip smile warmly at each of his guests, always with an outstretched hand. She couldn't stop herself from noticing the muscles in his shoulders and back flexing against the slim-cut dress shirt, or the way the upper sleeves strained across his biceps. He ran his fingers through his thick, dark hair in an attempt to control a wayward lock.

"Looks like we're running low on cookies," said Pam, one of the college interns. The interruption made Annie jump.

"Oh, let me get those." Annie hurried into the kitchen, chastising herself for letting her mind get so carried away by Kip's…assets. She opened the white bakery box and carefully arranged the red, white, and blue iced cookies on the antique silver tray—another find from her mother's attic—when she felt a brush of air against her neck.

"Great party, Coach. You outdid yourself," Kip whispered in her ear, his body so close to hers she could almost feel him. "Let me get that for you." Kip reached around Annie, coming even closer, and lifted the heavy tray with one hand. Once again her eyes were drawn to his strong, bulging muscles.

"Thanks," she mumbled.

Kip took a step back and held the tray in both hands, looking down at the arrangement. "I was thinking we should go out and celebrate tonight. Today was a huge hit."

"Celebrate?"

"Yeah. You've worked really hard…got the press here, even the *Baltimore Sun*. Several people have promised contributions to the campaign. It's been really great. We need to celebrate."

"Okay. That sounds fun."

Kip smiled and pressed close to Annie. She felt her pulse quicken. "Great. Let's make plans after this is over."

"I'll let the staff know," Annie said, trying to keep the quiver out of her voice.

"I was hoping it would just be the two of us."

"Oh, I don't think so. No, but thank you."

Kip huffed a lungful of air and walked out of the kitchen, tray in hand. Annie fell back against the countertop, her fingers knotted together and palms sweating. She'd made the right decision. It wasn't appropriate for her go on what essentially would be a date with her boss, but she couldn't deny the nearness of him, his tantalizing smile, and his spicy maleness made it difficult to say no. She took another moment to collect herself before rejoining the party.

"Congressman Porter, it's so nice to meet you. I'm Rene Hoffer and this is my sister, Lori Richardson." Two attractive, fifty-something women walked up to Kip and Tom as they finished their conversation with the mayor of Shady Beach.

"Hello, ladies. So nice to meet you. This is my chief of staff, Tom Garrett. Do you live here in Shady Beach?" Kip asked.

Tom and Kip shook hands with the sisters as Rene replied, "No, actually, I live in Denver and Lori lives in Baltimore. I'm visiting her this week."

"We were having lunch down the street and then were looking in some shops, and noticed a party going on," Lori said.

"We don't like to miss a party," Rene barked with a laugh, teetering on her strappy heels.

Tom steadied her by grabbing her elbow. "I'm sorry we can't offer you some rum punch. We're only serving the straight stuff."

"No worries, darling." Rene opened her Versace bag and exposed a shiny silver flask.

"We're always prepared...like Girl Scouts." The sisters leaned into each other and giggled. "Plus we wanted to check out the store," Lori said.

Kip cocked one eyebrow. "The store?"

Rene laughed and placed her hand on his forearm. "Yes, our grandfather and great-grandfather had a store at this location for several decades. Darlington Hardware."

"Oh, of course. I used to go there with my dad when I was young. It must have closed when I was about ten or eleven," Kip said.

"That's right. Well, we've been working on our family's genealogy and discovered through my great-aunt that our great-grandfather was a bootlegger during Prohibition. He sold homemade moonshine to the Washington elite," Lori whispered, as though revealing a national secret.

Rene interrupted and once again placed her hand on Kip's arm. It occurred to Kip that the clearly intoxicated woman might actually need his support to steady herself as she leaned in and spoke just above a hush. "He kept his whiskey stashed in the broom closet in the back room. There was a false wall in the back of the closet that the police never discovered in all that time."

"Why are you whispering?" Lori said, releasing a small chuckle. "It's not like it's a big secret. Not anymore anyway."

"I think you were the only one whispering," Rene replied.

Lori turned to Kip and said, "Do you think we could look in the closet to see if the false wall is still there?"

Kip turned to Tom, a bewildered expression on his face. "Do you know anything about a broom closet?"

"I think there might be one in the kitchen. We can take a look." Tom extended his arm, pointing the ladies in the right direction.

"Now, won't this be fun? The four of us in a closet. This could get interesting." Rene reached down and squeezed Kip's rear-end, making him jump.

"Whoa there…careful." Kip took a step back, but Rene followed forward, wrapping her outstretched arms around his waist. "Sorry, darling, you're just too handsome for your own good." Kip gently removed her hands and tucked them down by her sides while giving a concerned look at Tom. Tom replied with a nod and a crooked grin, rubbing his fingers together behind his other hand. Kip furrowed his brows with a slight shake of his head, but allowed himself to be led through a doorway toward the back. The sisters twittered and whispered to each other as they followed Kip down a narrow hallway toward the kitchen.

"There are actually two closets in the kitchen. One is really small, but the other is a walk-in Annie's set up as a supply closet," Tom said.

"I have a marvelous idea. Why don't you and Lori check out the broom closet while Kip and I investigate the walk-in?" Rene didn't wait for an answer. She pulled Kip by the hand into the larger space.

Once inside, Kip pulled out the portable shelving lining the room in search of a trap door or loose wallboard.

"Can you see anything?" Rene said as she leaned over Kip, who was crouching in a corner.

"Not yet, but maybe it's one of those walls you have to tap in just the right place to open," Kip said, knocking his fist in several places. The potentially historical significance of his campaign headquarters had piqued his interest in spite of himself. "It does sound hollow behind this wall."

"Do you have any tools handy?" With a tiny snicker, Rene continued. "Silly question. I'm sure you do."

Kip stood and eased around Rene and climbed from behind the shelf. "I'll get something to pry open the wall." He walked down the hall to where Tom and Lori were snug inside the empty broom closet. He signaled to Tom to join him in the kitchen. When he did, Kip whispered, "Jesus, she's all over me back there."

"Bro, come on. Financial support can come from anywhere. Just make her happy and then get her to write a check."

Kip released a loud sigh and ran his fingers through his thick hair. "Where's a tool kit?"

Tom opened a few drawers and pulled out a screwdriver, which Kip snatched out of his hand before stalking back toward the supply room.

"I think if I slide the screwdriver into this space I can force this open." Using the shank of the screwdriver as leverage, Kip was able to pull up a section of wallboard, revealing an open cavity behind. Once he could get his hand behind the board, he grabbed it and pulled. All at once, the drywall in Kip's hand gave way and they found themselves looking at the cleverly disguised hiding place with several shelves, about six inches wide. A few dusty ceramic bottles remained. Rene slid in front of him and bent over, pressing her butt against his crotch.

"Amazing. This is so great," Rene said. She abruptly rose and turned to face him.

Kip took a step backward but continued staring into the dark space. "Yeah, it's amazing these bottles are still here after so long."

"I wasn't talking about the bottles." Rene stepped closer and deftly unbuckled Kip's belt as her other hand massaged his inner thighs.

"Uh…Rene, I—" Kip jumped when he heard a loud crash behind them. He pushed Rene's hands away and re-buckled his belt. "Take all the time you want in here. I, um…gotta go." Kip rushed from behind the shelf, nearly tripping over a large stack of paper plates and cups strewn across the floor.

NINE

An hour later the campaign office was empty and several volunteers were picking up cups and plates, washing out the punch bowl and sweeping the floor. Even Tom and Kip pitched in to clean the space where so many people had come to show their support for Kip's re-election bid. Shortly after the supply room debacle, Kip was able to avoid the tipsy twins until they stumbled out the front door. He'd looked throughout the office for Annie, but quickly realized it must have been she who had walked in on Rene's failed attempt to seduce him and then left in a huff.

Once the office was cleaned and the last volunteer walked out the back door, Kip sent Annie a text.

Hey where'd u go?

He waited several minutes and when he got no reply he tried again.

The volunteers are going to dinner. U coming?

Again, with no reply, he finally texted, It's not what u think.

Kip took one last look at his silent phone before slamming out the back door. He marched to his Lexus and revved the engine while dialing Annie's number. It came as no surprise that she didn't answer, but he hung up and dialed one more time anyway. When she didn't pick up, he skidded out of the parking lot, gravel flying, and pointed his car toward DC.

Push, pull. Push, pull. Annie ran the vacuum cleaner over the same spot on the carpet as if she were under a spell. Since arriving home from Shady Beach, she'd been furiously cleaning—not only the living room, kitchen, and her bedroom, but Kate's as well. Images of that nipped and tucked cougar giving Kip the blow job of his life inside the supply room coursed through her brain. How could he be so reckless? What if a reporter had walked in? What was he thinking? It was one thing to flirt with those old bats to secure campaign financing, but unzipping his pants to get what he needed? Annie flipped off the switch and grabbed a dust rag, feverishly rubbing the top of the coffee table. She wasn't naïve; she knew all too well this stuff went on, but she never dreamed when she walked into the closet to get more plates and cups she'd find her boss getting sucked off behind the shelves.

Annie walked into the kitchen and furiously began dropping dishes into the dishwasher. It wasn't her imagination—she knew what she saw. But earlier she'd seen how he looked at her when she showed him the office. And then in the kitchen he'd leaned in close and seemed disappointed when she suggested the staff join them at the celebratory dinner.

"I'm an idiot," she scolded herself. She'd been flattered by his attention, but knew better than to fall for a politician's charms. Speaking of politicians, Annie felt her phone vibrate and noticed a call coming through from her father. She chose to let it go to voice mail, making it the third message he had left that week. She didn't want to listen to his sickening sweet rhetoric again. *How about we meet for a drink after work this week, honey? I'd love to hear about your new job.* The last thing she wanted to do was discuss her career with her father. *Hi, Annie bug, hope you can make it to brunch tomorrow.* She had been avoiding brunch as much as possible. He must have been caught in another compromising situation, but for the life of her she couldn't remember reading anything online. Surely it would make the news soon…there was no other explanation for his efforts.

And now she felt déjà vu with her new boss. Were they all alike? How could she work for someone like that? As a campaign manager, she was supposed to believe in the candidate she represented. How could she be expected to tout Kip's qualities to the public when she had such doubts? Honesty and trust were important to her and she wasn't about to compromise her principles.

She'd quit—that was the only answer.

Annie snapped the dishwasher door shut and fired up her laptop, quickly writing a letter of resignation right then and there. It wasn't too late for him to find another campaign manager and she could get right back to job hunting. Maybe by now some of the companies she'd applied to would have openings. It wasn't unheard of to quit two jobs within a couple of months of each other, was it?

As Annie was pulling the resignation letter out of her printer, the doorbell rang. For what felt like the thousandth time that day, her heart skipped a beat. Who could be bothering her now? She tossed the letter on the kitchen counter and rushed to the door. When she looked through the peep hole she drew in a ragged breath. Kip Porter was standing on the other side of the door, pacing in a circle.

"What do you want?" she shouted through the door.

"I want to talk to you."

"I'm busy."

Kip slapped his palm against the door and pressed his eye against the peep hole. "I can stand out here and let your neighbors hear us or you can let me in. Either way, we're going to talk."

Annie turned and threw her back against the door, releasing a pent-up sigh. It looked as though she had no choice but to let the sleaze-ball in. She unlocked the deadbolt and opened the door, inviting him in with a sweep of her hand.

Kip stepped into Annie's living room and looked around at the tastefully designed furnishings, taking a moment to study the old movie posters framed on the walls. She stood near the door with her arms crossed over her chest, waiting for him to say something.

"Nice. I like your apartment."

Kip's shirt sleeves were rolled up and he had removed his tie, and Annie noticed his typically groomed hair was a bit disheveled. His hands were tucked deep inside his pants pockets and he seemed to be pushing something on the floor with his toe.

She was losing patience. "Well?" she said as she grabbed the dust rag and began rubbing the coffee table once more.

"Well I've been texting and calling you."

"I turned off my phone."

Kip resumed studying something on the floor. "I was hoping we'd still get to go out to celebrate. It was a great turnout."

Annie dropped her hands to her sides, forming a fist in each, and marched to the kitchen. "Why aren't you there?" She pulled a bottle of wine out of the refrigerator, splashed a generous amount into a glass and turned around, leaning her elbows on the bar separating the two rooms. She took a long drink. "Oh, yeah, you already celebrated."

"No, I helped clean up after the party and came directly here." Kip walked to the opposite end of the counter. "Can I have one of those?"

Annie turned in a huff and grabbed a wine glass from the cabinet, then slammed it shut. A puddle of wine sloshed onto the counter as she filled his glass, creating a large stain on the resignation letter. She noticed Kip's attention drawn to the spill and then to the letter before him. She snatched it up before he could study it any further.

"I wasn't talking about going out to dinner. I was talking about the little celebration you received in the supply closet."

"What's that?" Kip grabbed a handful of air as Annie stepped back, the resignation letter firmly in her grasp. Kip walked around the end of the counter, coming within a few inches of Annie. He reached out his hand but she dodged him. "It wasn't what you think," he said, once more grabbing at air.

"Why do you always say that after I've caught you in a compromising position with a woman?" Annie circled around Kip and headed for the living room.

"Because you keep jumping to conclusions," he said, following close behind.

She turned and poked her finger into Kip's chest. "I'm not jumping to conclusions. I heard your belt buckle unlatch and Miss Busy Hands say you were amazing. I know what I heard."

Kip reached out again and grabbed hold of Annie's wrist—the one holding the letter. "There's the problem. You heard it, but you didn't see it."

"That's because you were hiding behind a shelf. Did you really think that would give you enough privacy?"

"We weren't hiding. There was nothing to hide."

"Really? Do I look stupid to you?"

Kip pulled Annie closer. A smile slowly grew on his face as he looked at her through hooded eyelids. "Stupid is not the word I'd use." His eyes trailed down the length of her body.

Annie followed the path of his gaze to her clothes. She was wearing an old cami, which gave a generous view of her cleavage, a pair of faded shorts that were too short, and a yellowed pair of athletic socks that should have been thrown out long ago.

"Oh, please." She reached out and tilted his chin up. "Eyes up here, Porter."

"Easier said than done." He smiled brightly, his eyes penetrating hers.

"Seriously? Oh, my God, that's your problem." Annie pulled away and walked back into the kitchen with Kip trailing close behind. She turned abruptly to find him at her heels.

"I don't have a problem," Kip said, towering above her with his arms crossed.

"Get real. What you did was disgusting, not to mention just plain… dangerous. What if someone had walked in—other than me?"

Kip brought his face down to hers and said through gritted teeth, "Nothing happened. If you had stuck around, you would have heard me re-buckling my belt and getting out of there."

"Only because you were caught."

"Damn it, Annie, I didn't do anything! I didn't encourage her, I didn't lead her into a closet, and I certainly didn't let her give me a blowjob," he said.

Annie couldn't help feeling satisfied that Mr. Calm-Cool-and-Collected was finally starting to crack under the pressure. "You expect me to believe that?"

"What's with you?"

Annie picked up her wine glass and drained the golden liquid. "How am I supposed to work for someone who has no regard for propriety? Someone who will do anything—I mean anything—to get ahead?"

Kip stepped closer, his face red and his breathing shallow. "For the last time, you've got this all wrong. You've got me all wrong."

Annie looked up at Kip hovering above her. Their eyes locked, and again she was keenly aware of her racing pulse. "I...don't know what to believe," she whispered.

"Say you'll stick around." The resignation letter slipped easily out of her hand and Kip quickly tore it into pieces. "And I'll prove to you I'm not that guy."

With their eyes locked a moment longer, Annie found herself speechless, swimming in the pools of his crystal blue eyes. Kip must have taken her silence for defiance and stepped back, shaking his head. He punched his thigh with his fist and stalked out of the apartment, letting the door slam behind him.

TEN

Monday morning, as Annie sat in traffic along Constitution Avenue, she couldn't seem to calm the jitters coursing through her limbs. After Kip's hasty departure—and for the rest of the weekend—she had rewound and replayed their argument several times, wrestling with the possibility that maybe she had misinterpreted what she'd heard in the supply room. While sitting at a traffic light, she gripped and ungripped the steering wheel, considering that maybe it was just as he had said: he hadn't encouraged that woman to unbuckle his belt. An annoying pop song came on the radio and Annie punched at the buttons, up and down the dial, finally giving up and slapping the power button off. The traffic light turned green and Annie laid on her horn. "Move it," she mumbled, charging around the car ahead of her and nearly colliding with another car in the left lane. Once she parked, she sat for a moment and realized maybe the best thing to do was apologize. The thought of job hunting all over again made her crazy and she really couldn't afford to lose this one. She would take the high road and say she was sorry for her part in the confrontation. Annie climbed out of the car, threw back her shoulders, and marched up the street toward the capitol building.

When she walked into the congressional office, several staff members were huddled in twos and threes. Tom had his hip propped on the receptionist's desk, talking on his cell phone, and Kip was nowhere in sight. She let out a long, slow sigh, greeted his assistant, and began going over his schedule for the week.

At exactly eight fifty-nine, everyone meandered into the conference room and Annie sat in a chair as far from Kip's usual seat as possible. She placed her leather bag on the floor and as she bent over to retrieve her laptop, she heard two young interns talking to her left.

"Seriously, dude, that old lady was all over me. I had to peel her off."

"No way."

"Yep and I saw her sister grab Blake's ass." The pair began laughing. When they resumed talking, they were so quiet Annie couldn't hear the rest of the story.

After lifting the screen, she flicked her hair over her shoulder and began tapping the keys when she heard murmurings of "good morning" and "how's everyone doing." She looked toward the head of the table and found Kip looking at her, a serious, unreadable expression on his face. Annie felt her cheeks grow warm and refocused her concentration on her laptop screen.

"Okay, guys, let's get started. I've got a meeting in forty-five minutes." Kip unbuttoned his jacket and sat in the leather chair, clearing his throat as he rolled closer to the table. "I want to begin by thanking Annie for organizing such a great grand opening on Saturday."

The room erupted with enthusiastic clapping and Annie nervously glanced around at the room full of smiling faces. Finally, her eyes settled on Kip, who seemed to be beaming. "It was a big success. Lots of interesting people stopped by—"

A burst of laughter came from Annie's left. One of the interns said, "You can say that again."

"Did I miss something?" Tom asked.

"Sorry, Tom, we're just laughing about those older ladies from Baltimore. They were out of control. They even invited Blake and me to a party at their house."

Those who had attended the opening started talking among themselves, comparing stories of the now-infamous sisters. Annie wanted to crawl under the table, she was so embarrassed. She had misread what had happened in the closet, she was sure of it. She apprehensively looked at

Kip, who gave her a shrug and that wry smile. Feeling somewhat forgiven, she felt sure she'd be vindicated when she gave her campaign report.

"Kip, I've arranged for several campaign appearances for you next week and have already cleared the dates with your secretary."

"I'm sure Kip will be too busy next week. Let's put those off for a while." Tom reached across the table and patronizingly patted her hand. "You just man the phones at campaign headquarters. That would be best."

"But, there are some important meetings and events he should attend if he wants to increase his edge in the polls."

"His *edge* is just fine. Let's move on." Tom silenced her with his scowl as he nodded to Kip to continue the meeting. Wasn't she hired to run his campaign? If so, why wasn't Tom letting her do her job? As soon as the meeting ended, she would talk to Kip alone.

After the meeting was over, everyone rushed from the room to begin the week's work, while Annie took her time placing her laptop back in its tote. She stood up, straightened her blouse, then walked into the outer office where she found Kip and Tom in discussion. She kept her distance until they'd finished their conversation, but couldn't help overhearing.

"Bro, you've got to get moving on this."

"I'm on it. You just do what you need to do." Kip's face was red. Was it anger Annie saw in his usually composed features?

"Hey, it's not my name on the bill."

"I hear ya, but—" Kip stopped suddenly, turning his gaze on Annie.

Tom looked at Annie and then again at Kip. "Well, okay then," he said, "I guess I better get to work. Are we still on for lunch?"

"Sure thing." Kip patted Tom on the back before walking over to Annie, who was almost compulsively readjusting the strap on her messenger bag.

"I didn't mean to interrupt."

"You didn't. We were finished."

Annie shifted her weight from one foot to the other, glanced over her shoulder, then focused on Kip's tie. "Um…I owe you an apology."

Kip shrugged. "That's okay."

With a tilt of her head, Annie walked toward Kip's office, signaling him to follow. Once inside, she continued: "I was way off base and should have taken you at your word. I'm really sorry."

"It's okay. I probably would have jumped to the same conclusion if I were you." He took a step closer and Annie drew in a breath. Her attraction to him was undeniable—but inappropriate. They needed to maintain a professional relationship.

"I wanted to talk with you about some of these appearances. It's important you're seen in your district, attend various functions. You don't want to slip in the polls."

"It's still early. No worries."

"But, Kip." She stopped when Kip sat behind his desk and focused his attention on his computer screen. Gathering her messenger bag in her arms, Annie turned toward the door. "Well, I guess I better get over to campaign headquarters. I've got some press releases to get out."

"I guess this means you're not quitting?" He drew his eyes away from the screen and paralyzed her with his gaze.

"Um...no, I'll stay on."

"Any chance we can get that cup of coffee sometime?"

Anne squeezed her eyes shut, took a deep breath, then matched his gaze. "Yes, maybe, sometime."

Before Kip could say another word, she rushed out of his office.

ELEVEN

"We're in for a steamy day, folks, with temperatures reaching into the mid-to upper nineties in the District and only a few degrees cooler along the bay. Winds will be out of the south at ten to twenty miles an hour with a risk of scattered thunderstorms this afternoon." The local meteorologist was rattling off the morning's weather report for the fifth time in an hour—an hour in which Annie had changed her outfit three times and was considering a fourth. She stood in front of the full length mirror attached to her bedroom door and sighed heavily as she tugged at the hem of her pale blue skirt.

"Too short," she mumbled, yanking down the side zipper and stepping out of the garment. It dropped in a heap on the floor.

She ransacked her closet again, pulling out a floral sundress and holding it in her right hand as she stared absently at a navy blue shift in the other.

"What do you wear to a chicken farm?" she asked the empty room.

She shoved both dresses back in the closet and retrieved a red sleeveless dress from her bed, where it lay buried under a pile of discarded clothes, and pulled it over her head. Turning left and right, she inspected her reflection before slipping on a pair of wedge sandals. A diamond pendant, tennis bracelet, and gold hoops completed the ensemble. Still, Annie wasn't sure if she was over-dressed or under-dressed or not dressed right at all. With a final glance in the mirror, she snatched a white sweater off her bed, picked up her leather bag, and walked out the door. Her cell phone alerted her to a text message as soon as she stepped into the hallway, its shrill ding echoing off the walls.

Ready to visit the crazy cat lady?

She pressed the elevator button, her mouth curling into an amused grin, and tapped out a quick response to Kip.

Yep. Did u take ur Benadryl?

As she stepped through the double doors, she received his reply.

Wouldn't leave home without it.

It had been four days since she'd seen Kip at the staff meeting and she was looking forward to this field trip. His district included three counties and dozens of small towns, but the only area she had become familiar with was Shady Beach. She looked forward to seeing the rest of the area he represented and teaching him a lesson about the importance of following up with constituents. As she dropped her cell phone into her messenger bag, it dinged once more.

Want a ride?

Annie stopped in the lobby of her apartment building and stared at the screen while twisting a lock of hair around her finger, letting it go, and twisting it again. The plan had been to meet at the campaign office, and then ride to Martha Mahan's together—only a ten-minute drive. If she accepted his offer, they would be riding together—alone—for over an hour. She tapped out a response to his text.

Already in the car. Meet you at headquarters.

Kip's black Lexus pulled to the curb and she knew she was busted. The passenger side window rolled down to reveal a smiling Kip inside who asked, "Having car trouble?"

The ride out of DC across the Bay Bridge had been pleasant, if somewhat awkward, with Annie and Kip sticking strictly to office topics—exactly the professional relationship she'd asked for. Neither one strayed from safe subjects, keeping the mood all business. It wasn't until they came to the peaceful countryside that Kip became playful, making quips about the simple life outside the city.

"Now look, Coach, we're about to go through the big metropolis of Normansville. Don't blink or you'll miss it." They stopped at an intersection with a tackle store on one corner, a convenience store on another, and two-story farmhouses completing the junction.

"Bet you can't guess who founded this little hamlet," Kip said.

Annie rolled her eyes. "Ummm...would it be someone named Norman?"

"Ding, ding, ding. We have a winner." Even if they both laughed a little too hard at the joke, the result was that any pretense or uneasiness evaporated.

Martha Mahan lived along a narrow road a quarter mile from her nearest neighbor, surrounded by fields of tall green cornstalks on three sides of her single-story home. Kip pulled his Lexus into the gravel driveway and Annie snorted a laugh when she saw several cat-themed yard ornaments gracing Ms. Mahan's impeccably manicured lawn.

Kip arched his brow and looked at Annie with a wide-eyed gaze.

"Let's hope these concrete cats are the only ones she has," Annie said.

"I don't have a good feeling about this." Kip tapped Annie's hand and said, "Stay right there."

He walked around the front of the car and opened Annie's door, extending his hand. "You're two for two, Porter."

"Huh?"

"Twice we've ridden together and twice you've opened my door."

Kip leaned his elbow on the edge of the door while maintaining his grip on Annie's delicate hand. "Is that a problem?"

"No problem." Annie stifled a grin and then quietly thanked him, gently pulling her hand from his. Was he truly a gentleman or just trying to butter her up?

They walked up the short cement sidewalk and had just taken a step onto the stoop when the front door flew open and several cats in varying colors came charging out, singing a chorus of meows. A thin, slightly hunched woman with frizzy, shoulder-length gray hair stepped outside, followed by two more cats slinking close to her bright blue running shoes.

She was wearing a pink snap-front seersucker house dress and two plastic beaded necklaces—one red and one yellow.

"Well, I never thought I'd see the day. It's about time you got here." She put her hands on her narrow hips and smacked her lips into a pucker, looking Kip over from head to toe. "You look exactly like your pictures. That doesn't always happen. I was figuring you'd be an older man—you know, one who puts that Just for Men in his hair to fool people about his age. Urmph."

Kip shook his head as if to clear his befuddled mind, and extended his hand to the weathered old lady. "Ms. Mahan...it's a pleasure to meet you. This is my campaign manager, Annie Merriman."

After Martha let go of the vise-like grip she had on Kip's hand, she reached out and took Annie's hand more gently. But with surprising strength, she pulled Annie close to her; she studied every inch of Annie's face before dropping her hand like she had been burned.

"Pretty," she said, and then turned back to Kip.

"Well now...down to business. You smell that?" Martha extended her arm and waved it over her head.

"Uh, no ma'am, I don't smell anything," Kip said.

"Oh, come now, surely you smell that horrendous odor. Follow me." The old lady marched down the steps and treaded across her lawn, her gaggle of cats never far behind.

Annie and Kip followed her around the corner of the house to a side yard where a garden swing sat under a spreading oak tree and a plot of colorful annuals lined the foundation.

"What a lovely yard you have, Ms. Mahan," Annie said, looking around at the perfectly groomed garden.

"I wish I could enjoy it, but I can't take the smell most days."

Kip, Annie, and Martha stood in the side yard, their faces kissed by the soft breeze blowing across the cornfield. Annie was mesmerized by the quiet clattering of cornstalks swaying in the wind and the warmth of the bright, cloudless sky.

Martha walked a few feet closer to the field and then turned back to face Annie and Kip, her hands on her hips once more. "Looks like you came on the wrong day. The wind is coming from the south and Len Heldreth's farm is north of here. I don't know what that old man is doing over there, but it smells like raw sewage."

Kip stepped toward the old woman. "Ma'am, you mentioned on the phone that this Mr. Heldreth has a chicken farm? Is that all he raises?"

"Chickens…that's all anyone raises around here, young man. He sells them to Pardo Chicken down the shore. I quit buying that brand since that smell started. I don't want to go to the emergency room to find out I'm dying from one of his salmonella-infested birds."

"Yes, ma'am. Well, Ms. Merriman and I have an appointment with an inspector from the USDA this afternoon." Kip pulled up his jacket sleeve and glanced at his watch. A long-haired gray tabby wrapped itself around Kip's ankles and he took a step back. "We're uh…" The cat wouldn't be deterred and wrapped himself around Kip's other ankle, purring loudly. "We're going to pay a visit to Mr. Heldreth and try to get to the bottom of this."

"Toby likes ya." Martha's toothless grin spread across her face as she nodded toward the fluffy cat massaging Kip's ankles. "He's usually a standoffish one. That's a good sign."

"A good sign?" Kip inquired, doing his best to shake the furry feline from his legs.

"When a cat rubs on you as much as Toby is, it means luck is coming your way." She clapped her hands as if in applause and all the cats ran to her obediently.

"Well, um…" Kip's eyes began to water and he sniffled twice before letting out a loud sneeze. "Okay, then. We've got to get going to that meeting. I'll be in touch."

"Now, hold on there. Let me just warn ya. Len will probably say I'm just trying to stir up trouble because he broke my heart. But mind what I'm saying, it was the other way around. He's probably stinking the place up in hopes I'll go marching over there. But I won't do it. That man is crazy."

"Thanks for the warning, Ms. Mahan." Kip quickly shook Martha's hand and attempted to escape, but the old lady held firm.

"One more thing while I've got ya here. I don't like the idea of the pipeline coming through. And neither does anyone else around here."

"Oh?" Kip straightened his spine and took a step back. "I'm surprised to hear that."

"Urmph…I don't know why. That pipeline would be bad for the environment. Too risky. We don't need that thing leaking oil and killing our fish."

Kip cleared his throat and shot a confused look at Annie before turning back to Martha.

"Well, I will certainly look into your concerns, Ms. Mahan. Thank you for bringing them to my attention."

He turned and placed his left hand at the small of Annie's back, propelling her toward the car. Once inside, he turned the key and let loose three more sneezes in rapid succession. Annie rooted around in her purse, unearthing a wad of tissues. After blowing into the bundle, he leaned his head back against the seat and took a deep breath.

"I think we got out of there just in time before she came up with something else to complain about." His words were muffled by congestion.

"I thought you took Benadryl?"

"I did." He swiped at his nose once more and tossed the tissues behind him into the back seat.

"You weren't exaggerating, were you? You really are allergic."

"Unfortunately." Kip turned in his seat and draped his arm across the back of hers. "Can I say I told you so now?"

"Told me so?"

"Yes, I told you she was a crazy cat lady. She even thinks this farmer has a thing for her. I bet when we go over there, Len Heldreth will have a perfectly clean operation and he won't even know Martha Mahan's name."

Annie shrugged and rolled her eyes. "How about you save the I told you so until after we visit him?"

Kip's mouth twisted into a wry grin as he backed his car out of the gravel drive.

The same two-lane road that ran past Martha Mahan's led to Len Heldreth's farm, two-and-a-half miles northwest. The path wound past more cornfields with their enormous spider-like irrigation systems watering the loose, sandy soil. The land was flat, not a hill in sight, creating long vistas of adjoining corn and soybean fields. They passed several elongated steel buildings with screened windows and large fans at each end, lined up side-by-side. Kip pointed out they were chicken farms that dotted this part of the state.

Kip rolled his car to a stop beside a beat-up metal mailbox sitting at the end of a long gravel driveway, the number four-ninety-nine hand-painted on the side.

"This is it. Smell anything yet?" Kip winked at Annie as he turned into the driveway.

They followed the narrow lane into a wide, flat yard where a rusty tractor and a car up on cinder blocks sat in front of the old two-story house, which badly needed a coat of paint. The front porch was leaning to one side, causing the roof to tip forward, and weeds grew knee-high along the foundation. In the center of the yard was a tall dead tree. Annie and Kip stared at the scene through the windshield, their mouths hanging open in shock.

"Do you think Mrs. Bates is inside?" Annie whispered. She was rewarded with a low chuckle from Kip.

Kip turned off the car and climbed out hesitantly. In the passenger side mirror, Annie watched him move around the back of the car, stop to stifle a gag, and continue around to open her door, his face set as if fending off some kind of pain. When he opened her door, Annie was laughing at him. He reached for her hand and said, "Breath through your mouth if you know what's good for you."

His warning only made her laugh more, and as she sucked in a big breath, she felt her stomach flop and her gag reflex kick into gear.

"My God, what is that?" Annie bent over, her tongue coming out of her mouth, sure she was going to lose her breakfast.

Kip covered his mouth and laughed at Annie trying not to throw up. "Hey, don't say I didn't warn you."

The sour, sickly smell seemed to invade her entire body and she began looking around for its source as she placed her hand over her lower face.

"What is that?" Kip squeezed his nose between his fingers.

"It smells familiar, but I can't figure it out. It smells like—"

"Shit."

Annie followed the direction of Kip's stare and saw a small stream of thick, black sludge winding its way through the heavy grass.

"Oh, my God, what is that? Why, is that?" Annie took a few steps closer to the greasy creek and then cringed when she got a strong whiff of the putrid mess.

"I'm no expert, but I think Mr. Heldreth has a serious sewage problem. Come on." Kip wrapped his hand around Annie's elbow and led her toward the house, where an old, shriveled man stepped onto the porch.

"What can I do for ya?" His raspy voice boomed in the quiet as he adjusted the suspenders on his dirty tan work pants.

Kip released his grip on Annie's arm, but kept a hand pressed against his nose as he trampled through the thick weeds, extending his right hand toward the old farmer.

"Hello, Mr. Heldreth, I'm Congressman Kip Porter."

Rather than shake Kip's hand, the old man gave a quick wave and slid his hands deep in his pockets. "Out drumming up support, huh?"

"Not actually..." Kip cleared his throat. "My assistant and I are following up on a complaint we've had about the smell coming from your—"

"Has Martha Mahan been harassing you, too?"

Kip looked over his shoulder at Annie and tilted his head, signaling with his eyes that he had told her so. He turned back around and continued his conversation.

"What do you mean, Mr. Heldreth?"

"That old bat has been calling the county sheriff, the extension agent, the health department, and now you. Hell, I wouldn't be surprised if she's called the president." Len lumbered down his porch steps and walked behind his house, where six elongated, wooden chicken houses stood in a semi circle. Just like the man's home, the chicken houses were in desperate need of paint and were leaning in the same direction as the porch. Annie focused on one building whose screens were torn, an occasional feather floating from inside onto the afternoon breeze.

"She's been a thorn in my side since 1962," he grumbled, as he walked toward the closest barn. He opened a solid wood door to an inner screened door, beyond which thousands of white-feathered chickens could be seen pecking along the dirt floor. He waved his hand toward the mass of clucking. "Go on. See for yourself. I raise a fine crop of chickens and have never failed an inspection."

Kip and Annie walked up to the screened door and looked in at the noisy white birds milling about. There was an odor coming from inside, but nothing offensive. It had to have been the open sewage that Martha Mahan had been complaining about.

Annie looked over her shoulder when she heard the crunching of tires on the gravel drive and saw a black SUV with government plates pull into the yard. She nudged Kip and whispered, "USDA is here."

There was nothing wrong with the old man's hearing because he barked, "Good. Let 'em come. I've got nothing to hide."

For an old man, Mr. Heldreth marched at a surprisingly quick clip toward the federal inspector, leaving Annie and Kip outside the chicken barn. Annie looked up at Kip and shrugged.

"Let's take a look around," he said.

They walked along the weathered chicken house, more than the length of a football field, occasionally stopping to look inside the screened windows at the sea of poultry. Annie stopped and cupped her hands around her face to block out the sun as she looked more closely through the window.

"How many chickens do you suppose are in there?"

"No clue. We'll have to ask him," Kip replied, standing close to Annie at the window.

"I've got over fifteen thousand chickens in each house." Mr. Heldreth's booming voice startled Annie and Kip and they jumped back from the screen. Kip's foot landed with a squishing sound. He lifted it to find the sole of his shoe covered with a mushy, yellow-gray substance. He shot an angry look at Annie, who was hiding a laugh behind the back of her hand.

The farmer continued walking toward Annie and Kip, looking down at Kip's raised foot. "Well, now, looks like you stepped in it." He chuckled and turned to the inspector, who was following close behind while tapping something onto an iPad.

"Mr. Heldreth," the inspector said, looking up from his tablet. "Everything seems to be fine with your operation, but you need to address the sewage issue."

The farmer scratched his head and looked toward the front of his house where the river of sewage lay. "I've been trying to get that fixed for a couple of years, but to be honest with you, I don't have the money. According to a plumber I had out here a few years ago, it's going to cost me about ten thousand dollars to get a new system installed. I just don't have the money for it."

"Let Congressman Porter talk to the folks at the county level and see if there isn't a grant or low-interest loan you could apply for. I'm sure there's something that can be done." Annie looked to Kip for validation, but only received a stern glare instead.

Len shook the inspector's hand and began walking him toward his vehicle, barking over his shoulder to Kip, "There's a hose round back."

Kip pursed his lips together and exhaled through his nose like a raging bull. He stalked to the spigot, where a faded garden hose snaked across the ground. Annie tiptoed behind him, careful not to step on any other gooey substances, silently hiding her laughter and keeping her head tipped down.

Kip snatched the hose from the ground. "Maybe you should have asked me before you volunteered my services. If you haven't noticed, I'm rather busy these days." He turned the rusty faucet handle as a wayward stream of water hit him square in the eye. Several misty jets sprang from cracks in the old hose, dampening his clothing and hair.

Annie couldn't hold back any longer and burst out laughing.

"Don't you see? If you make a few calls and get his problems solved…" Annie continued to laugh between words. "You'll be a local hero. We can get a lot of free press coverage and a much needed campaign boost." She leaned over to turn off the water, but before she could reach the handle, Kip wrapped an arm around her waist and pulled her against him.

"Do you see something funny?" Kip held her back tight against him, the hose close to her face. Cool mist coated her skin. The flow of water at the end of the hose gurgled over, creating a puddle at her feet.

Annie continued laughing, closing her eyes and turning her head side to side to avoid a direct hit from the water. She reached out and wrapped her hands around the hose in an effort to aim it at Kip's face. A tug of war began, each trying to gain control. At one point, Annie won the battle, jerking the hose from Kip's hands and turning to face him with her arm outstretched as if the hose had become a saber.

"Stay back, Porter, or you'll get it." She waved the hose like a fencer ready to do battle.

"Put it down." With his hands up in surrender, Kip inched toward Annie. "Don't do anything you'll regret."

"I rarely have regrets," she replied, retreating with baby steps. Kip lunged toward her and she pressed her thumb over the flow, letting a heavy spray soak the full length of his sleeve.

"Now you've done it," Kip said, joining Annie in raucous laughter while snatching the hose from her hand. He pulled her against him and sprayed a stream of water down the back of her dress, the shocking cold causing her to press tight against him.

"Say uncle," he laughed while holding the hose near her head.

"You wouldn't dare," she said, grabbing toward the hose only to catch a handful of air.

"Try me." Kip brought the hose closer to her head, the water streaming down his already-soaked arm.

Annie shrieked in between attempts to reach the hose, "Okay...I give...uncle...Just don't spray my hair."

Kip dropped the hose to his side, letting the water flow away from them while keeping Annie firmly planted against his chest. Their laughter faded and their eyes locked, and Kip dropped the hose on the ground, sliding his now free hand into the thick curls at the base of Annie's neck.

"Fine. I'll do it your way and make some calls."

He pulled her tighter against him at the waist. Slowly, he bent down, his eyes locked on Annie's parted lips, and brushed his mouth against hers.

"Well, I see you found the hose." They jumped apart at the sound of farmer Heldreth's booming voice.

Annie stepped back, her eyes locked on Kip's as she registered the disappointment on his face. He bent over, picked up the hose, and finished cleaning the chicken waste from his shoe. Annie turned and made her way to the car, swiping excess water from the back of her dress while a silly grin spread across her face.

TWELVE

When they'd reached the end of the drive, Kip put his car in park and turned toward Annie, a mischievous grin on his face. "I don't know about you, but I'm in the mood for chicken."

Annie burst out laughing, bending her left knee onto the seat and turning to look at Kip. "Are you serious? You have an appetite after that?"

He inched closer to her. "Sure. Don't you?"

"Uh…not exactly."

"Well, I'm starved. How about we pick up subs and have a picnic down by the water?"

Annie put both feet back on the floor and looked out the passenger side window, seeming captivated by the swaying stalks of corn.

"Coach?" Kip lightly tapped her shoulder, bringing her out of her reflections.

Annie looked at Kip with a hesitant smile and said, "Sure. We can have a quick lunch and then I better get back to headquarters." Crossing her arms, she turned her attention to the scene outside her window as Kip put the car in drive.

Twenty minutes later, they were cruising down another country road, Keith Urban on the radio singing about a long hot summer, the spicy smell of Italian subs filling the car's interior. The air conditioning blasted through the vents and made Annie's long curls billow around her shoulders.

Neither one had said much since leaving the farm and Kip was growing uncomfortable with the silence.

"This park we're going to is nice. Picnic tables under tall pines right along the sand."

Annie responded with a brief smile and continued her musings out the window.

"You like Italian subs, right?" He still got no response. "At least I didn't make you get chicken."

Once more Annie tossed him a quick smile without a word.

Kip drummed his fingers on the steering wheel and released a loud sigh. "Come on, Coach, what did I do this time?"

"You didn't do anything," she said.

"So why the silent treatment?"

Annie looked down at her lap where her fingers were twisting in knots, and slowly replied just above a whisper, "We shouldn't have come out here."

"Why?"

"You were right. Martha Mahan is a bit crazy and this was a waste of your time. Someone in your office could have called the health department and taken care of everything."

"She might have been crazy, but she was right about the smell. It was a good decision to come out here."

"I'm sure you have much more important things to do than tramp around in chicken shit."

"Something I'll never forget." Kip shook his head and leaned his right elbow on the console, briefly taking his eyes off the road. "It wasn't a waste of time."

"Are you sure?" Annie asked.

"Positive. I thought it was a great way to spend the day," he replied. His soft expression seemed to caress Annie where she sat.

"Since you're so busy, I'll be glad to call the local authorities to help Mr. Heldreth."

"I'd appreciate that."

Annie slowly pulled away from his gaze, looking out the windshield, then suddenly gripped the dashboard. "A deer," she shouted.

Standing in the middle of the road was a tall buck defiantly staring them down. Kip pressed his foot to the brake with all his might and swerved to the right to avoid hitting the impressive animal. His front left bumper clipped the deer and it charged away into a soybean field as Kip careened off the road, hitting an underground culvert. The vehicle bounced back onto the shoulder and Kip was eventually able to bring the car to a halt along the side of the road, but not before a loud blast sounded from underneath the car. When they were finally still, the passenger's side was leaning at a definite tilt.

"Are you okay?" he asked, brushing his finger along Annie's cheek.

With confusion etched across her face, Annie nodded her head and climbed out of the car. Kip joined her at the front of the Lexus and they stared slack-jawed at the blown tire and crumpled bumper.

"Damn…a flat tire." Kip stared at the shredded tire while scratching his head.

"You better hope that's all it is. Come on, let's get the jack." Annie marched toward the trunk of the car, leaving Kip standing in place, still scratching his head.

"What? We're not going to change this. I'll call a tow truck."

Coming to a sudden stop, Annie turned and with a tilt of her head said, "A tow truck? Wouldn't it be easier to just change the tire?"

"Not really."

"Have you ever changed a tire?" Annie squinted her eyes at Kip with a smirk.

"What…like you have?"

"Oh, my God, are you serious?" Annie walked to the back of the car and signaled for Kip to pop the trunk. "Didn't they teach you that in Boy Scouts?"

Kip reached into the back of the trunk and lifted the carpet to find the spare tire, jack, and tire iron underneath.

"No, I didn't learn auto mechanics in Boy Scouts," he said flatly.

Annie threw back her head. "Hah, well then, it's time you learned." His dad had tried several times to teach him to change a tire, but Kip refused. He had higher hopes for himself and figured he'd save such menial tasks for others to do.

She bent over and turned the wing nut holding the spare in place while barking orders at Kip to take out the jack and tire iron. "Here." She shoved the donut into his arms and led him toward the front of the car. In short order she showed him how to place the jack under the car and turn the crank to lift it high enough to remove the tire. Once the blown tire was off and lying in the grass, Annie tucked her skirt under her and dropped beside the car.

"What the hell are you doing?" Kip reached for her as she reclined onto her back and slid under the car.

"I'm checking the tie rod and ball joints."

Kip tugged on her ankles, trying to pull her out from under the car. She kicked at his hands, freeing her ankles from his grip.

"Stop, Porter," she shouted. "Ah ha! Just what I was afraid of. The jam nut on your tie rod is hanging." She scooted from under the car and sat up, brushing off the palms of her hands. "You do need to be towed. You're not driving this car."

Kip tucked his hands under her arms and lifted her to her feet. "This is a joke, right?" He glared down at her. "You're just messing with me."

Emphatically, Annie shook her head. "No joke. You can't drive this car."

"How do you know?"

Annie brushed the grit from the back of her skirt and then lifted her hair off her sweaty neck, holding it in a pile atop her head. "I used to date an auto mechanic in high school. On Saturdays, I'd go over to his house and watch him work on his car."

"Really? An auto mechanic."

"I did." She held up two fingers. "Scouts honor. Call a tow truck. You'll see I'm right."

As her hair cascaded to the center of her back, she sashayed to the back of the car and lifted the trunk's carpet, dragging it several feet into the grassy field along the side of the road. Kip watched with his hands on his hips and a crease between his brows as Annie walked back to the car and retrieved the deli bag from the back seat. Little Miss Know-It-All had just schooled him on auto repair. He wondered what other talents she had.

"Might as well eat since we're going to be here a while." She plopped her rear-end on the carpet, extended her slim legs in the grass, and patted the small square of carpet beside her. She unbuckled her sandals, tossing them aside, and arched a brow at Kip. "You're the one who wanted to have a picnic," she said, waving a butcher paper-wrapped sub in the air.

Annie felt the sting and quickly slapped the mosquito nibbling on her calf. They'd been sitting in the grassy field for over an hour waiting for the tow truck to arrive. The subs had long ago been eaten, but they lounged on the trunk carpet sipping what was left of their fountain drinks.

"Damn, it's hot." Kip began unbuttoning his shirt and pulling the tail out of his pants. "I've got to get out of these clothes."

Purposely looking the opposite direction, Annie fought the urge to take a glimpse of a shirtless Kip, but instead looked out at the baking weeds in the field. She jerked upright when she heard his belt buckle clink.

"What are you doing?" she shrieked.

"I'm getting out of these clothes. I'm burning up." Kip tramped to the car, walking around to the driver's side back door, and leaned inside where Annie couldn't see. She strained her neck and rose up on her knees, stretching to see what he was doing. A few minutes later he returned to their makeshift picnic spot wearing gym shorts, a T-shirt, and sneakers. Annie dropped back onto the carpet and pulled up a few blades of grass as Kip dropped beside her.

"Disappointed?" he whispered in her ear.

"Huh?"

"You heard me."

"Why would I be disappointed?"

"You were hoping I was going to strip down." He wiggled his eyebrows and nudged his shoulder into hers.

"Oh, please." She went back to weeding the field, furiously yanking blades of grass and letting them flutter in the humid breeze.

"Come on, Coach. I saw the look on your face when I started unbuttoning my shirt."

"Get over yourself." She shoved back and then stood up, brushing the dust from her dress. "Should you call them again to see where the truck is?"

"What, don't you like our little picnic?"

"Porter…seriously, we need to get back." Annie glared at Kip where he lay on the carpet, resting his head in his hands.

"Relax, it will be here soon. Come lay down with me." He patted his hand on the carpet and gave her his most salacious grin.

"Not a chance."

"Come on…what are you afraid of?"

Annie stared at Kip, taking a tendril in her hand and twisting it tightly around her finger. She glanced over her shoulder at the car and then back at him, now lying on his side with his head resting on his hand. He patted the carpet once more and invited her over with a swoosh of his hand.

"Fine," she said, joining him on the carpet and mimicking his relaxed position.

"Tell me about the mechanic."

"I already told you. We dated in high school and he taught me all about cars."

"Nah…there's got to be more to the story." Annie watched Kip's soft lips curl at the corners. The memory of him leaning in to kiss her earlier in the day flashed through her mind. She sighed and flipped flat on her back.

"Not really. My father hated him…thought he wasn't a good influence. We didn't date long."

"This is the first I've heard about your dad. You've never mentioned your family actually. What do they do?"

"Oh, um…" Annie closed her eyes against the bright sun. "My dad is an attorney and my mom is a professional party giver." Not a total lie.

"Sound like interesting people. I'd like to meet them."

"Um, they're not that interesting."

"Okay." Kip threw his head back and chuckled. "That's it? What about siblings?"

"I have two older sisters and a younger brother." She rushed her answer and then sprang to her feet. "Don't you think it's strange not a single car has gone by? Should we call someone to come pick us up?"

"We're in the middle of nowhere. I wouldn't know what to tell them."

Annie crossed her arms, seeming skeptical of his answer. "Come on, Porter, you have to know where we are. You've lived here your whole life."

Kip came to his feet and spread his arms wide. "It all looks the same… everywhere…with no landmarks. I don't even think this road has a name."

"Why don't I believe you?" She furrowed her brows and stared at the humor in his eyes.

"Would I lie?" A rolling crack of thunder shook the ground, followed by a blinding flash of lightning. Kip snatched the carpet from the ground, wrapped his hand around Annie's upper arm, and said "See? There's your confirmation," as they rushed through heavy raindrops toward the car.

THIRTEEN

"Drenched again." Annie laughed while looking down at her rain-soaked dress clinging to her skin. Pea-sized raindrops pelted the windshield, making it impossible to see the lush fields beyond. Kip stretched to the back seat to retrieve a towel from his gym bag, affording Annie an extended glimpse at his firm abs peeking out below his T-shirt. Pulling her eyes away was a struggle, but she managed to do so as he handed the fluffy towel to her.

"Looks like our picnic is a washout," Kip said.

"And so are we." Annie mussed Kip's hair with the towel, laughing at the mess she made of his usually perfect coif.

"Not us."

"You're kidding, right? Look at us. We're soaked."

"That's not what I meant." Kip looked intently into Annie's eyes and she felt her jaw go slack. Things were getting too heated, too intimate between them and she had to stop the momentum. He was her boss, an elected official, and he was attempting to cross the proverbial line where scandal took place, careers ended, and hearts got broken. He seemed to sense her unease and broke his gaze, looking at himself in the rear-view mirror. He tugged on his short cropped hair so that each strand stood at attention. "You think the voters would like this look?"

Annie replied with a forced chuckle, "Definitely not," smoothing his hair back into place.

A deafening crack followed by a brilliant streak of lightning shook the car, causing Annie to shriek and cover her ears.

"That was close," Kip said, leaning his elbow on the console while raking a finger down Annie's bare arm. "You okay?"

"I hate thunderstorms."

"Well, maybe I should find a way to take your mind off it." He reached out toward Annie's shoulder and she jerked back against the passenger door.

"Listen…we need to keep this professional."

"And what if I don't want to?" His searing gaze singed Annie's skin, making her feel feverish. Somehow she'd have to get back to business and get his mind on track.

"Let's talk about the pipeline."

"Let's not."

"What did Martha say today? No one in her area supports the bill."

Kip pulled his eyes away from Annie and sighed heavily, leaning against the driver's side door. He drummed his fingers on the steering wheel while looking through the blurry windshield.

"She doesn't know what she's talking about," he said.

"Are you sure? What do the polls say?" This time it was Annie's turn to lean her elbow on the console, drilling her eyes into Kip's profile.

"I don't think there have been any polls on the subject."

"Really? I'm surprised. That's something I can handle when I get back to the office."

"It won't be necessary."

"Why?"

Kip's head snapped in Annie's direction, his brows furrowed angrily. "Because the research indicates the pipeline will be a huge boost to the economy in the area. Tom has all the reports concerning economic and environmental impacts. Trust me; it's a good thing."

"Okay, okay," Annie said, holding up her hands defensively. "Don't freak out. I just thought it would make sense to get a read on what your constituents think." She took a steadying breath. Something had been nagging her and now seemed as good a time as any to bring it up. "You know, I could be doing so much more as your campaign manager, but I get the feeling Tom doesn't want to give up control."

"He's my chief of staff."

"I know, but sometimes I get the impression he's in control of everything—you, me, the campaign."

"Oh, really?" Kip flashed her a quick glance and then looked away, running his hand through his hair. "Fine, go ahead and conduct a survey. You'll see an overwhelmingly positive response to the pipeline."

"Okay then." Annie bent over and reached into her tote bag, pulling out a handful of envelopes and papers. "How about we go over some of these invitations you've received? We're stuck here so we might as well get some work done."

Kip tipped the seat back into a slight recline, stretched out his legs, and released an audible sigh. "You're a slave driver, Coach. Let's have at it."

"Great. Okay." The first invitation Annie pulled out was an engraved invitation tucked inside a creamy envelope. "Let's see. This is an invitation to the Friends of the Bay annual dinner dance at the Chesapeake Country Club."

"I think I'm busy." Kip stared through the windshield at the rain still pummeling the landscape continuing to tap out a beat on the steering wheel.

"Okay. How about this one?" Annie pulled a photocopied page out of an envelope and read, "You are cordially invited to attend the ribbon cutting ceremony for Pets Galore on Saturday, July 14 at 2:00 in downtown Calvertshire."

"Uh…no…you know what happens when I get around anything furry."

"Okay, we're zero for two. You need to get out there—go to some of these events. How about this one? It's an invitation to the Rivermen's Club annual crab feast. It's this Saturday at the—"

"I know where it is," he barked.

Snapping her head in his direction, Annie found Kip pensively looking out the steamed up windshield, tapping his knuckles against the window.

His silence was in such contrast to his earlier jovialness, she worried she'd said something wrong.

"So, what do you think?"

It took Kip a few moments to acknowledge Annie's question, finally pulling himself away from his private reflection. "I think we go zero for three."

"Why?"

"Not interested," he replied with a deep crevice forming between his eyes. "I'm not going."

Annie dropped the stack of invitations back into her bag and swiveled to rest on her left hip, facing him square on. "Okay, spill it, Porter. What's this all about? Why don't you want to spend time with your constituents?"

"I'm just busy, that's all."

"I don't buy it. You got awfully quiet when I read the crab feast invite."

He threw himself back against the headrest and studied the ceiling, turning introspective once again. Annie couldn't pull her eyes away from the ever-changing kaleidoscope of emotions scattering his face. One moment he looked sad, the next second he looked angry, all the while withdrawing to his private thoughts.

She reached out, laying her hand on his arm and said, "Talk to me."

As if in slow motion, Kip turned his head, his eyes gravitating to her hand delicately wrapped around his wrist. He captured her hand in his and pulled it onto his lap, keeping his glacial stare locked on her.

"Just don't want to go…isn't that enough?"

"It's in your hometown. Wouldn't you know lots of people?"

"I'd know everyone."

"So?" Annie kept her eyes locked on his. Kip rotated toward her, placing his other hand on hers. "I'll make a deal with you. I'll go if you go with me…and it can't be a campaign appearance. Just regular old Kip taking Annie to a crab feast."

"I don't understand."

He tugged at their joined hands, pulling her closer to him, "If you want to make this one for three, you just have to do it my way. Will you come with me?"

Annie felt like she was floating in a sea of crystal blue, unable to swim away. Kip's intensive gaze, his firm grasp on her hand, his tender, pleading request was too much to resist. She was entering dangerous waters but couldn't stop herself from diving in.

"Yes."

A shrill ding split the quiet and Kip reached for his cell phone tucked deep in his front pocket, finding a text from Tom.

Where are you?

Car broke down…with Annie.

Perfect. Any luck?

First date confirmed.

Now we're getting somewhere.

You bet. Talk 2 u later.

As Kip dropped the cell phone in a cup holder, a pair of bright headlights shone through the windshield. A pick-up truck pulled alongside the car and Kip jumped out to talk to the driver.

"Having car trouble?" the man asked.

"Yeah, we hit a deer."

"Hey, you're Congressman Porter, aren't ya? Can I give you a ride somewhere?"

"Nah, we're waiting on a tow truck."

"Seriously, I'd be glad to drive you somewhere. You live around here?"

"Nah, I live in Washington."

"I'm heading over there in about a half hour. I just have to stop at my house before I deliver these parts to a contractor working on the capitol dome. I can take you."

Kip scratched his head looking over the bed of the truck as rain continued beating down. He offered his hand to the driver and said, "I appreciate that, but I'm sure the tow truck will be here soon. Thanks."

Kip climbed back into the car, his semi-dry clothes now wet all over again, and reached for the towel draped across the back of his seat.

"What did he say?" Annie asked.

"He said he would have been glad to give us a ride back to DC if it had been earlier in the day, but he had to get home...his wife has to leave for work." No way was he going back to DC in that guy's pick-up truck. He was finally making headway with Annie.

"Oh, no. We're having the worst luck."

"Which makes no sense because Martha Mahan was sure that cat was going to bring me luck." Kip laughed and reached for Annie's hand. She busied herself looking at the navigational system, touching the screen, then digging through the glove compartment.

"Looking for something?"

"I'm just checking out your car." She lifted some receipts and the owner's manual and then let out a tiny shriek. "Hey...you've been holding out on me."

As if she'd discovered buried treasure, Annie triumphantly held up a candy bar before ripping the package open and taking a bite. She chewed slowly, rolling her eyes until her lids dropped, and then moaned with ecstasy. "Mmm...so good. Wans sum," she slurred between chews, holding out the candy bar.

Kip noticed a puddle of melting chocolate at the edge of her mouth and he leaned toward Annie. "I'd like a taste," he whispered, keeping his eyes on the candy bar.

As Annie looked at the candy bar, pulling the wrapper down to expose more of the creamy milk chocolate, Kip inched closer and placed his lips over the corner of her mouth, kissing away the chocolate threatening to slide down her chin.

Instead of pulling away as Kip had expected, she held stock-still, momentarily halting her chewing as her eyes grew large.

"Mmm...delicious," he said, brushing his lips across hers. Kip pulled back just enough to see Annie swallow the candy bar, her eyes dropping to his mouth. She ran her tongue over her lips and he couldn't hold back another second. He slid his hand behind her head and pressed his lips to hers. She didn't resist, but it took a few seconds for a response. Hesitantly, Annie kissed him back, opening her lips to his probing tongue, and then sliding her free hand up his chest and across his shoulder. She continued to hold the melting candy bar in her other hand like a torch in the night. Without releasing his lips from hers Kip said, "Let me help you with that." He took the candy bar out of her hand, dropped it in a cup holder, and then wrapped his arm around her waist, pulling her tight against his chest. While the storm raged on outside the steamy car, their kiss became equally heated.

It was as if all the fight had gone out of Annie. She sagged against him and slid her now free hand under his arm to his back, gently grazing her nails along his spine. Her tongue dove deeper, his lips locked over hers, their breathing grew shallow, and a loud horn broke the intensity. Annie and Kip jumped back from one another and looked through the windshield at a double set of headlights bearing down on the car. The tow truck had arrived—finally.

"Couldn't he have waited a little longer?" Kip sighed. He looked over at Annie, who was fiddling with her hair and smoothing out her skirt before opening her door. He reached out and grabbed her wrist before she could get away, giving her a sweet smile. What he got in return was another one of Annie's stony stares.

Kip sat in his leather chair, elbows on his desk and head in his hands, trying to study a recent Supreme Court ruling on immigration. His mind was anywhere but on the document in front of him. Since the electric kiss less than twenty-four hours ago, he had wrestled with his original intentions and the feelings he was now having. It was supposed to have been just a matter of getting an introduction to Senator Cooper, but now all he wanted to do was kiss that soft, sexy mouth again and forget the senatorial support. He knew he was falling for Annie the moment she walked into the first staff meeting, but had convinced himself it was just his desire to clinch a vote. Now, he felt guilty about hiring her under false pretenses. She was working hard, taking her role seriously, and making a real difference. It was getting harder and harder to look her in the eye.

"Well, look who decided to come back to the real world." Tom had silently entered Kip's office and dropped into the chair in front of his desk.

"Yeah, I'm back from the land of Oz," Kip said, slamming the notebook shut.

"You were gone most of the day. How did it go?"

"Well. We were able to pinpoint the problem at the farm and work out a solution with the county."

Tom stood up abruptly and laid his hands on the desk, the better to leer down at Kip. "I'm talking about how things went with Annie. You said you have a date lined up. When?"

"Saturday we're going to a crab feast."

"With her family?"

"No, over in Shady Beach."

Tom spun away from the desk and ran his hands through his hair. "Bro, you're supposed to get an introduction to her father, get in good with him. What the hell's the problem?"

Kip leaned back in his chair and smiled up at Tom. "It's been a bigger challenge than I thought."

"Yeah, and you seem to be enjoying it."

With his fingers laced across his stomach, Kip rocked back and forth in his chair and replied with a satisfied grin, "Yeah, I have."

"Kip," Tom punched his fist into his hand and spun, coming behind the desk, "what the fuck are you doing? Time is of the essence. The bill comes up for vote in three weeks. Quit fucking around and get the introduction."

Bringing himself to his full six-two height, Kip turned to face his chief of staff. "How would you like me to go about it? 'Annie, we hired you because I need your dad's support on the pipeline bill if it's going to get through the Senate Appropriations committee.'"

"Why not? Whatever works." Tom glared right back.

"I can't do that."

"Can't because you're being a huge pussy, or because you've suddenly grown a strong moral center? She's just a means to an end—and a nice little end, I must say."

Kip let the image of another term in office take shape in his mind. "You're not wrong about that."

"Then get it done already," Tom huffed, turning toward the door. "Fuck the girl if you have to. Just get her father's vote."

FOURTEEN

Stretching like a cat, arms extended to their limits, with a flex of her feet, Annie climbed out of the deep cocoon of sleep, waking to sunlight streaming through her bedroom blinds. She sat up and snatched her cell phone from its power cord while tapping the screen in hopes of finding a missed call or text. Nothing. A small stream of disappointment coursed through her, but she quickly shook it off. She couldn't expect to hear from him every day.

Since their amazing kiss had been interrupted, she'd wavered between picking up where they had left off and keeping a safe distance from Kip. Today, she didn't have any choice; she was going to the crab feast with him and she wasn't sure how she could possibly keep her distance—or if she even wanted to. Several times since they'd been stranded along the side of the road, Kip had sent her a text or call pretending to need some important information, only to end up engaging her in brief conversations about anything but the "pressing" topic. While in a committee meeting yesterday, he had sent her quotes from the discussion and then added funny commentary, forcing her to hide her laughter behind a series of violent coughs.

Bored? She texted.

With you? Never!

I meant with the meeting.

Yes…come rescue me.

She scrolled through some of the texts she had received since Wednesday night, when they'd finally made it back to DC in the cab of the tow truck. Kip had charmed the driver into taking the Lexus to the dealership rather than the local repair shop and had thrown in an extra hundred dollars as added persuasion. Annie tucked down into the sheets, biting her bottom lip as she continued scrolling and rereading.

Just received confirmation: it was indeed the jam nut.

Was there ever a doubt?

If there was, I'll never admit it.

Any other mechanical problems you need to me to check?

Umm…I don't think I should answer that.

Annie smiled, absently chewing on her thumbnail. Everything had changed since their adventure out to Heldreth's farm and if she was honest, it scared her. After she and Kate said goodbye to their trivia team Thursday night, they stuck around for one more beer and Annie couldn't stop her perpetual grin each time she received a text.

"What is going on? Why do you look like you just swallowed a canary?" Kate asked, grabbing Annie's phone from her hand. "Who have you been texting all night?" With a couple of taps to the screen, Kate sagged against the booth and sighed. "Oh…so your lack of concentration tonight was because of a certain congressman, huh?"

Annie swiped her cell phone out of Kate's hand and dropped it on the table as if she'd been shocked. When the phone dinged once more, Annie splayed her hands on the table, fighting the urge to read Kip's latest text.

"Aren't you going to see what he said?"

"Kate, this is crazy…what am I doing? He's my boss."

"Well, if you're not going to read it, I am." Kate picked up the phone and read out loud, "'Wear something simple; we might get messy.'" She leaned forward, eyes bulging and said, "Messy? I've got to hear this."

Annie laughed and took the phone from Kate, glancing down at the text. "We're going to a crab feast tomorrow. Get your mind out of the gutter."

"That sounds tame. Why are you worried?"

"It's not an official appearance. It's a date. I shouldn't be going on a date with my boss."

"Why not? He's single; you're single. There's nothing wrong with that. Where in the HR manual does it say you can't go to a crab feast with your boss?"

"There is no HR manual," Annie mumbled, continuing to glance at her phone.

"Exactly."

"A politician is the last person I should get involved with. Look at my mother's miserable life."

"Don't you think you're jumping the gun? It's just a date."

Maybe Kate was right. It was just a date—didn't mean anything. Besides, it had been awhile since she had such ardent male attention. Not wanting to end the string of texts, Annie picked up her phone and typed what do you mean by simple?

Within seconds her phone dinged with Kip's reply. That thing you were wearing when I came to your apartment would work, minus the socks.

She remembered the way he had looked at her that day, shamelessly raking his eyes over her exposed cleavage and legs, and she couldn't stop her lips from curling into a grin.

I'm not sure that would be a wise choice.

Why?

You might not be able to concentrate on breaking open those crabs.

I could do it with my eyes closed.

I'll bet you could.

Ms. Merriman, I'm not sure we're talking about picking crabs anymore.

When Annie saw "Ms. Merriman," she felt a crushing weight of guilt press on her chest. She had to tell him the truth about who she was. She couldn't keep up the ruse much longer. Surely he would understand the reason she'd lied. As soon as the time felt right, she would tell the truth. For now, she'd end the texting before it went too far.

That's exactly what I was referring to.

Darn it.

Hey, gotta go. TTYL.

On Friday he had sent her several texts, but as of this morning she hadn't heard a word. The crab feast started at five o'clock and they had agreed to meet at the club, since Kip was spending the weekend at his cabin. Annie threw her legs over the side of the bed and leaped to the floor. She needed to do laundry if she was going to find something perfectly "simple" to wear that evening.

The smell of salty, spicy crabs in make-shift steamers fashioned from fifty-gallon drums and the sweetness of barbecuing chicken filled the air as Annie and Kip walked across the gravel lot toward a long pavilion adorned with the Rivermen's Club crest hanging below the roof's eaves. They were hand-in-hand, approaching dozens of men and women talking in groups while seagulls squawked amid strains of country music coming from mounted speakers. They had pulled into the parking lot at the same time and Kip greeted Annie with a brief kiss before taking her hand in his, leading her toward the party.

"I think we're the youngest ones here," he said in Annie's ear.

"No, you're wrong." She pointed toward a colorful metal structure with winding tube slides and two sets of swings where at least a dozen kids ran and played. "Maybe you'd be more comfortable over there."

Kip stopped and let out a low whistle. "Look at that. That's an improvement over the playground that used to be here."

"So you've been here before?" Annie's forehead creased in confusion.

"Every year until my dad passed away." He ended the conversation with a tug of her hand and began introducing her to friends and relatives he'd grown up around. There was a lot of back slapping from the men who had been longtime friends of his father's and hugs from their wives. While Annie chatted with two women who had known his family long before "Kip and his brothers had even been thought of," Kip filled two red plastic cups from the cold keg resting in a tub of ice.

"We were just about to tell Annie some stories about when you were a boy, Kip," one of the gray-haired ladies said with mischief in her eyes.

"Like the time you broke Virgil's prop, running his boat aground."
The ladies laughed and Kip's face cycled through several shades of red as
he wrapped an arm around Annie, steering her away.

"I don't need my sterling reputation ruined on my first date."

The women continued cackling as Annie protested his leading her
away. "Wait now, maybe I want to hear that story."

"Trust me; you don't," he mumbled against her temple, then smiled
warmly at the women. He gave them a wave and said, "Nice talking to you."

"Oh, come on, Porter, don't be such a spoil sport." Annie laughed,
noticing his obvious discomfort. "This must be some story to get a reaction
like that."

Kip squeezed her close, planted a kiss in her hair, and said, "Not one
of my finer moments."

An hour after they had made their rounds and Kip had introduced Annie
to nearly everyone there, a blue pick-up truck pulled into the parking lot,
followed by a heavy blast of the truck's horn. They had just sat down to a
large pile of steaming crabs mounded on the picnic table between them
and Annie noticed a huge smile spread across Kip's face.

"My mom and brother are here." He climbed over the bench seat and
rushed around the table to help Annie crawl over the wooden slat where
she'd been sitting. "I guess I should have warned you."

"No problem...I'd love to meet your family." Annie hoped her enthusiastic response covered up the onslaught of nerves quivering through
her body, making her knees go weak. Kip grabbed her hand and Annie
found herself gripping it tighter, as if it were a lifeline. With each step that
drew them closer to Kip's mother and brother, Annie took deep breaths
to quiet her jitters.

"Hey, you made it." Kip released Annie's hand and drew his mother
in for a warm hug. He greeted his brother with a handshake and pat on
the back.

"Sorry we're late," his brother said.

The affection they had for one another was evident, with sincere smiles and frequent touching, and Annie suddenly felt out of place. Though it had only lasted a moment, she felt like an eternity had passed before Kip wrapped an arm around her waist and pulled her into their circle.

"This is Annie."

She looked up and found Kip beaming. Before she looked away, his brother drew her into a bear hug.

"Come here, girl. I'm Rob. Great to finally meet you."

"Finally?" Annie murmured.

"And I'm Kip's mom. Call me Helen, please." His mother wrapped her arms around Annie's shoulders, gave her a gentle hug, then cupped Annie's face in her hands. "Aren't you the prettiest thing?"

"Thank you," Annie whispered. Her throat had inexplicably clogged with emotion and she felt her eyes welling up. She'd never felt such kindness from virtual strangers. Thankfully, Kip's mother dropped her grip on Annie's cheeks and she was able to step back, dropping her head to hide the tears threatening to fall.

"Come on. Annie and I were about to crack open some crabs." Kip's arm once more circled Annie's waist and he pulled her tight against him, nearly lifting her off the ground. The smile he gave her was pure delight and she felt her earlier nerves melting away.

Returning to the weathered picnic table, Rob and Kip began their expert tutorial on how to open up the red, hot crabs to find the succulent white meat inside. But after Annie nearly gagged when she saw the yellowish goo also inside, Kip took over opening the bodies.

"That looks like the same stuff you stepped in at the farm," she said. They burst out laughing at the memory and then quickly worked out a system for picking crabs: Annie pulled off the claws and broke them open with a hard thwack of the wooden hammer, while Kip snapped the body into quarters and pulled out the lumps.

Several times, friends of Kip's father stopped by their table and commented how nice it was to have Kip back at the annual event, making him promise to return next year. The men praised Kip's hard work in

Congress and expressed the pride his father would have had, making Kip's face blush a bright red.

It wasn't until Annie walked over to get two water bottles from the icy cooler that she heard the first disparaging words about Kip. She took her time retrieving the water while listening to three men, huddled together in consultation.

"We need to talk to him."

"Not today, Bill. Can't you see the boy's on a date? Leave him alone for now."

"Let me tell ya somethin', his daddy would not be any happier about this pipeline than we are. He needs to know the people around here don't want it, no matter how many jobs it brings. Frankly, I don't think it'll create much of anything in the way of permanent employment," said the man named Bill.

"I'm thinking about selling and moving to the Midwest. My farm won't be worth a damn once that pipeline comes through," said another man.

"I've heard the company running the show has a terrible reputation for shoddy workmanship," the third man commented.

"He's probably been offered a bribe or something. I can't believe he's behind this."

"They need to put it somewhere else."

"I agree with ya, Bill, but leave Kip alone today. We'll talk to him soon."

Annie strolled back to the table and pointed out the men to Kip, reporting what they'd said. Kip just laughed. "The loud mouth is Bill Fletcher. I don't pay any attention to what he says. All he does is complain. Here, open up." Kip had a large, flaky lump of crabmeat between his fingers, which he dropped into Annie's mouth.

Most of the rest of the day was spent huddled around the mountain of crabs at the picnic table, listening to stories about Kip's childhood and football experiences. The warmth and love Annie witnessed between Kip and his family was a sharp contrast to the relationship she currently had with her father, and she found herself wishing she'd had a life like this. By the time Kip's mother hugged Annie goodbye, she felt like part of the family.

Shoulder-to-shoulder, their hands behind them on the dried boards, leaning back as the last light faded, Annie and Kip sat silently, drinking in the tranquility of the twilight. The sun sank behind the stand of trees across the river as the sound of tires crunching on gravel disturbed the quiet. Most of guests had said goodbye, leaving only a handful of folks sitting inside the pavilion. Rob and three of his friends were gathered around the keg, finishing off what was left of the beer. Helen had caught a ride with a friend back to her house, and Annie and Kip were dangling their toes in the still, cool water. They had strolled down to the dock where two cabin cruisers and a small fishing skiff were tied to the weathered pilings, and she sighed at the perfection of this day.

Kip gave her shoulder a nudge and said, "I hear the wheels turning. What are you thinking about?"

I'm falling in love with you, your family, your life… "Oh, just thinking how pretty the water is this time of night."

"Like glass." Kip sat upright and wrapped his arm around her shoulder, turning her against him, and tipped her chin up with his hand. "Did you have a good time today?"

"The best." Annie placed her hands on his shoulders and slowly trailed them around his neck as Kip wrapped her in a gentle embrace, capturing her lips against his. Tickling her mouth open with his tongue, Annie welcomed his warm, luscious kiss; she felt like she was floating away. She could never remember a time when a kiss could make her soar, but that's what Kip's did to her. After several moments, they leaned their foreheads together, catching their breath, gazing deep in each other's eyes. "And to think you didn't even want to come today," Annie said as she planted a quick kiss on his lips.

Kip drew back and dropped his hold on her, standing up quickly. His hands dove deep in his pockets and he shrugged his shoulders toward the water.

Annie climbed to her feet and placed her hand on the small of his back. "Did I say something wrong?"

Kip shook his head, continuing to stare out into the water. He tilted his head and looked at Annie, "You didn't say anything wrong. I guess I owe you an explanation."

Annie dropped her hand from his back and took a step back, confusion swirling in her mind as she tried to make sense of the sad expression that had overtaken Kip's face.

"Today was the first time I've been at this picnic since my dad died three years ago. I haven't wanted to come…because…well, I should thank you for coming with me."

"Why haven't you wanted to come?" Annie placed her hand on his wrist, tugging gently until he pulled his hand out of his pocket. She grasped his hand between hers.

"Three years ago at this crab feast, my dad had a heart attack and died…right next to the grill."

"Oh, Kip." Annie slid her arms around his waist and looked up into his clouded eyes.

"I was helping him grill chicken when he fell over. I thought the heat had gotten to him. The first thing I did was pour water over his head. When he didn't move, I knew something was really wrong."

Laying her head against his chest, feeling the quick beat of his heart, Annie held him until he finally circled his arms around her, pulling her tight against him. "I'm sorry," she murmured.

"I've been afraid to come—afraid of the memories. But having you here with me today made it so much easier. My mom was really happy we came."

Annie drew back enough to look up at Kip. "I love your mom and Rob is so funny. I'm so glad I got to spend time with them today."

"So am I." Kip lifted Annie in his arms, leaving her feet to dangle. "When do I get to meet your parents?"

"What?" She suddenly felt trapped in his firm hold. "Why would you—"

"I mean, fair's fair. You met my family today." Kip tightened his grip against her protests.

"That's different. They just happened to be here. Besides—" Annie wiggled her hips, trying her best to get free. "Put me down."

"No. Why won't you introduce me to your parents?"

"Come on, Porter. It's not like we're dating."

"We could be." Annie stopped fighting her entrapment. "I mean today was great and I like spending time with you."

"Today was great, but meeting my parents—it's just—too soon." Kip finally lowered her to the weathered dock and brushed a dark tendril from her cheek.

"Too soon, huh? Okay. If you say so."

"You know I'm right; besides you're my—"

"Your boss. I know. You remind me every day."

"Well—"

"We'll drop it for now. Come on. I'm taking you out on that river."

"What? Are you nuts? It's dark out there."

"Nah, there's enough light. I want to show you where I live."

Kip eased himself off the dock into the small fishing skiff and reached up to help Annie climb aboard. She lay on her stomach and dangled her legs over the side of the dock, cringing at the fact that she was giving Kip a front row seat to her rear-end.

"Nice shorts, Coach." He laughed as his hands gripped each side of her waist, lifting her safely into the boat.

"Keep your eyes where they belong, Porter."

"Can't do it."

The skiff was nothing more than a large rowboat with a small outboard engine, which Kip quickly started after tossing the ropes onto the dock. Annie sat facing him with a firm grip on the sides of the boat.

"Whose boat is this?" she asked.

"Don't know."

"Kip, you stole someone's boat?" Her head bobbed back and forth, looking toward the shore.

"I'm borrowing it. We're just going around that point and we'll be back before it gets too dark. It'll never be missed."

The boat moved slowly through the water and Annie watched Kip's face in the waning light, feeling a swell of emotion. God, he was handsome, with his cheeks lightly sunburned and his short hair blowing in the breeze. Her eyes trailed down to his thick biceps straining against his T-shirt sleeves, then down to his muscular legs with just the right amount of hair. Her fingers were itching to reach out and stroke his thighs, mere inches from hers.

"Got something on your mind, Coach?" Kip chuckled, his eyebrows arched in merriment.

"I…um…I'm just enjoying the ride."

Kip laughed and floored the engine, making the bow of the boat rise and Annie release a squeal. He took the vessel around the point into a cove where several large homes dotted the shoreline. Only one tiny cottage stood alone among its opulent neighbors and Annie was happy to learn it belonged to Kip.

"I was hoping that was yours," she said.

"I bet." He turned the boat sharply, heading back around the point.

"Seriously…I was. It just looks like the kind of cabin you'd expect to find around here. It's perfect."

She could see the pleasure on Kip's face, almost awash with relief.

"You'll have to come over sometime," he shouted over the roar of the engine.

"Maybe I will."

A few hundred yards from the dock where their trip began, Annie stood up and said, "I've always wanted to do this." She turned to face the bow, holding on to the sides of the boat to steady herself and then climbed on the metal cross beam at the front of the boat. Balancing like a gymnast, Annie stood up, threw her arms out and yelled, "I'm king of the world!"

Kip laughed and yelled back, "What are you doing?"

She looked over her shoulder at Kip, giving him a wink while the boat rocked side to side. "Like in *Titanic*, silly."

"Sit down before you f—"

All at once, Annie lost her footing and tumbled over the side, creating a loud splash. Kip turned off the engine and jumped over the side, giving the boat a hard shove toward shore. Annie came out of the water sputtering and laughing while Kip swam to her. He gathered her in his arms and lifted her up to face him.

"You're crazy, you know that?" He laughed and hugged her tight against him.

"That's not how it happened in the movie."

"Good thing." The water was shoulder-deep where Kip stood on the sandy bottom. "They would have drowned."

Annie draped her arms over his shoulders and wrapped her legs around his waist. "They did drown at the end—well, Jack did."

"Yeah, but not before that scene in the antique car."

"Of course you'd remember that part."

"Of course." Before Annie could say another word, Kip wrapped a hand around the back of her head and pulled her in for a kiss. She tightened her hold around his neck and held fast, opening her lips, inviting him to slip inside. Their tongues mingled and the kiss deepened, their lips pressed tightly to one another. Annie's heart was racing, her desiring surging; she never wanted this to end. She felt Kip's hands engulf her rear-end and pull her tight against his firm abs while his thumbs dipped inside her denim shorts. She reached down and grabbed a handful of T-shirt and pulled upward, exposing his bare skin, and her smile grew against his lips when she felt his hand reach under her tank top to graze across the thin fabric of her bra. He slid his hands around her bra strap only to sigh when he didn't find a clasp at her back.

Annie laughed and whispered in his ear, "It opens in the front."

"Trying to trick me, huh?" Kip unlatched the clasp with two fingers and covered one breast with his large hand.

"Perfect," he said against her lips before he plunged his tongue into her welcoming mouth once again. Annie lifted his sopping T-shirt and ran her hands across his washboard abs and matched his passion, kiss for kiss. She snaked her hands around to his back and slipped them inside his waistband, pressing her bare breasts to his chest. The skin-to-skin sensation left her breathless. Kip lifted her higher and began nibbling on her collarbone, on a quest to explore even lower, when suddenly they were bathed in a white, hot light.

"What're y'all doing out there?" A group of men cackled as the spotlight zeroed in on Annie and Kip.

"Turn off that damn spotlight, Rob," Kip yelled over his shoulder, not letting go of Annie. She pulled down her tank top and tried to pull out of Kip's arms, only to feel him tighten his hold.

"Just making sure you two were alright. The boat came back without ya." Once more a burst of laughter could be heard from the shore and Annie dropped her head against Kip's shoulder, feeling totally demoralized.

"Turn. Off. That. Damn. Light," Kip roared, turning to face his brother and his drunken friends.

Rob shouted, "Okay, buddy. Will do. Have fun." Another burst of laughter and they were thrown back into darkness.

Annie pushed out of his arms and swam furiously back to shore with Kip close at her heels. When her feet hit the sandy bottom, she ran toward the grassy edge while wringing the water out of her drenched shirt. She turned back to the water and clasped her bra closed as Kip walked up to her, reaching out his arms.

Annie snapped around and marched up the grassy knoll toward the pavilion and snatched her flip flops, keys, and phone off the picnic table where she'd left them. In her periphery, she noticed Kip nose-to-nose with Rob, gritting out a stern rebuke. As she reached her car, Kip ran up behind her and grabbed the hem of her shirt, making her stop mid-stride.

"Come here." He pulled her back against his chest and locked his hands in front of her. "I'm sorry," he muttered against her ear.

More embarrassed than she could ever remember, all she wanted to do was leave, but Kip wasn't loosening his grip. She'd nearly had sex with her boss in a river and she just wanted to crawl into her car and get as far away as she could.

"I've gotta go," she said, ducking under his arms. "Really."

"Annie, come on, don't leave. I'm sorry about my asshole brother."

She placed her hand against his chest and looked up at his stricken expression. "It's late. I have a long drive."

"Stay at my place." Kip drew her close, pulling her in with his hands on her hips and his eyes locked on hers. Annie chewed on her bottom lip, trying to break the hold his eyes had on her.

She took a few steps back, out of his reach, and said, "Absolutely not. I had a great time and everything, but no thank you." Annie pulled open the door and climbed in her car, but before she could shut the door, Kip grabbed it and leaned in close to her.

"Let me make this up to you."

With his furrowed brow and pleading gaze, Annie felt her resolve melting, but knew it would be wrong to continue. It was obvious he was as upset as she was and she couldn't blame him for what had happened, but that didn't make up for the fact that he was her boss. Her lips curled into a soft smile. "That's very sweet of you, but I think it's best I go." Annie turned over the engine and backed out of the parking space. As she pulled out of the parking lot, she could still see his silhouette in her rearview mirror, watching her drive away.

FIFTEEN

Annie rushed up the congressional steps twenty minutes earlier than necessary for the weekly staff meeting. She had tossed and turned all night thinking about seeing Kip again. He had spent Sunday at his mom's house, helping Rob replace some guttering damaged by a downed tree during a recent thunderstorm, but took frequent breaks to text her. He apologized several times for how their evening had ended and vowed to make Rob pay. Annie couldn't stop smiling as she entered the office already buzzing with activity. The first person she saw was Tom, leaning over Kip's assistant's desk, looking at something on her computer screen. When he saw her enter, he greeted her with a warm, "Good morning."

"Hey, Tom, I wanted to talk to you about something, if you have a minute," Annie said, dropping her satchel in an empty chair. As Tom walked from behind the desk, she quickly surveyed the office looking for Kip.

"Sure. What's up?"

"I just wanted to tell you I'm going to conduct a poll regarding key issues before we get any deeper into the campaign. You know—things like immigration policy, the environment, government spending, and the pipeline."

Tom's head snapped up from perusing his cell phone and he struck Annie with a hard glare. "The pipeline? Why?"

Annie crossed her arms over her chest. "It's an important issue and we just want to see what Kip's constituents are thinking."

"We? Who's we?"

"Kip and me. We talked about it last week. When we met with Martha Mahan, she said none of her neighbors are happy about the pipeline and Kip was surprised to hear that. So I suggested we conduct a poll."

Tom let out a humorless laugh. "Isn't Martha Mahan the crazy cat lady? Are you going to believe her?"

"That's why I want to do this poll."

Tom's eyes grew dark, but he kept a practiced grin on his face. "Your time would be better spent putting up campaign signs. Stay away from issues and leave polling to me."

A cold shiver ran down Annie's spine. Had he just issued a threat? Tom hovered over her, emphasizing his command with a steady glare. She'd never felt such a cold, unwelcome response from him, but couldn't let it deter her from doing the job she'd been hired to do.

"Surely, you're not paying me to simply put up campaign signs."

"We're paying you to run the campaign office. That's it." Tom walked away, shaking his head, and said over his shoulder, "Stick to what you do best."

Annie dropped her arms, sighing loudly, and wondered why the sudden change in Tom. While she stood staring at Tom's back, she felt a brush of air against her cheek and heard Kip whisper, "Good morning, sweetheart." He kept right on walking into his office and picked up his telephone, watching Annie through the doorway. Flustered and feeling her face grow warm, Annie grabbed her bag and walked into the conference room, ready for the meeting to begin.

The staff and interns began shuffling into the room, taking the empty seats surrounding Annie, with a low hum of conversation among them. A light clinking sound dragged her attention away from her laptop and she found a delicate, floral tea cup and saucer placed on the table in front of her.

"Earl Grey with one sugar. That's how you take it, right?"

Annie slowly looked over her right shoulder to find Kip standing behind her with a donut resting on a white paper plate in his hand.

"I'm sorry we don't have any scones. This was the next best thing."

Annie bit the corner of her bottom lip and looked up at Kip from beneath hooded eyelids. She felt the pull of his charm and cleared her throat, doing her best to appear unaffected.

"This'll work. Thank you."

Kip responded with a tiny grin and then took his seat at the front of the room.

Annie kept her head bowed, trying to hide the silly grin she couldn't erase, doing her best not to look at Kip. When she was finally able to strike a poker face, she looked up and saw those around her staring slack-jawed at the refreshments in front of her. Her earlier thrill was replaced by utter mortification. Everyone around her had seen Kip's little gesture and she felt as though a neon sign was flashing overhead: Kip and Annie Have a Thing Going On. She wanted to crawl under the table, but instead shot a look at Kip meant to tell him his gesture was *not* okay. The only reply she received was a wink. *Not helping, Kip.*

Forty-five minutes later, as everyone rushed out of the room, Kip walked over to Annie and said loud enough for those around to hear, "Annie, may I see you in my office for a few minutes, please?"

She obediently followed him into his office with her head bowed, avoiding the stares she was sure she'd find if she looked up. The door closed with a click of the lock and Annie was pulled into Kip's arms, his mouth firmly engulfing hers, while his hands gripped her behind and pressed her tightly against him.

Kip tore his mouth from hers and trailed delicate kisses down her neck. "Damn...I've...missed...you."

A war was going on between Annie's brain and her libido, but she finally pushed Kip away long enough to chastise him for his earlier actions. "What were you trying to do in there? Advertise us? Everyone was staring at me."

With a hearty laugh, Kip resumed his ministrations to her neck and said, "Didn't you like your tea?"

"Kip!"

He leaned back and grasped Annie's face in his hands. "I don't care who knows about us. In fact, I think I'll go out there right now and make an announcement."

He turned toward the door and Annie grabbed his arm. "Don't you dare. Besides, there is no *us*."

"Why are you fighting this?" Gathering Annie's hands in his, he brushed feather-light kisses across her knuckles making her knees go weak. "I like you. You like me. Us."

Getting sucked into Kip's whirlpool of sexiness would not be a good idea. How could they possibly work together and date at the same time? Would they be able to keep it from the staff? This was a bad idea, but with each tender kiss, she caved just a little more.

"I'll make a deal with you." Kip's brows arched and he nailed her with his sultry gaze, keeping up his knuckle delight. Annie sighed as she continued. "Let's just keep this—whatever this is—to ourselves and see where it goes. It's too soon—and frankly inappropriate—to call us *us*."

"Okay, okay." Kip enveloped her in his arms, planting a breathless kiss on her lips. "You win for now."

"Good." Annie wrenched free of his embrace, straightened her blouse, and resumed her earlier professional self. "We need to talk."

"Are you breaking up with me already?" Kip tapped a quick kiss on her forehead and chuckled as he circled round his desk.

"About my responsibilities…that's what we need to talk about."

"Okay, shoot." He rocked back in his chair, fingers entwined across his stomach, and smiled seductively. Annie could see he wasn't in the mood to talk business, but she forged ahead.

"I spoke with Tom this morning about the poll we discussed. He told me my time would be better spent running the campaign office and putting out signs." She stopped when Kip snorted a laugh. "Do you think this is funny?"

"Um…" He cleared his throat and took on a serious expression. "No, not at all. Continue."

"I have much more to offer than just spiking signs in the ground. There is so much to do, but I've been getting resistance from Tom and you frankly."

"Me?"

"Yes, you've turned down nearly every invitation you've received—all but the crab feast."

"That was a good decision on my part, don't you think?" Kip gave her another sexy smile and Annie fought the tingle creeping low in her belly. She had to keep her mind on the business at hand and not think about what almost happened in the river.

"Yes. Your presence was very well received and should bolster support."

"That's not what I meant."

"The point is, I could conduct the poll, send out press releases, and plan fundraisers if you'd give me the go ahead. Maybe even arrange a debate. There are many opportunities to get out in front of the voters, if you'd just cooperate." Annie grew frustrated when Kip didn't reply, but simply stared at her with longing in his eyes. She stood up and brushed the wrinkles from her skirt. "You're lagging behind your challenger in the general election. You can't hide away here on Capitol Hill and expect to get elected."

"Lagging behind?" That seemed to get his attention. Kip stood up and flattened his hands on his desk. "Since when?"

"Ever since I took the job, two months ago, you've been behind. I told Tom about it and he said he'd talk to you. Don't you ever look at the numbers yourself?"

"Not lately. I've relied on you and Tom to deal with it."

"Maybe you should talk to him. We can turn these numbers around if you'll let me do my job."

Kip came around to the front of the desk and perched on the edge, drawing Annie in his arms. "Okay. I'll talk to him. Do what you need to do."

"So, I can conduct the issues poll and RSVP yes to some of the more important events?"

"Mm hm." Kip ran his hand up her back, keeping his crystal eyes locked on her, making her brain shut down. "Tell me where to be and when, and I'll be there. I'm putty in your hands."

SIXTEEN

Annie slipped her hand through Kip's arm, seeking a steadying force as she walked up the elevated plank to the sleek yacht moored along the Potomac River. White monuments and government buildings illuminated in the distance as the last rays of sunshine sank below the horizon. She teetered on her four inch heals while holding the hem of her mini cocktail dress against the breeze gusting off the river.

"Very fancy, Porter. I can see why you'd pass up the opening of the county fair to attend this swanky event."

"Couldn't pass up the opportunity to show off my girl." Kip gave her a wink as they stepped onto the gleaming teak deck.

"You're showing off your campaign manager, remember?"

"If you say so, Coach."

They hadn't made anything official, but in the past two weeks they'd had dinner twice. Each time she was alone with him, he became harder to resist. Tonight would be especially hard. She'd always been a sucker for a guy in a black tux and Kip wore his especially well. When an invitation to this private donor event crossed Kip's desk, she didn't hesitate to accept on his behalf.

"Kip, darling, you made it." Amelia Wentworth, the host of the event, sidled up to Kip, brushing her over-exposed cleavage against his arm. "And you brought your lovely campaign manager. How delightful."

"Hello, Mrs. Wentworth." Annie extended her hand in greeting. "It's so nice to see you again."

"And you, dear. I must thank you for getting your boss to this party. So many important people he must meet, you know." She gazed up at Kip with a school girl giggle and wrapped her manicured hand around his elbow. "Let me introduce you. You don't mind, do you, dear?"

Well, so much for spending the evening together. Before Annie could say a word, Kip shrugged and was pulled away.

Across the deck in front of a large window was a bar. Just because she was left on her own didn't mean she shouldn't enjoy herself. She crossed the deck and ordered a Cosmo, smiling at the unfamiliar faces around her. Through the window she could see Kip, head bowed, in what looked like a serious discussion with Amelia, Tom, and a tall, gray-haired man. Mr. Wentworth, perhaps? It didn't look like the kind of chat she should interrupt, so she decided a tour around the yacht was in order.

As she walked along the outer rail toward the bow of the boat, she nearly collided with her parents, who were stepping through a side door.

"Ann. What a nice surprise!" Her mother gathered her in a brief hug and trailed her eyes down the length of Annie's body. "You look fabulous. I don't think I've seen you at a black tie event in ages."

"I haven't been invited to many lately."

"Hello, Annie bug." George Cooper planted a quick kiss on Annie's temple. His use of her childhood nickname made her blood boil. He was good at pulling out the "Annie bug" when he wanted something.

"Hello, Dad." Annie took a long drink of her cocktail and focused on her mother. "You look beautiful as always, Mom."

"Thank you. Your father bought this for me." Marjorie Cooper's hand swept down the length of her black lace gown. "He has great taste, don't you think?"

"He does."

"So, are you here alone?" Her mother looked over Annie's shoulder expectantly.

"No, I'm here with my boss, but he's talking with Mrs. Wentworth."

"Oh," Marjorie whispered. "Should we act like we don't know you?"

Annie laughed and gave her mother's hand a squeeze. "That might be best. I still haven't told him the truth." Soon she would have to confess if they continued to see each other outside the office.

"Why in the world would you give him a false name in the first place?"

"Shhh." Annie held her finger to her lips and glanced over her shoulder. "Well, Dad, if you must know. It's not easy being George Cooper's daughter." Annie looked away over the water and drained the rest of her glass.

"Why would you say—"

"Maybe I should thank you. If I hadn't left Howard, Wolfe, and Richards—because of yours and Mr. Wolfe's shady dealings—I wouldn't have found this job—a job I got all on my own without your influence." The Cosmo had given Annie just enough courage to say what she'd been holding in for too long. Now seemed like as good a time as any to let her father know how his behavior had affected her life.

"I've never been involved with that crook."

"You say. And, I'm making a real impact as Congressman Porter's campaign manager. His poll numbers are rising and he's getting noticed in the press. All because of me—not you, meddling in my business."

"Annie, when are you going to forgive me? So, I've called in a few favors in the past. Life's hard. I thought I was helping. You asked me five years ago to stay out of your business and I have."

"Whatever," Annie mumbled, while tipping up the empty cocktail glass to her lips. "I need another drink."

"Listen, Annie bug." Her father's tender tone made Annie look him in the eyes, imploring her to hear him out. "I'm sorry. I don't know what else to say. But, let me just tell you that politics can be a nasty business. That's why I tried to keep you out of it. But, if you ever need anything, any advice or help, don't hesitate to call me."

"I'm doing fine on my own."

"I'm sure you are. You're a very intelligent, capable woman and Congressman Porter should be proud to have you on staff. Just keep in mind, I'm only a phone call away."

Damn it. Why did her father have to be so...so...kind? Annie looked over her shoulder at the rippling tide, fighting back the tears welling in her eyes. Why was he being so helpful? And, why the compliments? George Cooper didn't compliment his children. Why did he have to do it now when mascara threatened to ruin her make-up?

"Well, Marjorie, how about you and I get another drink?" At least George Cooper knew when to make an exit. He tapped another kiss on Annie's temple and led her mother toward the back of the yacht.

"As I've told you, over and over, I don't like how this is going." Kip tipped back his tumbler, letting the dark liquor hit the back of his throat. "I don't like their control over me—us," he whispered at Tom, as an older couple passed them on the foredeck.

"We're in too deep, bro. The Wentworths are expecting this deal to go through. They've invested too much time and money in you."

"Maybe I'll refuse their donations. Maybe that will give them a clear signal I want out." Kip looked into his empty glass, needing a refill fast. He should have gone to the county fair instead of this nightmare wrapped in a cocktail party. From the moment he stepped on the deck, the Wentworths had been all over him. In fact, not only the Wentworths, but Tom as well. Why was Tom so invested in this bill getting passed?

"Don't fuck this up, bro." Tom reached for the doorknob to walk back inside the cabin, but stopped. "Kip, Senator Cooper is here. And, he's talking to Annie. Get over there and get an introduction."

"I'm done with this. Understand?" Kip walked through the cabin door, away from where Annie spoke with her parents. She was still hiding her identity and the last thing he wanted was to make an awkward situation for her. Sure, he was supposed to be seducing an introduction out of her, but the reality was he only wanted to seduce her—introduction or not. He couldn't stop thinking of her and wanted more. He wanted them to be *us*.

With her Cosmo freshly refilled and her parents off talking to another couple, Annie set out to find Kip. She'd come as his date, after all, and didn't really want to spend the evening alone. She entered the main cabin, where she'd earlier seen him speaking with the Wentworths and Tom, but didn't recognize him in the crowd. While she was inside, she decided to seek out the restroom before resuming her search. She wandered down a long hallway to her left, passing a galley kitchen and a small office before finding the restroom at the end of the hall. A door was ajar across the hall and a familiar voice came from inside. Annie stepped closer and leaned against the wall to listen.

"Don't worry. I'll make it happen." Tom's tone was strained, as if he was held in a vise. "Just…just…ah!"

"Ooh, you like that, do you?" That sticky sweet voice could be none other than Amelia Wentworth. What in the world was Tom doing in there with her?

"Darlin', you know I do."

Annie's answer came quick enough when she pushed the door open enough to peek inside. Tom had his back to the wall with his erection firmly in Amelia's tight fist.

"So, tell me again," Amelia Wentworth threatened. "There will be no roadblocks, right?"

"Right," Tom whimpered.

"That's want I want to hear."

"Remind me," Tom moaned, "what's in it for me again?"

"Don't worry, you'll be generously rewarded."

Annie rushed down the hallway, determined to find Kip.

"There you are." Kip placed his hand on the small of her back, rubbing her dress's silky black fabric clinging to her perfect figure. He couldn't take another minute of this party, preferring instead to be alone with Annie. "How about we blow this joint? I've had enough."

"Sure. If you want, but—"

"I haven't spent a moment with you. Let's get out of here."

Thanks to Amelia Wentworth, the whole evening was ruined. Annie looked so gorgeous when he'd picked her up and he really wanted to show her his classier side. No beer and crabs. Tonight was supposed to be about champagne and caviar, and rubbing elbows with the Washington elite—a world with which she'd be most familiar. Why did Amelia have to pull him into the cabin as soon as he arrived to apply her special brand of pressure when all he wanted to do was show Annie a good time? Even though luring an introduction to her father was the central focus, Kip was quickly losing interest in the whole scheme—especially after tonight.

He opened her car door, assisting her in, and slammed it shut.

"I have to tell you something." Annie placed her hand on his shoulder once Kip was behind the wheel.

"Man, it's good to be out of there. I should've listened to you, Coach, and gone to the fair." He shifted in his seat and reached for her hand. "You look beautiful. I'm sorry to cut our night short."

"I don't mind. I didn't know anyone anyway."

Kip turned the ignition key and backed out of the parking space. As they wound through the marina toward the exit, he thought about how he could wrangle an invitation up to Annie's apartment. The more time they spent together, the more he wanted her. He wanted to get lost in her amazing kisses and forget he ever met the Wentworths.

"I know why we came to this party." Kip locked up the brakes, throwing Annie against her seat belt.

"What do you mean?" He wrenched the car into park and turned to her, eyes dark and brows furrowed. Had she overheard something at the party?

"Or, I should say, I know why Tom was so anxious for us to accept the invitation. I know what's going on with Amelia Wentworth."

"You do?" A cold sweat formed on Kip's brow. How did she find out about the pipeline scheme? Had she been eavesdropping? When Annie nodded her head, Kip sighed heavily and raked his hand through his perfectly groomed hair. Maybe it was time to confess. "I owe you an explanation. It's gone too far."

"I'll say. I couldn't believe what I saw in that little room. I think they were about to go at it."

"What?" Kip whipped around and stared at Annie, completely confused. "Who?"

"I was going into the bathroom when I heard Tom talking with someone in the room across the hall. I know it was wrong, but I stood outside and listened. Then, I looked inside and they were at the start of something...sexual." Annie shivered.

No way. There was no doubt Tom enjoyed his fair share of women, but he certainly wouldn't be sexually involved with Amelia Wentworth. There was no reason.

"You're jumping to conclusions, again."

"I'm not. Believe me. I'm right this time. I heard her say she would give him his reward." She shivered again and chuckled. "I wonder what that reward might be."

"You need glasses, Coach." Kip's flat tone reflected no humor. Once again, Annie misinterpreted something she saw. Since the day he met her, she'd been suspicious of his behavior. Now she was turning those suspicions on Tom.

"I know what I saw." Annie pressed her back against the seat and crossed her arms over her chest.

"There's nothing going on between Tom and Amelia Wentworth."

"How do you know?"

"Because I know Tom and there's no reason for him to do that with Amelia."

"Obviously, you didn't know about it and are finding it hard to believe. But, it's true."

Kip thrust the car in drive, letting gravel fly as they pulled out of the marina. Why the hell was Annie stirring up trouble? They have enough trouble as it is. "She's twice his age."

"With more money than God."

"So, you think Mrs. Wentworth is paying him to have sex with her?" The traffic light turned from yellow to red, but Kip blazed right through the intersection.

"I don't know what their arrangement is, but they definitely have one. You better look into this, Porter. This whole thing could come back to bite you."

"I can handle my own staff, thank you."

"Apparently you can't because your chief of staff is screwing around with a very wealthy donor—one I've noticed has been very generous with your campaign."

Kip swerved the car into a no-parking zone and killed the engine. "What are you trying to say? That I've pimped out my chief of staff to bring in donations?"

"Oh, my God, of course not. But, it's evident you didn't know anything about this and it wouldn't be the first time a congressman got in hot water over shady dealings going on behind his back." It finally hit Kip like a ten-pound sledge hammer right between the eyes. Tom *did* have something going on with Amelia. It made perfect sense. But, what exactly? Tom had been hell-bent on getting the pipeline contract to Wentworth Global and lately had been completely unreasonable when it came to the bill. What was in it for him?

"I don't want to see you get in trouble because of something Tom did," Annie said.

"I'll talk to him." Kip merged back into the heavy Saturday night traffic, figuring out the best way to handle Tom.

"Here we are." Annie pointed toward an open parking space. Kip pulled the Lexus to the curb outside her apartment and cut the engine. He reached behind her head and pulled her in for a long, gut-wrenching kiss. All week he'd dreamed of this moment when he'd take her home, kiss her deeply, and then ask to come in. They'd go upstairs and finally follow through with what he was sure they both wanted. Now that Annie had exposed Tom and Amelia, all Kip could do was think of how he planned to handle it. His dream of waking up in Annie's arms evaporated.

"Would you like to come up?" Annie's playful tone nearly brought him out of his rage.

"Babe." Kip sighed. "Any other night, believe me, I'd love to come up." He brushed a dark tendril behind her ear and drank in her natural beauty. Damn it, he was falling and didn't know how to stop it. "Can I have a rain check? I have to talk to Tom."

"So you'd rather spend time with your chief of staff over your campaign manager, huh? Okay, Porter. Don't let it be said I didn't offer." Annie chuckled and reached for the door handle.

"Hey." Kip reached for her hand and tugged her into a tight embrace. "I'm sorry. I'll make this right. You'll see." And, he would. He'd get himself out of this mess with the Wentworths and do his best to win over Annie.

"So serious." She pouted like a child and then laughed. "It's okay, Porter. We'll get together another time. No worries." Annie rubbed the wrinkle between his brow with the pad of her thumb and then pecked a kiss on his lips. "I'll see you on Monday."

SEVENTEEN

"Good morning." Annie breezed through the office toward the conference room when she was stopped by Kip's assistant.

"Kip postponed the staff meeting. Didn't you get the text?"

"I don't think so." She frantically scrolled through her texts and emails. "Isn't he here?"

"He's in with Tom, but asked that you wait for him in his office."

Annie and the receptionist snapped their attention toward Tom's door when a loud shout came from within. Indecipherable, but clearly angry, Tom's voice traveled through the heavy wooden door. Annie shrugged her shoulders and walked into Kip's office. Obviously, he was confronting Tom with what Annie witnessed at the yacht party and it wasn't going over well. She sat on the office couch and flipped open her laptop, ready to go over debate questions with Kip.

"See if you can get me an appointment with the speaker," Kip barked at his assistant as he entered his office. He closed the door with force and stalked across his office without speaking to Annie.

After several silent minutes, Annie said, "I take it things didn't go well with Tom this morning." Annie set her laptop on the coffee table and moved to the chair in front of Kip's desk. He didn't reply, still fuming from his encounter with Tom. Instead, he tapped away on his keyboard and kept his gaze directed at the computer screen. She wasn't sure if she should stay or go. After several minutes, Kip hit the send button and settled back into his leather chair with a heavy sigh.

"Hi." He gave Annie a small grin as he rubbed the back of his neck.

"Bad morning?"

"Something like that."

"If you want me to go, we can talk later." Annie rose from her chair and Kip rushed around his desk, pulling her into his arms.

"Don't go." His request was more of a plea and Annie sensed he needed her to stay. She wrapped her arms around his neck and held tight. Kip sighed, lightened his hold, and then pressed a tender kiss on her lips. He kissed her hesitantly, as if he were asking permission, pain showing in his eyes. Whatever had happened between him and Tom, it had obviously left him upset. Annie wanted to kiss away his stress and disappointment. She rubbed the tension in his neck while capturing his mouth, letting him know with her kiss she was there for him. He was hurting, she could see it, and she wanted more than anything to be the one to help.

"Do you want to talk about what happened with Tom?" Annie feathered delicate kisses on his cheeks, his forehead, and his nose as she offered her support. Kip sagged in her arms, gliding his hands lower.

"No. Just kiss me." Kip palmed her bottom, pressing her tightly against him as he plunged his tongue between her lips. He kissed her as if he drew strength from her exhaled breath.

"Kip," Annie murmured against his lips. "I'm here for you."

Lifting her feet off the floor, Kip carried Annie to the leather couch along the wall where he laid her against the armrest and settled his heavy body beside hers. He smothered her lips against his in a feverish kiss and slipped his hand under her skirt, massaging her thigh as his hand trailed higher. Her thoughts screamed, "Stop," but her hands operated of their own volition. He needed her and she couldn't resist him. She tugged at his shirt hem, freeing the fabric from his pants so she could run her hands over his taut back and contoured chest.

Kip leaned up, locking her eyes with his, and slowly unbuttoned her blouse. "I need you, Annie." The desire in his eyes melted Annie's reserve, sending a deep aching need inside her. She cupped his face in her hands and kissed him tenderly. Kip unhooked her bra, shoving it aside, and covered her breasts with his mouth, devouring each hungrily. She looked up at the coffered ceiling as he nibbled down her neck, reminding herself this shouldn't be happening, but she was too weak to stop it. When Kip's hand slid higher up her thigh, the war was over and Annie's desire had won. She quickly unbuttoned Kip's shirt and felt her breath hitch in her throat at the sight of his magnificently firm body. He'd obviously kept in shape since his football days and Annie couldn't resist pressing her mouth against his thick pecs, tasting the sweetness of his skin.

Kip tugged down her panties and gently slid his finger inside, and Annie gasped from the sensation.

"You can tell me to stop," Kip murmured against her mouth, but Annie shook her head while unlatching his belt buckle. "Thank God." Kip laughed and sucked her into a lusciously suffocating kiss. He reached into his back pocket to pull out his wallet and from it, a condom. He sat up to roll it on and then reached behind Annie, lifting her onto his lap. While she straddled him, Kip raised the mass of curls from her neck, grazing his lips down her tingling skin to her aching breasts. She couldn't wait much longer and was relieved when he lifted her hips and entered her. With her heart pounding out of her chest and desire pulsing throughout her body, Annie gave herself completely to Kip, all inhibitions and concerns thrown to the wind. Resting on his sinewy thighs, with his hands and mouth all over her body and her hands gripping his strong shoulders, Kip and Annie were in perfect sync, riding the wave of ecstasy together. They muffled their screams with a deep kiss and Annie collapsed in his arms.

For a few minutes, they lay chest-to-chest, trying to catch their breath, gently stroking each other's damp skin. Kip planted several tiny kisses on her shoulder while caressing her back as Annie nuzzled her face in the crook of his neck, drinking in his masculine smell. A loud shrill noise snapped their languor and Kip reached behind Annie to his cell phone on the coffee table.

He tapped on the screen and blurted, "Damn it. I have a hearing in ten minutes."

Kip lifted Annie off of his lap and deposited her on the end of the couch like a sack of potatoes being dropped off the back of a truck. He grabbed his pants from where they'd puddled at his feet and walked to his adjoining bathroom without casting Annie so much as a backward glance. In an instant, the needful, sensuous, connection between them evaporated and Annie felt deflated.

As if in a trance, she grabbed her panties off the floor and slowly pulled them up under her skirt. One by one she buttoned her blouse, then lifted her hips to tuck it into her waistband. She shrunk against the arm of the couch and threw her arm over her eyes, releasing a quivering sigh. What had just happened? Annie lifted herself off the sofa, feeling the afterglow of great sex, but totally humiliated. She pulled a hair band out of her purse, gathered her thick curls into a ponytail, and checked her reflection in her compact mirror. Her lipstick was smudged and her mascara had smeared, but quick action with a tissue had her looking as she had before walking into his office.

Annie lifted her satchel strap onto her shoulder and smiled as Kip rushed out of the bathroom, hoping their earlier passion wasn't forgotten. He brushed a kiss across her temple and said "I'll call you," then left the door standing open as he hurried out of his office.

With a loud bang, Annie slammed the oven door closed and picked up the large stainless bowl. She stirred the thick batter with a wooden spoon, periodically dipping in a finger and extracting a large glob of cookie dough, which she promptly inserted in her mouth.

"Will there be enough dough left to even bake the cookies?" Emberly's voice echoed through the laptop. As soon as Annie walked into her apartment, she had put in a Skype call to her old friend, knowing it was late afternoon in Rome. After Kip's brush off, she couldn't face the day, so she called Pam in the campaign office and told her she wasn't feeling well. Instead, she retreated to her apartment and went into a baking frenzy. A pan of brownies baked in the oven while she prepared a double batch of peanut butter cookies.

Annie shouted from the kitchen, "If not, I'll make some more." She laughed and then slapped her hands down on the counter, looking at Emberly's face on the screen. "Maybe I should travel the world with you and Nico."

"Why?"

"Because I'd be away from all this."

"What happened? Why are you home baking like a fiend instead of working at the campaign office?"

While Annie filled Emberly in on her morning, she furiously plopped large spoonfuls of dough on a cookie sheet. "He just left me standing there while his staff stared at me, knowing I'd just screwed my boss on his leather couch." She walked to the other side of the counter and dropped onto a bar stool, dragging the laptop around to face her. She swiped a cookie dough ball off the metal pan, leaned her elbows on the counter, and chewed the sweet concoction. "I'm no better than the sluts you see on TV, forever scandalized because of an affair with a politician. I'm no better than the woman my father was caught with. God, what was I thinking?"

"I think you're exaggerating." Emberly held up her finger when her desk phone rang. "Hold on. I need to take this."

"Just wait until the news gets out," Annie mumbled to herself, as she scooped up another tablespoon of dough.

While Emberly took her call, Annie dropped her head in her hands, remembering the humiliation she felt after Kip had walked out. Three sets of eyes had stared accusingly back at her. She was certain they knew after he left her standing all flushed in his office. She dragged her fingers through her hair, pulling the strands away from her face, making her eyebrows lift painfully.

"What are you doing?" Emberly had returned.

"Maybe I can have plastic surgery. I've changed my last name, maybe I can change my face and move to Alaska, where no one will know me or recognize me. If I show my face on Capitol Hill again, they'll all whisper behind my back, 'There's that skank, Annie. Wonder which congressman she's planning to do today?'."

"Annie, come on." Emberly laughed. "You're making too much out of this. I'm sure his staff didn't know what went on in the office. From everything you've told me, he sounds like a nice guy."

"Nice guy?" Annie dropped her hair and snapped to attention. "The guy has his way with me in his office—on a Monday morning, mind you—and then throws out the old 'I'll call you' line, and you say he sounds pretty nice? It's time to call it quits and find a job far, far from Washington."

"Wait." Emberly held up her hand to the screen and Annie saw the concern in her eyes. "Okay, so maybe it wasn't the best time or place for—well—you know, but you're both single. There's nothing in the manual that says you can't date your boss."

"You sound like Kate. But, FYI, I don't think he had dating on his mind."

"Why he rushed out of there, I can't say. But, give it a day or two and see what happens. It's not like he's going to leak it to the press."

"God, I hope not. That would be the worst publicity."

"See. No one will know."

"But that doesn't answer why he rushed out of there the way he did."

Annie picked up the cookie sheet, cleared off a row of dough, and held the blob up to her lips.

"Some advice?" Emberly tapped her fingertip against the screen. "I'd drop that dough back on the tray. If he does call, hoping to see you tonight, you'll want to still fit in your clothes."

"Good point." The dough landed with a plop on the tray.

Eighteen

Kip didn't make the call until noon on Tuesday. On Monday he had rushed from a hearing to a committee meeting to a press conference, with no time for lunch or even a quick call to Annie.

At least that's what he'd been telling himself.

He'd spent his evening making fundraising calls on behalf of the party and then immersed himself in reading some pending bills before collapsing on his office couch. At midnight he was still wide awake thinking about what had transpired that morning. He hadn't intended on having sex with her in his office— but, after his fight with Tom, he couldn't resist her tender, caring touch. With each kiss and caress, he knew he couldn't hold back. Then again, maybe Tom's words—*fuck her if you have to*—were the reason he'd taken advantage of her, and now he felt like a heel. The truth was, if he had it all to do again, he wouldn't. Annie was too sweet, too clever, too damned wonderful to be treated that way. As soon as he had rushed out of his office, the guilt started eating away at him.

Kip rolled on his side and punched the pillow several times until he flopped back on the couch. He couldn't believe he had gotten himself in this mess. If only Tom hadn't met her in that bar and convinced him they should hire her to get to her dad. But if Tom hadn't met her, Kip wouldn't have either. This whole plot was screwed up. Tomorrow he'd quit being a coward and tell Annie the truth about knowing her identity. And then maybe his conscience would leave him alone.

Kip was ripped from a deep, dreamless sleep when he felt something hit the bottom of his bare foot. He sat up abruptly, rubbing the sand from his eyes, and found Tom leering down at him, fully dressed in a gray suit with a red tie, wearing a crooked grin.

"What are you doing sleeping in your office? Haven't you been home?"

Swinging his legs to the floor while flinging off the plaid fleece throw, Kip yawned deeply and then rested his elbows on his knees. "Yeah, I wanted to get caught up on some stuff and it got late. Didn't feel like driving back to my apartment."

"You look like hell. Better get moving."

"What time is it?" Kip stood and reached for the shirt and pants he had flung across the coffee table.

"It's seven and we have a meeting with the speaker at nine," Tom said. He walked out of Kip's office and started a pot of coffee in the reception area. As he dumped a bag of grounds into the machine, he said over his shoulder, "I think the speaker wants to talk about the Appropriations Committee position that's coming available. When we get the pipeline bill passed, you should gain some real clout—be able to name your positions."

"I'll be glad when it's over."

When Tom came back into the office and handed Kip a mug of coffee, he stared at the cup and thought about Annie and her love of tea cups. He shook his head slightly and grinned at the memory of her long explanation of the benefit of china. Kip picked up his phone, quickly scrolling through his messages.

"I'm going to tell her," Kip said, finally looking clearly at Tom.

"Tell who what?"

"I'm going to tell Annie the truth—that we've known who she is from the beginning."

"You can't." Tom stepped closer to Kip—only the coffee table stood between them.

"Why? You said the other day we need to do whatever it takes, even if that means telling her the truth."

"I didn't mean it. You know she'll flip if you tell her." Tom began laps around an invisible track in the center of the room. "You have to keep getting closer to her. Let her think you're in love. She's the only way you can get to her dad."

"No, there has to be another way. Besides, we can probably get enough votes on the Senate side." Kip took another sip of coffee as Tom wore a path in the carpet.

"It's not just the Senate votes. The contract has to go to Wentworth Global. You know what they can do for your career."

"Or yours?" Kip scratched his head, his brows furrowed. "Why the hell did you promise Amelia they'd get the contract? Once it passes the House and Senate, the contract will go out for bid. It shouldn't be our concern at that point. The Appropriations Committee should decide who gets the bid. The only thing I wanted was to be sure local people get hired for the project."

"And they will with Wentworth. It's all set. Don't rock the boat now just because that hot little girl has gotten under your skin."

"The way Amelia's gotten under yours?" Kip dropped back to the couch and ran both hands through his hair. "This is so messed up."

Tom leaned down, bringing himself to Kip's eye level. "Listen, bro, you can't tell Annie the truth. Just get in good with her dad and float the idea of Wentworth past him."

"I'm going to tell her. I can't keep up this lie any longer."

"Would you just listen to me for once?" Tom's shout reverberated off the walls. "It's crucial Wentworth gets the bid. Don't fuck this up." Tom picked up a photo of Maryland's winning football team and shoved it in Kip's face. "Remember this? We were a team, remember? We need to work together and stick to the original game plan. That's how you win. That's how we've always won."

"This isn't a football game. These are people's lives, Tom. We can't—"

But before Kip could finish, Tom heaved the photo to the floor, splintering the glass in a crystalline spider web.

"Look, I don't know what the hell's the matter with you this morning," Kip said, straining to control the volume, "but I'm going to hit the treadmill and take a shower. I'll be back before nine." Kip brushed past a furious, shaking Tom and walked out of the office.

Three miles later, Kip hung his towel on the hook outside the shower stall and angled his sweat soaked body under the steaming hot water. He stood with his face to the spray, letting the hot water scald his skin. The whole time he had been running, he kept replaying the scene with Tom. He'd dragged both of them deeper into this mess than Kip liked. "It's my name on that bill, not his. What's Amelia promised him?" The mumbled words bounced off the tiled walls. He thought of Annie's comment that Tom seemed to be in charge. If he was honest with himself, he'd always let Tom be in control. It was an old habit from their football days; one it seemed neither one of them was in much of a rush to break.

Six months ago, Tom had presented Kip with the idea of the pipeline. He'd introduced Kip to some very powerful people who wanted to expand the project, and Tom thought it would be Kip's ticket to political stardom if he got it run through his district. Tom told him if he could get this deal to go through, Kip's future in the party was secure. All those nights they'd dreamed about climbing the political ladder over cold beers was finally within reach with this bill. Tom would be Kip's wingman all the way to the White House. But the memory of the small gifts and benefits they'd received along the way, as well as the promise of future funding from private donors, created a burning in Kip's gut. He suspected the Wentworths had offered more than what Tom was sharing. Suspicion and guilt tingled up his spine and he couldn't help but think about one of the last conversations he'd had with his dad before he died.

It had been a cloudless Saturday in June and they were sitting out on the pier in front of the cabin, dropping crabbing cages into the murky water. Kip was a rookie congressman, only in office six months. Although his dad had campaigned for him and volunteered as much as he could, they'd never really had a conversation about his new career.

His dad had pulled up a cage, dumped a cluster of crabs into a plastic bucket, then dropped it back to the riverbed. He kept his head down and appeared to be concentrating on the crabbing when he broke the silence by saying, "You know, Kip, I've never told you how proud I am of you." He cleared his throat and then continued, still looking down into the water. "You've grown into a good man and I'm real impressed with your success."

Kip's father, though occasionally affectionate with his boys, had never been one to verbalize his feelings. When Kip made the all-state high school football team three years in a row, all he'd gotten was a silent pat on the back. When he was an All-American at Maryland, he got a simple, "Congratulations." He had always felt his parents were proud of him, but it caught him off guard when his father expressed his pride in such uncertain terms.

"You've been elected to follow the wishes of the people in this area—represent their needs. Being an elected official can bring a lot of temptations that can pull you away from your honorable intentions. You need to keep your eyes open and listen to your gut. If something doesn't sit well with you, you should steer clear. You understand what I'm saying, son?"

Kip smiled at his dad and laid his hand across his shoulder. "I understand. I went into this for the right reasons, Dad. Don't worry."

"I never had a doubt. Just remember to always keep your integrity intact. Be honest, be fair, and treat people the way you'd like to be treated. At the end of the day, that's all that's really important."

"I'll remember," Kip had said.

And he did.

As the water slapped against his cheeks he could feel tears stinging his eyes. What would his father think if he knew what Kip was involved with? He'd never felt so low in his life. He could no longer trust Tom, he'd lied to the sweetest girl he'd ever met, and he had the feeling he was being dragged down a dark, shadowy alley. He had to find a way out.

The moment Kip and Tom came out of the Speaker of the House's office, the congressman rushed back to his office and slammed the door behind him. He'd had a hard time concentrating on their discussion; his mind was focused on Annie and what he would say to her. What he did remember from the meeting was the speaker's praise for Kip's loyalty to the party and how the passing of this pipeline bill would benefit him. No matter, he still felt he needed to be honest with Annie and hoped he could spin it in a way that wouldn't hurt her. She picked up on the third ring.

"Hello," she said.

"Hey...I'm so sorry it's taken me this long to call. I've had a crazy twenty-four hours." Kip's opening line was met with dead silence. He counted to ten and then continued. "Yeah, um, I went from one meeting to the other yesterday, did some fundraising calls in the evening, and ended up sleeping on the couch in my office. Didn't even make it home."

"Okay," Annie said, short, quiet, undecipherable.

Kip wasn't making progress this way. He dropped his voice just above a whisper, his voice gravelly with emotion, "Listen, I'm sorry. I should have sent you a text at the very least. I have no viable excuse."

"Try one."

"Okay." Kip cleared his throat while pinching the bridge of his nose. "The truth is, I feel bad about what happened yesterday morning." He heard a puff of air through the phone and could just picture Annie rolling her eyes in disbelief. "Don't get me wrong, it was amazing—you were amazing—but you deserve more than just a romp on my couch." This time he heard an intake of breath and feared she would hang up. "Wait, that came out wrong. What I mean is that you're a beautiful, smart, classy woman and what I should have done is waited until the right time and the right place. You deserved better. But obviously I couldn't resist you and wasn't thinking with my head."

"Well, Porter, that's the most believable thing you've said so far."

Kip released a chuckle and flopped into his chair, his legs giving way beneath him. "So, am I forgiven?"

Several seconds went by before Annie said, "This time."

"Whew...you had me scared for a minute."

"Good."

"Where are you right now? At the campaign office?"

"No, I'm working from home today. Pam can handle headquarters while I go over the poll results from here."

"You didn't waste any time."

"You gave me the go ahead."

"I did. You're right." Kip scratched the back of his head, dreading Tom's reaction. Well, he'd just have to get over the fact that Kip was taking back control of his career.

"Could I come over? There's something I need to talk to you about."

"Sure. Have you had lunch?"

"Honestly, I can't remember the last time I ate." "Okay, then, you can join me—I was just about to eat."

"Be there in twenty."

Kip was greeted at the door by a smiling Annie wearing a Kiss the Cook apron, her hair drawn up in a pony tail and a spicy-cinnamon smell in the air.

"May I?" He tapped her apron with his index finger and leaned down, pressing his lips to hers before she could answer. "Mmm...you taste good."

"Sugar," Annie mumbled against his lips.

"I love it when you call me that." They laughed together as Annie led him to an expertly set table with a white cloth draping to the floor, pale grey placemats with matching napkins bunched into rings, and a small flower arrangement in the center.

"Have a seat. Everything's ready." Annie flitted to the kitchen and removed two plates from the refrigerator, placing each on the table. "Would you like something other than water?"

"No...this is fine." Kip stared wide-eyed at the elaborate arrangement and the silver-rimmed china topped with chicken salad on a bed of lettuce, fresh sliced tomatoes and mozzarella, and two deviled eggs. He shook away his confusion and then looked at Annie, who had begun eating.

"When did you do all this?"

"Oh, I made the chicken salad and deviled eggs yesterday, and I made the caprese salad after you called."

"But the table—"

"Oh, that's nothing." Kip watched as Annie stacked a piece of tomato on the cheese and gingerly popped them in her mouth. This woman was too good to be true. He had already recognized her decorating talents, but she could cook, too.

"Aren't you going to eat?" she asked.

"Sorry…I'm just amazed, I guess."

"It's a stress reliever." Her face flushed and she looked away. "Cooking, that is."

"Seems like a great stress reliever. I didn't know you could cook along with all your other talents."

Annie quickly covered her mouth with her napkin, laughing with her mouth full. She swallowed with a visible gulp and said, "Which talents are those, Porter?"

"I'm serious. You're smart, creative, have great decorating taste, can throw a great party, and you cook."

"You haven't tasted it yet."

Kip shook away his amazement and plunged his fork into the chicken salad. One bite and he thought he would moan out loud. It was delicious—beyond delicious. "This is so good—really." He picked up Annie's hand, giving it a quick kiss, before she dragged it away and tucked it in her lap. They resumed eating in silence, and but he couldn't keep his eyes off the amazing woman across from him. He'd do anything not to hurt her, but feared he'd do just that when he remembered the reason he'd come to see her.

"I need to talk to you about something," Kip said.

"Okay, let me clear the plates and get dessert out of the oven."

"You made dessert? Ms. Merriman, you constantly surprise me."

"Oh." Annie came up short, briefly stopping her trek to the kitchen. "It's nothing fancy. Just a quick peach cobbler. I bought the peaches from a farm stand on my way back from the campaign office last week. They're amazing." She slid thick oven mitts onto her hands and reached in for the bubbling dessert. "That's where the tomatoes came from. Weren't they good? I love farm fresh produce, don't you?"

Kip noticed Annie working at warp speed, talking non-stop, scooping cobbler into bowls and covering them with a long spray of whipped cream. It looked as though her hands were shaking and he suddenly had a case of déjà vu. He'd seen this nervous, chattering behavior from her before, but couldn't understand what was causing it this time.

She floated into the room, carrying a bowl in each hand, and walked over to the couch. "How about we have dessert over here."

Kip joined her and watched as she tugged the skirt of her sleeveless dress and flipped her ponytail behind her back. He took a small bite before setting the bowl on the coffee table.

"Delicious. Thank you." Kip cleared his throat and rubbed his palms together. With a deep breath, he turned and looked pointedly at Annie. "What I wanted to talk to you about w—"

"Wait, could I go first? There's something I need to tell you." Annie's bowl clattered on the coffee table, making him jump. She gave Kip a sheepish grin and folded her hands in her lap, keeping her gaze focused on it. "There's something you need to know about me. I haven't been completely honest with you."

"How so?"

"I don't like keeping secrets." A flush of guilt burned in Kip's gut. Had she figured out their scheme?

Annie popped to her feet and retrieved the newspaper from a basket near the door. When she returned to the sofa, she handed the paper to Kip and tapped on the headline story: Local Accounting Exec Indicted on Corruption Charges. "See that?"

Kip skimmed over the story, confusion rolling through his mind. He turned to Annie, his brow furrowed, and shrugged.

"That man who was indicted, John Wolfe? I used to work for him."

"Okay."

"I don't know if Tom ever told you, but I met him in a bar right after I quit my job."

"Actually, he did tell me that, which was what I—"

"That day, John Wolfe had offered me a promotion to head a new governmental auditing department. The firm was bidding on a government contract and I thought it seemed underhanded."

"Annie, it's okay because—"

"The reason I thought it was underhanded is because my father sits on the Senate Appropriations Committee." Annie took the newspaper from Kip and dropped it on the floor beside her. She grabbed both of his hands in hers and looked at him with watery eyes. "My last name is not Merriman. It's Cooper. I lied to you and Tom and I feel terrible about it."

"It's okay…I know—"

"You see, all my life I've had to deal with being George Cooper's daughter: the special treatment, the manipulation, even the humiliation from his sordid behavior. You would think it would be a good thing, but it isn't. People expect things from me, special favors because of my dad. I've stopped counting how many times I just wanted to be someone other than his daughter. My whole life my father has essentially ignored me and my siblings and embarrassed the whole family with his antics, but he continuously interferes behind the scenes. I guess he thinks…" Annie fingered a long curl behind her ear and released a heavy sigh. "Never mind what he thinks. The day I met Tom—and believe me, he met me at a really low point in my life—I decided to use my middle name as my last name. I didn't want him or anyone else to know who I was. I'm so sorry."

Kip could see that Annie was on the verge of tears, her eyes welling up. He pulled her to him and wrapped his arms around her. He held her to his chest until she released a cleansing breath and sat back. "Over the phone you said I deserved better than what happened in your office. And you deserve better from me. That's why I'm coming clean. By disguising my real name, I thought I could prove to you and myself that I could do a good job without any prior expectations. I would be crushed if I thought I was hired just because I was Senator Cooper's daughter. Do you understand?"

A heavy, sickening feeling caved in on Kip and he realized there was no way he could tell Annie the truth. Her thick dark lashes were wet with unshed tears and her pleading expression was nearly his undoing. Only he and Tom knew the truth and he was sure they could keep it from Annie. There was no point in sharing their prior knowledge with her now. Kip placed his hands on her face and tenderly kissed her quivering lips.

"Of course I understand. I get it."

"You do? I mean, if it's easier you can still call me Annie Merriman—around the staff I mean."

"That makes sense."

"Or you decide...whatever you call me is okay by me."

"That's fine. We'll stick to Merriman in the office. You're doing an incredible job and it doesn't matter what your real name is."

Annie threw herself against Kip, wrapping her arms tight around his neck. "Thank you for understanding. No more lies between us."

Kip swallowed the lump in his throat and locked his lips against hers, hoping she didn't recognize the guilt on his face. At some point he'd have to tell her the truth, but couldn't bring himself to do it now. He never wanted to see tears in her eyes again. Maybe luck would be on his side and he'd never have to confess.

"What time do you have to be back?" she asked, her lips still pressed to his.

"Not until three."

"Mmm." Annie resumed their luscious kiss and the removal of his tie. "That should be enough time for you to redeem yourself."

"We better not," he said, his eyes dark and hooded.

"But I have a nice soft bed," she replied with a song in her voice.

"But I don't have any condoms."

Annie undid another button while grazing her lips from his cheek to his ear. "But I do."

Kip tipped back, his brows arched and lips pursed.

She dropped her hands from his buttons. "Oh, come on, cowboy… surely you know this isn't my first rodeo?"

"Is that what this is?" Kip's hands had dropped to his sides and he cast a serious look at Annie.

"Well…no," she said, keeping her gaze down as she began re-buttoning his shirt. "What is it to you?"

Kip tipped her chin up with his fingers and said, "I was hoping we could see each other…exclusively."

"Yeah?"

"Yeah. My granny would have called it going steady. Would you go steady with me, Annie Merriman Cooper?"

Annie laughed and threw her arms around his neck, coming nose-to-nose with Kip. "Will you give me your class ring?"

"If I can find it, it's yours." Kip snaked his hand under her dress and ran his finger along the inside of her thong.

"Then the answer is yes."

Kip sealed the deal by covering her mouth with his, drawing her in to a deep, wet kiss. He tugged the zipper down the length of her back and murmured in her ear, "Now, what were you saying about a nice, soft bed?"

Nineteen

"Oww, damn it." Annie sat on her bed and looked at the broken nail she'd just received from the stubborn zipper on her suitcase, which she knew she'd packed too full. When Kip had asked her on Wednesday to spend the weekend with him at his river cabin, he had been vague about the itinerary. She decided to pack several outfits, both casual and dressy, along with bathing suits, shorts, T-shirts, and three different options for sleepwear. *Hopefully, I won't be wearing any of them*, she thought with a wicked grin.

As she finished filing her nail, her cell phone alerted her to a call from Kip.

"Hi," she answered, tossing the file back into the drawer.

"Hey, I've circled your block twice and can't find a parking place."

"No worries, I'm ready. I'll be down in a minute." With one last tug to the zipper, the suitcase was secure and she was ready for her weekend.

Kip double-parked outside Annie's apartment in his new Ford Escape Hybrid and honked the horn with gusto when Annie emerged from the building. He climbed out of the car, forcing drivers to veer around him, and rushed to Annie, who was dragging the heavy suitcase behind her.

"What's in here, a dead body?" Kip hefted the suitcase into the SUV and tapped the rear bumper with his leg.

"Porter, you leased a sensible, energy efficient car! I'm so proud of you." Annie threw up her hand in a high-five and Kip smacked his hand against hers, while wrapping his other arm around her waist, lifting her feet off the ground.

"I got the message loud and clear, Coach. I should be a better steward of the taxpayers' money. It's less expensive and made in America—maybe."

He drove them out of the city, away from the noise and crowds, across the Bay Bridge spanning the sparkling Chesapeake below to a land far-removed by more than just miles. They held hands as they passed farms and fields with fresh country air blowing through their opened windows, until they pulled into the gravel, tree-lined drive of Kip's river cabin.

After depositing her enormous suitcase inside the door, Kip stood back as Annie surveyed the cabin that time had forgotten with its wood paneled walls, brown plaid furniture, and shag carpet. She turned her back to Kip and stifled a laugh over the hideous furnishings.

"Nice, huh?" Kip leaned against the doorway with a smirk on his face.

"Well, now, I think it has a certain charm." She smiled a little too brightly.

"Oh, is that what you'd call it?"

"It has that warm, lived-in feeling," Annie said, as she wrung her hands together before pulling on the cord of a bamboo shade. She gave it a hard tug and found an ancient air conditioner sitting in the window.

Kip laughed and sauntered toward her. "What this place needs is the Annie touch. Maybe when the campaign is over you can help me update it."

"I would love that. This would be such a fun project." Annie rubbed her palms together and smiled broadly at Kip, her eyes sparkling.

"I want you to be comfortable here." Kip gathered her in his arms and brushed his lips across hers.

"As long as you're here with me, I'll be comfortable," Annie whispered, rising up on her tiptoes to return the kiss. She dropped back on her heels and grabbed Kip's hands, pulling him behind her. "Show me everything."

"Okay, turn around and you'll see the kitchen."

Annie circled the seventies sofa and saw old wood cabinets lining the wall with aluminum edged Formica counter tops. The table looked like something from a sixties sitcom and the vintage flooring had gone out of style with bell bottoms and peace signs, but the appliances were surprisingly modern stainless steel. "Very unique."

"Way to put a positive spin on it, Coach."

"Thanks. So, if I go straight ahead it takes me where?" She looked over her shoulder at Kip standing behind her and caught a mischievous twinkle in his eye.

"The most important room in the house," he murmured against her hair. "Start walking."

Through the doorway beyond the kitchen were two rooms on either side of the hall with the bathroom directly between. Kip placed his hands on Annie's shoulders and directed her to enter the bedroom on the left. It was another wood-paneled room, but it had updated furniture and modern linens. She felt a wash of relief that at least the bedroom wasn't so bad.

"So I was thinking, since it was such a long drive, before we go out to dinner we should have a nap." Kip engulfed Annie against his chest, wrapping his arms around her waist from behind, while nuzzling warm kisses down her neck. "What do you say to that?"

"I say I'm suddenly feeling very sleepy. A nap would do the trick."

Later that evening, Kip took her to a seafood restaurant along the river where they sat on the deck under a garland of clear light bulbs strung between weathered posts. They ate oyster stew and crab cakes with farm fresh corn-on-the-cob, and washed it all down with a locally-made craft beer. A gray-bearded man played classic rock on his beat-up guitar inside near the bar, and the music floated through the air to their table. Crickets were singing in the tall grass, a light breeze was blowing, and Annie felt a rush of contentment when she looked across the candlelit table at Kip.

"What's going on in that beautiful head of yours?" Kip pushed his empty plate aside and covered her hands with his, leaning in close.

Annie placed her elbows on the table and leaned to within inches of Kip's face. "I'm thinking there couldn't be a more perfect evening than this one." Her gaze washed over Kip's gorgeous face, memorizing each curve and contour, as her heart swelled with emotion.

"Just think—it's not over yet." Kip smiled and placed a tender kiss on her hands. "Ready to go back?"

On the short return trip to the cabin, Annie's thoughts were on the night ahead. Sure, they'd made love that afternoon and did indeed take a nap, but something about the way Kip looked at her through dinner and the way he'd said the night wasn't over, made her think she should consider pulling out the sexy negligee she packed. Would it send too strong a message? They had such a fun, flirty relationship and she didn't want him to think she was hoping for more than what it was.

Kip answered her question rather quickly when he began lighting candles scattered throughout the bedroom. While he fiddled with the dials on an old stereo in the living room, Annie slipped into the bathroom and slid the short silver silk over her head. She released her ponytail from a hair band and raked her fingers through her long curls. As she walked back into the bedroom, she heard the soft strains of smooth jazz and felt a shiver of anticipation tingle down her spine. Kip was lounging on the unmade bed, his head resting against his folded arms with a sheet barely covering the lower half of his naked body. Annie drew in a quivering breath at the sight of his mouthwatering form.

"Wow," Kip said, rolling onto his side and propping his head on his hand. "Don't you look beautiful?" He folded the sheet back and patted the mattress.

"I figured two can play this romance game." Why were her knees shaking? It wasn't like it was their first time. Annie tentatively climbed in beside Kip, never taking her eyes off his hooded gaze and the tiny grin on his face.

"Mmm, you smell so good." Kip drew her against him while burying his face in her hair. His hand slid up under her hem line, where he caressed her bare skin. "Thanks for making it easy, babe."

Annie laughed and rolled onto her back. His little comment helped break the nervous state she'd been in. "I aim to please."

"And you always do." Kip smothered her with a kiss, his fingers pulling the spaghetti strap off her shoulder and releasing a breast from its lacy cup. He nibbled and pecked his way from her lips to her breast, tenderly teasing her nipple with the roll of his tongue. Annie arched upward, giving him freer access, inviting him to take all he wanted. She ran her fingers through his hair, cradling his head as he took control of her body. Running her fingertips down his back to his butt, she cupped his rear with its downy soft hair sprinkled across his well-defined muscles. Her hands inched along to his front, where she gathered his erection in her hands.

Kip grasped her hand. "Slow down, baby. There's no rush." His command was soft and full of emotion, and Annie sank into the mattress, content to let him set the pace. He opened his eyes and held her gaze as he kissed her, devouring her mouth, watching the fire surely flaring in her eyes.

"Ah, Annie," he murmured as he blazed a trail with his tongue between her breasts to her navel while his hands captured her thighs, lifting them to rest on his wide shoulders. The touch of his fingers, his tongue, was too much.

"Kip," she moaned.

"Shhh, I'm here." Kip continued his delicate, intimate assault and Annie was nearing an excruciatingly wonderful explosion. His touch was slow, tender, unhurried precision, and it was driving her mad.

Annie wiggled her legs off his shoulders and slid deeper beneath him, taking his face in her hands. "I want you with me."

"I'm with you." He entered her with painstaking slowness, methodically building to a crescendo that sent them both reeling, gasping for air and clinging to each other. As they slowly descended their mountaintop, Kip brushed Annie's damp hair from her forehead, tapping tiny kisses where it had lain.

"Annie...ah, Annie." He exhaled and buried his face in the pillow with his cheek pressed to hers.

"Kip," she murmured while running her hands over his back. "I—" Kip lifted up his face and buried her lips under his. Annie swallowed the thought, saving it for later. I love you—damn it.

Saturday morning, Annie woke to the strong, smoky smell of bacon frying and the sound of Kip singing in the kitchen. She lay there smiling; her handsome, smart, sexy guy could also carry a tune. She jumped out of bed and caught Kip laying placemats on his Formica table with a water glass full of wildflowers in the center. He turned with a start when he realized she was in the room. He shrugged and threw up his hands.

"It's not Martha Stewart or Annie Cooper, but it's the best I could do."

"How nice. I'm impressed. When did you have time to do all this?" She tucked herself against his chest and slid her arms around his waist.

"While you were snoring away in there."

"Snoring?" Annie's head snapped off his chest. "I don't snore," she protested.

"Did I say snore? Purr maybe. That's it. You purr in your sleep."

"Oh, stop it." She playfully slapped her hand over his heart and looked over her shoulder. "What are you making?" She dipped her finger in a glass bowl of batter and plunged it in her mouth. "Pancakes?"

"Not just any pancakes. Cinnamon, apple, caramel pancakes."

"What?"

"A Porter family tradition. My dad created the recipe when I was a kid. He was the pancake expert in our house and we had them every time we came out here."

"Sounds delicious…and fattening."

"Fattening, pff." Kip gave a quick pat to Annie's rear end. "You don't have to worry about that."

With deft, professional ease, Kip cooked a dozen pancakes, flipping them onto a round plate with flourish and placing them on the table. When Annie took the first bite, she rolled her eyes in ecstasy. "You're killing me. These are delicious." She shoved another big bite in her mouth and looked up to find Kip staring at her, a humorous expression on his face. She gestured for him to start eating by rolling her hand in the air and Kip laughed as he picked up his fork.

With the last sip of her coffee, Annie leaned against the chair back, more than satisfied with the incredible breakfast. Kip was at the sink, filling it with hot sudsy water.

"Let me do that," she said.

"Nah, I got it. Relax."

"You're spoiling me, Porter."

"That's the plan."

Annie got up and padded across the floor, her bare feet slapping against the cool linoleum. She picked up a towel and began drying the dishes resting in the rack.

"So, are you up for a day on the water?" Kip flashed a smile as he rinsed a frying pan.

"Sure, what did you have in mind?"

"I'm going to borrow Rob's boat and take you out on the bay. How does that sound?"

"Sounds great."

Kip leaned down and pecked a kiss on her forehead. "It will be."

They spent the whole day out on the water on Rob's boat, which had been docked at a local marina. Kip took them on an hour-long drive into the bay and pulled the open-bow boat into a cove, where Annie felt they were secluded from the rest of the world. While Kip dropped the anchor, Annie pulled colorful towels out of a beach bag and two water bottles from the cooler. Sunshine beat down from a cloudless sky, but thankfully there was a light breeze across the water.

While she slathered on a coat of sunscreen and Kip draped their towels across the vinyl seats lining the bow, Annie said, "I'd like to hear that story about breaking Virgil's propeller."

"Oh, no…no way."

"Why? What have you got to hide?" Annie teased him by squeezing a blob of sunscreen on Kip's chest.

"Hey." He snatched the bottle from her hands and patted the seat opposite him. "It's embarrassing."

"Oh, please…what's the story?"

"Promise not to laugh."

"I can't promise anything." Annie stretched her legs across the seat, picked up her water bottle, and pinned Kip with a look. "Go on… start talking."

"Fine. But I'll expect you to tell something personal after I'm done. Deal?"

"Maybe," she replied with a crooked grin.

"You're tough, Coach. Okay, the marina where Rob keeps his boat?" Kip continued after Annie quickly nodded her head. "That's Virgil's marina and I worked there every summer of high school, pumping gas, cleaning boats, stuff like that. Anyway, one summer I decided I was finally going to get laid by this hot chick from Delaware. I was sixteen, all my friends had done it—"

"Or so they said," Annie interjected.

"Right. And I decided that was going to be the summer it happened. Anyway, this hot chick from Delaware came down every weekend with her parents. Tiffany Sue Buttons."

Annie sat up and spurted out her water. "Seriously?"

"Yep, Tiffany Sue had the biggest breasts I'd ever seen and she made sure everyone knew it."

"A boob man, huh?" Annie tipped her sunglasses down and cast a look over the frames.

"You should know that by now." Kip mimicked her move, but leveled his gaze at her cleavage pressed inside her scant bikini top.

Annie flicked a handful of water at Kip and said, "Go on."

"As I was saying, she had flirted with me for a few weeks and all the guys at the marina encouraged me to take her out. So one Saturday night I asked Virgil if I could borrow one of his boats. I took her across the river into a cove."

"Please tell me we're not in the same cove."

"We're on the bay; that was on the river. So, it took a while—she had a lot to teach me—and it was getting dark. I forgot to drop the anchor and the boat drifted into shallow water. I guess Virgil was worried because we hadn't come back, so he came looking for us. We did it right there on the floor between the seats." Kip pointed to the floor and gave Annie a wink. "And just as I was pulling up my pants, I saw Virgil coming. I started the engine without realizing we had run aground. It damaged the prop and he had to tow us back."

"What did Virgil say to you? Was he mad?"

"No, he wasn't mad, but believe me he never let me forget it. All he said was, 'Now that you're a man, remember next time to borrow a cabin cruiser'."

Annie sat up and tucked her head into her knees, her shoulders shaking with laughter.

"Hey, it wasn't funny. It was embarrassing. The story spread throughout the marina and I was a joke the rest of the summer."

"Don't you wonder what he saw?"

"Probably all of it." Kip sat up and laid his hand on her knee. "Your turn. Got anything as humiliating as that one?"

"Hardly."

"Okay then…how many broken hearts have you left in your wake?" He struck her with an intensive gaze. Annie got up from her recline and wiggled to the edge of her seat, placing her hands on his thighs.

"None that I know of and I don't have anyone in my past as interesting as Tiffany Sue Buttons."

"I don't believe it." Kip leaned close and kissed the tip of Annie's nose.

"Believe it. I've had my heart broken a time or two—been played way too many times to count. For example…" Annie stopped momentarily to catch her breath, the memories still stinging after all these years. "In college, I dated a guy for a while who told me he was a journalism major whose life goal was to work at the *Washington Post*. As it turned out, he was a poli-sci major who wanted an internship in my father's office. When he didn't get it and I refused to talk to my dad, he dumped me."

"Ouch."

"Yeah. And I dated a guy a couple of years ago who after six months confessed he had a wife and two kids back in Connecticut."

"Annie, that's awful."

"And he had the nerve to ask if that would be a problem." She chuckled while looking over Kip's shoulder, avoiding his eyes. Kip pulled her over to his lap and wrapped his arms around her waist. "I don't get it."

"I guess I'm a bad judge of character or I have 'sucker' written across my forehead. For all I know you could be playing me right now." Annie cupped Kip's face in her hands. "Are you playing me, Porter?"

As though stung, Kip stared at her, his mouth agape. His eyes bore into hers as he said, "Why would you ask me that?"

"Oh, I don't know…former football player—player—get it?" She threw her head back with mock laughter. "What position did you play? Tight end?" She reached down to his butt and grabbed a handful.

"Easy now."

"I think that was the right position for you."

"If you're not careful, I'll lay you between the seats like Tiffany Sue."

"Ha! You wouldn't dare."

"Watch me." With lightening speed, Annie found herself flat on her back, the prickly outdoor carpet on the deck chafing her skin. Kip nuzzled against her neck, ravishing her with kisses.

Hours later they cruised back to the dock as the sun was sinking below the horizon. Most of the boaters had returned to the marina, the slips filled with vessels of every size. While Kip tied off the lines, Annie set the cooler and bag on the dock and then climbed onto the creaking boards. An old man dressed in baggy faded work pants and red suspenders limped toward them. Kip stepped onto the dock and jogged to the old man, gathering him in a bear hug. At least a head taller, Kip wrapped an arm around the small man's shoulder as they walked toward Annie.

"Look who I found! Annie, this is Virgil."

"It's so nice to meet you. I'm Annie." She reached out her hand in greeting and was yanked into Virgil's embrace. He was strong for such a small, elderly man.

"Damn, Kip, what line of shit did you give this beauty to get her to go out with you? Must've been good."

Kip's face grew red and he patted Virgil on his back, laughing.

"I heard you were at the crab feast, young lady. You're all the talk around here. Sorry I missed it," Virgil said with a twinkle in his eye.

Annie arched her brows at Kip. Surely Rob hadn't spread the story of them making out in the water. She was Tiffany Sue Buttons today in more ways than one.

"Kip, can I have a word with you?" Virgil didn't wait for an answer. He put his hand on Kip's back and began leading him down the dock.

Kip tossed Annie the keys and said, "I'll bring everything when I'm done."

When the men reached the end of the dock, Virgil turned and looked up at Kip with a shadow of seriousness across his face. "Son, you know your daddy and I were the best of friends and I think he'd want me to step in if I thought it necessary."

"Absolutely." Kip crossed his arms over his chest and mirrored Virgil's serious expression.

"Ken would be real proud of you the way you've handled your role as congressman. Most of the time, you've done right by the people around here. But, son, we have to talk about this pipeline. It's not good—not good at all."

Kip looked down at the man he'd grown to admire over the years. He'd not only been the best boss he'd ever had, he had become like a father to him since his dad died. Throughout his whole life, Kip had considered Virgil to be one of the wisest people he knew, strong in his beliefs, never wavering in his convictions.

"See now, Virgil, that's where we disagree. I see this pipeline as an opportunity for growth and economic stability in our district."

"How so?" Virgil shook his head, lifting his faded ball cap off his head and repositioning it.

"It's going to bring good jobs to the region. And think of all the possibilities after it's built. The pipeline will spur development, attract new companies to our area—"

"Frankly, son, it scares the hell out of me. I worry about an oil pipeline running less than three miles away from this water."

"Virgil, you have nothing to worry about. It's going to be built with the highest quality materials, far exceeding government standards."

"How can you be sure? I've lived on this river my whole life—born less than a mile down that way. I've made my living here, raised my family here, and…" Virgil sighed heavily and turned to look out at the still water. He appeared to be contemplating the setting sun while Kip scuffed his foot against the weathered wood. Finally, Virgil broke away from his reverie.

"It's taken years of effort to get the bay and its tributaries back to a somewhat healthy condition, and there's still more to do. If there were a leak or worse, a break in that pipeline, not only would it be an environmental disaster but an economic one, too. I'm begging you to reconsider." Virgil lifted himself to his full height to look Kip in the eye.

"I assure you that won't happen. I love this river, too. I wouldn't want anything to happen either," Kip replied.

"But why take the risk? This is a farming and fishing community. I don't think anyone wants the kind of growth you're talking about."

Kip looked down at the pack of Marlboros Virgil always had in his T-shirt pocket and the old Orioles ball cap he'd always worn. He might not be able to change Virgil's fashion sense, but he hoped he could change his way of thinking. "Virgil, change keeps us moving forward. It's good to diversify. A couple of years of drought could devastate this area. Wouldn't it be nice to know there would be some families who could survive a drought because they're livelihood was somehow related to the pipeline?"

Virgil sighed and again looked out at the quiet river. He shook his head a few times and turned back to Kip. "Look, I'm not the only one who feels this way. This isn't just some stubborn old man talking to you. You keep this up and you'll lose the election."

"That's not what our research shows."

"Your research is wrong. What about the petitions, the letters?"

"What petitions?"

"Son, there have been at least three petitions going around—at least I know I've signed three. Letters have been sent. People are up in arms about this."

"I haven't seen any petition or letters. I don't know what you're talking about."

"You better check with whoever opens your mail, because believe me, they've been sent. If you don't want a riot on the capitol steps, son, you better stop this bill."

TWENTY

Thank goodness Kip had given her the keys—it was sweltering inside the car. As soon as she climbed inside, she put down the windows and started the SUV, allowing the air conditioner to blast in her face. She glanced down at the dock and noticed Kip and Virgil talking and could see it was a serious discussion: no laughing, no patting each other on the back, the opposite of the way they had greeted each other a few minutes ago. Their conversation ended with a brief handshake and then Kip walked quickly up the dock, his head tilted down.

When he climbed in the car, Annie noticed his jaw muscle twitching. He didn't say a word as he charged out of the parking lot. They turned onto the narrow country road and Kip roared the engine, keeping his eyes pointed straight at the windshield.

"Is something wrong?" Annie asked, placing her hand on his arm.

"Everything's fine." Kip's clipped answer told her everything was not fine.

She propped her elbow against her door and twirled a piece of hair around her finger, let it drop, then twisted it again while she stared out the window at the flat fields.

"What do you think of the pipeline bill?" Kip asked, his voice deep and gritty.

"The pipeline? Well, to be honest, I haven't read up on it much. What I know is what you've told me. Why?"

"Virgil thinks it's a bad idea."

"Oh." Annie twirled another strand of hair so tight it stung her scalp. She let it drop and shifted in her seat to face Kip. "Remember what I overheard at the crab feast? Those men were grumbling about the pipeline, saying some rather unkind things about you."

"No, remind me."

Annie looked down at her lap, wringing her hands, wishing he hadn't asked. They'd had a perfect day and she didn't want to put him in a worse mood than he seemed to already be in.

"Tell me," Kip growled. "All of it."

"There were three men standing by the grill talking about how the pipeline was a terrible idea. They thought it was the wrong place for it. One man said he heard the company building it had a terrible safety record. Another guy said he was thinking of putting his farm up for sale and getting out of here before it came through. He thought maybe you'd been offered a bribe or something because he was shocked when he heard you were sponsoring the bill. He was going to talk to you that day, but one of the other guys told him to hold off until after the crab feast."

Kip didn't respond, just kept his eyes straight ahead, but Annie could see he was breathing heavily and the twitch in his jaw was getting stronger.

"Since you brought it up, the pipeline was one of the issues on the poll I wanted to talk to you about," she said.

"I want to know your opinion—based on what you know about it." Kip jerked the car to a stop at an intersection despite the green light ahead and looked at Annie. "What do you think?"

"Shouldn't you go on through the intersection?"

"No one's behind me. What's your opinion?"

Annie nibbled on her bottom lip and looked through the rear window. When she turned back, Kip was drilling her with piercing eyes and knitted brow. She cleared her throat and picked up twirling her hair again. "Like I said, I don't know much about it, but I agree with that gentleman at the picnic. It doesn't seem like the right place to build it. If they have to expand the pipeline, why not do it in a remote place that isn't near water? I mean, the bay and rivers are sources of drinking water, water for crops, fishing, shipping, recreation. If something happened, it would be devastating."

"Shit." Kip slammed his foot on the gas and squealed through the intersection.

They pulled in the drive a few minutes later, Kip still silently fuming, and he brought the car to a stop. He reached into the back seat, grabbed the cooler and bag, and went into the house ahead of Annie. When she reached the door, he was coming back out.

"I've got to talk to Tom," he said, brushing past her.

Kip walked down the lane with his cell phone pressed to his ear, and though Annie couldn't hear what was being said, she could see it was a heated discussion. His arms were flailing and his face was red. If only she knew what was going on.

She put the remaining food and drinks in the refrigerator, then took a shower. After she was dressed, she came into the kitchen and saw an open beer bottle on the table. The screen door slammed and Kip came in with grocery bags in his hands.

"I meant to stop at the store on our way back from the marina. I thought we'd grill tonight." He appeared relaxed, pleasant, as if nothing had happened earlier.

"That sounds good. Anything I can do?" Annie asked.

"Sure. Can you make a salad while I shower?"

"Okay."

"Thanks, babe." Kip dropped a quick kiss on her temple and brushed past her.

Throughout dinner, Annie waited for Kip to bring up what had happened earlier that day between him and Virgil and Tom, but he seemed to be avoiding any talk of the pipeline. It was as if he'd flipped the switch between his angry and happy self. After dinner, they sat on the screen porch, rocking back and forth on an old-fashioned glider. Annie's curiosity was getting the best of her.

"Everything okay with you and Tom? You seemed pretty angry when you were talking to him."

"Oh." Kip sighed. "Everything's fine. It's this damn pipeline. I'm sorry about earlier."

"It's okay. Anything I can do to help?"

"Nah, we're handling it. I was hoping you'd never see my quick temper."

"Too late...you've already turned that temper on me, remember?" She wrapped her arms around his waist and they both chuckled.

"I didn't want to deal with anything work related this weekend. Just wanted it to be about us."

"It has been. But, you and I need to talk about the poll results."

"Not this weekend, please," Kip said, as he tipped her chin up with his hand.

"Monday morning?"

"Absolutely. Monday morning, I'll be all yours," he said.

"What about right now?"

Kip's face erupted in a wide grin and he skimmed his lips across hers. "Definitely all yours."

Annie was trapped—trapped under the weight of a robust, delicious man—his arm draped protectively around her waist and his leg thrown over hers. Kip's shoulder was resting on her mass of hair and his warm breath was tickling her ear. She had to get up—nature was calling—but she didn't want to wake her sleeping giant. Ever so gently, she lifted his arm, placed it by his side, and slid out from under his leg. Painfully, she tugged her hair from beneath him and ran into the tiny bathroom outside his bedroom door. When Annie returned, she stood in the doorframe, drinking in the sight before her: Kip was dozing on his back with a peaceful expression, his lashes against his cheeks and his mouth gaping slightly. She felt a rush of emotion so intense it brought tears to her eyes. She'd just spent two days with him at his little cabin and she'd never been happier. It had been more perfect than she could have imagined.

Graceful as a cat, Annie crawled back into bed, tucked her shoulder under his arm, and rested her head against the soft dark hair on his chest. Kip sighed loudly, raised and lowered his knee, and then wrapped his arm around Annie, falling back into a deep sleep. She lay there looking up at the swirling ceiling fan click-click-clicking with each turn of the paddles. She splayed her fingers across Kip's chest, right over his heart, feeling its steady rhythm. "You have my heart, Kip Porter," she whispered softly. She leaned up and ran her lips gently over his chest while her hair veiled across his shoulders. After several moments, Kip stirred from his sleep and kissed Annie tenderly.

"Good morning, beautiful. How long have you been awake?" he asked in a groggy voice.

"Long enough to know this has been the best weekend ever." Annie's cell phone rang, the shrillness echoing off the bedroom walls.

"Uh oh, it's my mother. I forgot to call her." Annie sat up and tapped the phone screen, answering in her sweetest voice. "Hi, Mom. How are you this morning?"

"Ann, I was just setting the table for brunch and realized you didn't tell me whether you were coming or not."

Annie pinched the bridge of her nose and took a deep breath. "I'm so sorry, Mom. I forgot to call you. I can't come this morning."

"Oh? You haven't been to brunch in over a month. I was hoping you'd come this morning."

Annie glanced over at Kip, lying against a pile of pillows while he dragged his fingers up and down her back. He had a lazy smile and his blue eyes smoldered. She covered the phone with her hand and whispered to Kip, "How would you like to go with me to my parents' house for Sunday brunch next week?"

"Sounds great. Sure."

She pecked a kiss on the back of his hand and returned to her conversation. "Hey, Mom, count on me for brunch next week—for sure. In fact, I'd like to bring someone if that's okay."

"Of course," her mother responded with delight. "Who will you be bringing?"

"Kip Porter."

"Oh, how exciting. I had a feeling about him."

Annie laughed and rolled her eyes. "Okay, Mom, don't go crazy. We're just—well, I was going to say friends, but actually we've started dating."

"Ann, I'm thrilled. He's a very handsome man. Good for you."

"Thanks." Annie threw her hands in the air and looked to the ceiling. "Okay, I've got to go. I'll see you next week."

After Annie clicked off the call, Kip rose up and flipped her to her back. His eyes followed the back of his hand as he skimmed his fingers down her cheek, to her neck, to her breasts. "So, I'm going to meet the parents next week, huh?"

"Looks like it. Are you ready for that?" Annie wrapped her arms around his neck and focused on his reaction.

"I'm looking forward to it." Kip laid a long kiss against her lips.

"Surprisingly, so am I."

Across the bay, a world away from the quiet, riverside dawn, another couple laid side-by-side in luxurious cotton sheets beneath smoke rising toward the ceiling from a slim cigarette. Amelia Wentworth took another deep drag and let the gray smoke ribbon twirl above her while Tom tried to steady his breath, wiping sweat from his brow.

"Where does your husband think you are?" he panted.

"He thinks I'm at church, but he really doesn't care since he's playing golf."

Amelia leaned across Tom's chest and stubbed out the cigarette in an empty wine glass on the nightstand. "Okay, time to talk business."

"I've barely caught my breath and you want to talk business."

"Whether you realize this or not, my dear, this is all business. Now, we've got full congressional support and we're about 50-50 in the Senate. My sources tell me there may be a wind power farm in Nebraska tacked on to the bill, which might help. It will satisfy the alternative energy folks."

"True." Tom climbed out of bed and stepped into his boxers. His back was to Amelia and he felt himself stiffen when she said, "What about Appropriations? Any problem with us getting the bid?"

"Well, that may be our only glitch. We're having a problem getting an ally on the committee."

"Excuse me? I thought we'd have George Cooper in our pocket by now." Amelia rose up on her knees and burned an angry stare into Tom's back.

"Look, Amelia," Tom turned, letting his eyes wander down her incredibly well-preserved body. "I think we need to come up with another strategy, just in case we can't secure Senator Cooper's support."

"I should have known better than to get mixed up with a bunch of rookies."

"I'm just saying that if we had a couple more committee members on board, the decision would be more solid."

"Amateurs!" Amelia huffed before she shuffled on her bended knees to the edge of the bed, where she grabbed Tom between the legs. "Here's the strategy we're going to use. You're going to kick your boy's ass in gear and get George Cooper and the rest of the Appropriations Committee to grant us the bid, or I will pull all future financing from him, ruin his and your careers in the process, and you can forget about any other money coming your way. Do we have an understanding?"

TWENTY-ONE

"Kip, stop," Annie implored, though she exerted little effort as Kip nibbled on her neck and pressed her firmly against him with a hand on her bottom. His mouth covered hers, stifling her laughter, luring her in for a tantalizing kiss. Her resolve washed away and she wrapped her arms around his neck, molding her body to his. After a few moments, Annie finally tore her lips away. "If you keep this up, we'll end up back on that couch."

"Would that be so bad?" Kip looked down at her with laughter in his eyes. "It was a great way to start the week, as I recall."

"We can't spend every Monday morning on that couch."

"Why not?"

"Kip!" Annie scolded him, trying to wriggle out of his tight embrace.

"Okay, you're right. So let go of me if you don't want to go there."

Annie smothered a giggle against his chest. "I'm trying." Kip increased his grip on her, making it impossible to get away.

"You don't seem to be trying very hard, Ms. Cooper."

"Shhh! No one knows my real name." Annie stopped wiggling and glared hard at Kip. "Please, it will just be too confusing, raise too many questions with the staff."

"I know, babe, I haven't said anything. Your secret is safe." Kip kissed her forehead and took a step back, but didn't take his hands from around her waist. "We had a deal. It's all good."

"Okay, then. Tom should be in here any minute. You need to go sit down...behind your desk...where he won't see..." Annie raised her eyebrows and gazed pointedly below Kip's belt.

"Okay, Coach. I hear ya." He patted her on the bottom and walked around his desk, dropping into his leather chair.

"Right. It's time to get to work." Annie sat in the chair in front of Kip's desk and crossed her legs. She watched Kip's eyes focus on the rise of her skirt and she pulled down on the hem as best she could.

"That's not going to work, you know. I can still see your gorgeous legs," he said, with smoldering eyes.

"I'll be sure to wear pants in the future." Annie began rifling through a stack of papers on her lap, keeping her eyes cast downward, still feeling Kip's searing gaze.

"I missed you last night," Kip whispered.

"Stop!" Anne slammed the pile on her lap, but couldn't hold back a huge grin. "We're never going to get any work done."

"I mean it. I had trouble falling asleep. I missed that little purr thing you do."

"Kip." Her response came out breathless. She wished he'd quit looking at her with such earnest desire. His sexy voice and smoky gaze were driving her crazy.

"What are you doing tonight?"

Before she could answer, Tom swung the door wide and entered with an iPad in one hand and a coffee mug in the other. "I hope you didn't start without me."

"Oh, we definitely started," Kip said, hiding his mischievous grin behind his folded hands.

"Okay, then let's start again."

"Wish we could," Kip mumbled to himself. He sat up straight and wheeled his chair closer to the desk as he picked up a stapled packet of papers. "The floor is yours, Annie. Tell us about this poll."

"I just wanted to point out a few things that jumped out at me. Overall, you have a slight lead over your opponent, but there are some areas of concern which may need to be addressed. Currently you're trailing in the fifty to sixty-five age group by ten points and in the sixty-six and older, you're trailing by fifteen."

"Why do you suppose that is?" Kip asked.

"Weird. You captured that demographic with no problem in the last election," Tom said.

"If you look on page three you'll see the graph showing survey responses to several key issues. You're fine in these two age groups when it comes to your stance on immigration, defense spending, healthcare, and the economy. The biggest drop is in regard to the pipeline. You'll see a significant decline in support there."

"That can't be right. Who designed this poll?" Tom asked.

"I did," Annie answered.

Tom released a quick chuckle and settled back in his chair, draping his leg over his opposite knee. He straightened his tie and said, "How scientific could it have been?"

"I'll admit that it was put together rather quickly, but it's accurate information. Our volunteers did a great job asking the questions and they got some very frank, *unsolicited* responses."

"Like what?" Kip asked, as he stood and began slowly pacing behind his desk.

"Just what I told you over the weekend. They don't want the pipeline running through their area because they're afraid of an environmental disaster, afraid the pipe will leak."

"You two talked about this over the weekend? Without me. Since when are you conducting business over the weekend without my knowledge?" Tom slid to the edge of his seat, focusing his question to Kip. Annie was sitting to his right and felt as though he were blocking her out.

"We weren't conducting business. Just happened to talk about it briefly."

"What the hell is going on with you two?" Tom whispered through gritted teeth.

Annie slumped in her chair as she watched the color leave Kip's face.

"Spill it," Tom barked.

"Annie and I are dating," Kip blurted, tucking his hands deep in his pockets.

"Shit, I should've known. Who else knows?" Tom looked pointedly at Kip.

"No one. I didn't think the staff needed to know," Kip said.

"Well, hell, they already think there's something going on between you—the way you look at each other in staff meetings. You might as well come out with it." Tom jumped to his feet and glared at Kip across the desk.

"Fine. You can tell them." Kip sighed and ran a hand through his hair. "In the meantime, what about this pipeline bill?"

"I question Annie's results. The official poll numbers are showing strong support for the pipeline." Tom held up his tablet flashing a screen crowded with numbers. "I've got studies showing a low risk for environmental issues. I'm not sure where she came up with these bogus numbers. The company slated to do the work has a strong safety record."

"Have I seen that?" Kip asked.

"Of course. I email everything to you as I get it," Tom said.

"Really? Does that include letters and petitions against the pipeline?"

The room fell silent as Kip flattened his hands on the desk and leaned toward Tom, whose freckled complexion slowly grew to a deep pink from his neck to his cheeks. Tom pivoted and walked behind his chair, keeping his back to Kip.

"I give you everything you need to see."

"I want to see everything," Kip said.

Tom turned and placed his hands on the back of the chair. "You know that's impossible. That's why you have a staff—to read your correspondence, do research, keep you abreast of what's happening."

"Apparently, the staff hasn't been doing its job." Once again Kip's and Tom's eyes locked.

"Um, Tom." Annie cleared her throat as she rose from her chair. "Did I understand you correctly…someone's already been chosen to build the pipeline?"

"Wentworth Global," Tom answered at the same time as Kip said, "The contractor hasn't been determined."

Annie looked back and forth between Tom and Kip as if watching a tennis match. "Which is it?"

Kip stopped pacing and answered with a sigh. "It hasn't officially been determined—that's up to Appropriations, but Wentworth is the lead candidate to receive the bid. They've built pipelines all over the world."

"And they have an outstanding record of quality and safety. I think it's time for a PR campaign. Write a position paper and get it published in all the newspapers. Maybe hold a press conference touting the benefits of the bill. I don't think your constituents know how important it will be to your district, or how safe," Tom said.

"I'm not sure they can be convinced. It's personal with them," Annie said, stepping in front of Tom. "All the PR in the world isn't going to change their minds. If anything, it will make them angrier. The water is their livelihood, their way of life. If something happens, it will take years to recover."

"What the hell do you know about it? You're an accountant, not a political strategist or an environmental scientist. Stick to what you know."

Annie glared at him. "It doesn't take a rocket scientist to see this is a bad idea." She turned to Kip and said, "I'm sorry, Kip, but you know how Virgil feels and you know he's not alone."

"Who the hell is Virgil? You've known this chick for a month and you're going to let her call the shots?"

Kip came around the desk and gripped Tom's arm. "Come on, Tom. Annie has been vital to this campaign. She's the one over there talking to the people. She knows what's going on in their minds. Maybe I would have known too if you hadn't kept those petitions from me. If you'd get your head out of your ass, you'd see this was a bad idea."

"Aw, fuck. You're whipped. This wasn't in the plans, bro."

Kip dropped Tom's arm and ground his fist into his own hand, looking from Tom to Annie and back again. He wrapped his arm around Annie's waist and said, "I think Tom and I need to have a talk alone."

He reached down and handed Annie her messenger bag and stack of papers. Taking her by the hand, he guided her to the door and planted a light kiss on her lips. "I'll call you later."

Annie stood outside the door, stunned she'd been rushed out of the room so quickly. She looked around the reception area and noticed everyone looking at her. She shrugged her shoulders and said, "Kip and Tom have some things to talk about."

All eyes turned to the door when they heard Kip's booming voice, though the thick wood muffled his words. She gave a sheepish grin to the lingering staff and walked into the empty conference room. As soon as she shut the door, she dropped her bag on the table and tugged her fingers through her hair. So she hadn't misunderstood what she'd seen at the yacht party. Tom and Amelia were obviously working together to get the bid awarded to Wentworth Global. She was more confused now than before. Kip seemed surprised when she told him about the two of them. He insisted he was in control. If Kip was in charge, why did it seem like Tom was still calling all the shots? Even now, knowing how his constituents felt, Kip hadn't stood up to Tom or defended her research. And, what did Tom mean by "the plan?"

She settled in a chair, fired up her laptop, and typed "Wentworth Global" in the search box, needing to learn more about it. Several listings popped up on the screen and she began by tapping on Wentworth's official website. Photos of construction sites and gleaming office towers dotted the homepage. In the upper right hand corner was a photo of Mr. and Mrs. Wentworth. Annie had a flashback to the cocktail party on their yacht where she observed Kip in a serious conversation with them. Exactly how much influence did the Wentworths have on this pipeline deal? Over Kip and Tom?

Annie went back to the search list and tapped on an article about a Wentworth pipeline in Canada that had had a major leak in the first year of operation. They'd paid billions in lawsuits with several still pending. Annie printed out this article and any others she could find about Wentworth's workmanship. She also printed out several articles about the effects of oil spills on wetlands. Finally, she perused photos of the Wentworths at various political fundraising events, all smiles in their glittery attire. Most of the photos showed one or both of them posing beside key political figures. Several showed them at parties hosted by other wealthy donors, and the last picture she found was of Amelia Wentworth arm-in-arm with John Wolfe. A sharp prickle crept down Annie's spine. She stared at the beaming couple and felt renewed disgust for the seedy side of politics.

Annie caught a glimpse of the clock on the wall and realized the morning was getting away from her. She needed to drive over to campaign headquarters to plot out locations for new election signs and organize several neighborhood canvases. She tapped the stack of information against the table and put it all in a manila envelope. On her way out of the office she placed it in Kip's inter-office mail slot and glanced at his door, which remained closed. She concluded he must still be in with Tom and decided to tap out a text message to him rather than interrupt.

Put some important info in your box. Call me.

As soon as the door had shut behind Annie, Kip stalked back to Tom, who stood with his arms folded across his chest, leaning against his desk, shaking his head. "I can't believe this. You're actually having second thoughts about a bill that could have a major impact on your career and your wallet? What the hell is the matter with you?"

"We should never have gotten involved with the Wentworths. Should have done more research to gauge what the people think," Kip said. "I should've known what was going on with my own constituents."

"Shit, man, you know most voters don't know a damn thing about what's going on. All they care about is their next paycheck. This bill is going to help the folks in your area—you know that."

"Tom." Kip stepped within inches of him, his brow creased in a V. "It's a bad idea. I'm having second thoughts. I don't want to sponsor this bill. Get it?"

"I don't think you have any choice. We're in too deep." Tom emphasized each word with a finger poke to Kip's chest. "Piss off the Wentworths and you can kiss your career good-bye. *Get it?*"

"We're not in too deep. No money has changed hands—only a few dinners and trips. Unless you've promised Amelia something you shouldn't have. They can find some other sucker to run the pipeline through his district. I want out."

"I won't let you do that."

Kip grabbed Tom by the shirt, gathering a clump of necktie and cotton in his hand, and pulled him within inches of his face. "This isn't college football, Tom. You're not calling the plays anymore. I am. Either get on board or find another team."

Finally, Tom ended the stand-off. "You'll be laughed right off the hill." He pushed Kip's hand off his shirt. "Picture the headlines: Pussy Whipped Congressman Can't Handle it When the Going Gets Tough. Things haven't been the same since you met Annie, bro."

"You were the one who brought her on board."

"Just to get close to her father—remember? And, speaking of which, when's that going to happen?"

"It doesn't matter anymore. Stop and think about it: this is a bad bill. I don't want to be associated with something with such potential for disaster."

"I thought you were smarter, had some guts." Tom pushed past him and, as he reached the doorway, he left Kip with a parting shot. "Listen, bro, we've known each other a long time. The Kip I know would never let some bitch in a tight skirt lead him around by the balls."

"Oh, sorry, bro, I didn't realize we were talking about you and Amelia Wentworth. Who has who by the balls now?"

TWENTY-TWO

The heavy wooden door slammed shut, its sound reverberating throughout the hallowed office.

"Damn it!" Kip slammed his fist into his left hand and then shook out the pain. He dropped into his leather desk chair and opened a lower drawer, pulling out the fifth of Jack Daniel's he kept stashed inside. The burning elixir served as a celebratory libation as well as a stress-relieving tonic. Today, it would be used for the latter.

Kip splashed a generous amount of amber liquid in his coffee cup and took a quick shot, feeling it burn into his chest. How the hell had he gotten himself into this mess? This wasn't what he had signed up for when he decided to run for Congress. He stepped from behind his desk and picked up the team photo from his junior year—the year Maryland had won the league championship. In the front row, standing side-by-side like they had always been since the day they met at the first practice session their freshmen year, were him and Tom. The glass had not been replaced since the day Tom had thrown it to the floor in a burst of anger. Kip could count on one hand the number of times they had even raised their voices to one another, and now it seemed arguing was their only form of communication.

He laid the picture face-down on the credenza and picked up a photo of his family. It was a shot taken for the membership directory at his church when he was in high school. His mom and dad were sitting front and center surrounded by him, Rob, and David from behind. Kip couldn't remember the last time he'd crossed the threshold of his church—or any church for that matter—but he still held firm to the beliefs instilled in him, though lately he had wandered far from those values. He felt a crushing weight in his chest just thinking of what his dad would think of his choices—aspiring to promote his career with no regard for those it might hurt. It wasn't just wanting to rise through the ranks of politics; he had become greedy. He had lost all sense of himself.

Kip pulled his cell phone out of his pocket and saw a text from Annie.

Put some important info in your box. Call me.

He tapped the screen, pulling up several photos of Annie and the two of them he'd taken over the weekend. The weight in his chest lifted along with the corners of his mouth. It had been an amazing weekend—relaxing, fun, sexy, carefree. That's how Annie made him feel. That's how he always wanted to feel and he knew with Annie by his side it could be that way—always.

Kip tipped back the last of his whiskey, put his family portrait back on the credenza, and picked up his desk phone. He knew what had to be done.

"Good morning, this is Congressman Porter. Is the Speaker available, please?"

Annie threw her hands over her head and stretched long and hard, attempting to un-kink her muscles. She'd been at the computer all afternoon, graphing out locations for campaign signs and making a schedule for the volunteers coming in this weekend. Pushing her spine against the chair, she let her head fall back against her shoulders and her mouth open in a wide yawn. What she wouldn't give for a yoga session followed by a fruity cocktail.

She looked down at her phone. Still no word from Kip. Her old-fashioned self battled against her modern-woman self: should she call Kip or wait for him to call her? There was nothing wrong with her calling him—after all, he was her boyfriend. But then the voice of Marjorie Cooper rang through her head: "Ladies never call gentlemen." She drummed her nails against the desk a few seconds and then decided to listen to her modern-woman self, tapping Kip's name on her screen.

"Hi, babe," he answered on the third ring. She could hear the weariness in his voice. "I'm sorry I haven't called. It's been crazy."

She felt herself sag with relief. No more listening to her mother and her old-fashioned self. "That's okay. I just wanted to see how you're doing. It was a rough morning."

"It's been a rough day."

"Want to tell me about it?"

"Nothing to tell really."

Annie chewed on her lower lip while twisting a curl around her finger. After a few silent moments she said, "Did you get a chance to read the material I put I your box?"

Kip released a deep sigh. "No, but I'll get around to it."

"It's really important, Kip. It's about Wentworth Global and the safety of this pipeline."

"Okay."

"Okay?"

"I'm sorry. What do you want me to say?"

"Say you're going to read it, that you're going to consider dropping this bill. That you're going to stop shutting me out."

"Shutting you out?"

"I feel like..." Annie took a deep breath, attempting to control the quiver in her voice. "Whenever Tom is around you act like I'm not there... like what I have to say isn't important."

"That's not true."

"Isn't it? Why did you rush me out of the office this morning?"

"There's just some stuff between Tom and me."

"Like what?"

"Annie, I don't mean to shut you out, but sometimes Tom and I need to talk alone. That's all." The conversation stopped for a moment, neither one saying a word. Finally, Kip said, "I value your opinion. You're a smart woman and, whether you want to believe it or not, I'm listening."

"Thank you. I needed to hear that." Annie glanced down at her nails and waited for Kip to speak. After several moments she couldn't take the silence any longer. "So…how about I take you out to dinner? My treat."

"I wish I could." Kip released another loud sigh. "I have a meeting in about twenty minutes."

"At six o'clock?"

"It was the only time we could do it. Let's try again tomorrow."

Annie felt herself sag once more, but this time it was due to disappointment. Since spending the weekend with Kip, all she could think about was being with him every chance she got.

"That's fine." It wasn't, but she could hear the stress in his voice.

"Babe, I gotta go. We'll make plans for tomorrow—I promise."

"Okay. Talk to you later. Goodnight."

Kip ended the call without a response and Annie laid her elbows on the desk, pressing the cell phone against her forehead. He was having a bad day. She shouldn't let one flat phone call send her mind spinning with worry. He had a lot on his plate with the pipeline and she needed to give him space to work through it. This wasn't another one of her screwed-up relationships—Kip was different, and she needed to remember that. He was a good, honest man, and he was all hers.

Kip was greeted outside the Speaker of the House's office with a warm handshake and the offer of a cocktail.

"I'll have Jack and ginger if you've got it," Kip said.

"Sure thing." The Speaker packed the glass with ice and poured whiskey and ginger ale over the top. "Here you go. Have a seat. Tell me what's on your mind."

Kip took a long pull on his drink, letting the icy mix slide slowly down his throat. He placed the glass on the side table and cleared his throat. "Well, sir, I'm having second thoughts about the pipeline bill."

"Don't you think it's a little late for that?" the Speaker chuckled. "I mean, the vote is slated for next Tuesday. We've talked about this thing *ad nauseam.* You and Tom have done an enormous amount of work to make this thing happen. What's going on?"

"It's just that I've recently learned the majority of my constituents are opposed to the pipeline coming through my district, and I feel like I'd be doing them a disservice by not heeding their concerns."

"Shouldn't you have done your research before you even introduced the bill?"

Kip looked down into his drink, feeling like he was sitting in the principal's office, being punished for not doing his homework. "I thought we'd done a thorough job on the research, but apparently—"

"Look, Kip, let me give you a piece of advice. You're new at this—first time you've sponsored a bill on your own, right? And I'm sure you're just having a case of the jitters. This is a good bill and you've got plenty of support. Don't you think you'd have more opposition in Congress if it was a bad idea?"

"Yes, but—"

"You stand to gain enormous clout among your party and Congress as a whole. Don't forget that committee appointment we've talked about. You don't want to throw that all away, do you?"

"Well, no, but you see—"

"Relax. You have nothing to worry about. Next week at this time you and I will be celebrating your victory with a glass of champagne and a Cuban."

The Speaker stood and gestured for Kip to do the same. He rested his hand on Kip's shoulder as he escorted him to the door. "Let's get a tee time next week after this whole thing's over. Nothing like a day on the links to let off a little steam."

"Yes, sir. Thank you." Kip wandered out the door into the cold marble hallway as if in a fog. He stood for a moment looking one way, then the next, as if he didn't know the route back to his own office. Rather than return, he walked out of the building and strolled through the streets of Capitol Hill toward his small apartment.

Annie juggled the paper bag and drink carrier in one hand as she pushed the elevator button with the other. When she woke this morning, she vowed to cast any doubts aside and be a supportive girlfriend and team player. After the brief text session with Kip this morning, she decided to bring him lunch, knowing he probably wouldn't have time to take a break. He had back-to-back committee meetings today and several other meetings scattered throughout his schedule. She'd be surprised if she got that promised dinner with the way his agenda was shaping up.

She came into the office and flashed a smile at Kip's assistant as she walked toward his closed door. "Is he with anyone?" she asked.

"Actually, he's not here. He hasn't been in all morning."

"Isn't he supposed to be in a committee meeting?"

"He was, but he called about nine and asked me to clear his calendar. He didn't say where he'd be."

Annie turned in a circle, bewildered by the news. She looked around as if his assistant was wrong and Kip would come strolling in at any moment.

"Mind if I leave this on his desk? In case he comes back?" Annie asked, not waiting for the answer. She walked behind his desk and dropped the food bag on his chair where he couldn't miss it. She began looking at the papers scattered across the desk, not sure what she was looking for. Why hadn't he told her he would be out of the office? Did his absence have anything to do with the meeting he'd had last night? She was tired of feeling left out of the loop.

Kip pushed against the heavy weathered door and stepped into the dark tavern, temporarily blinded by the darkness. It was a bright afternoon outside and he felt like he had just entered a cave. He sat at the first barstool inside the door and ordered a beer.

"Hey, look what the cat dragged in." Kip swiveled the stool around to see where the greeting had come from. Sitting a few feet away under a neon Budweiser sign was Virgil and three of his father's old friends. "Come, join us," Virgil shouted.

"I tried calling you at the marina, but they said you were out." Kip dragged a chair from an adjacent table and sat down with the men he'd known his whole life. They were all members of the Rivermen's Club and regular fishing buddies of his dad's, and had been among Kip's staunchest supporters when he first ran for Congress. "I should have known you'd be here."

"You look like hell. What brings you to town?"

"Thanks, Virgil. You always know how to make a guy feel better."

Virgil laughed and slapped his knee. "I wouldn't want those Hollywood looks to go to your head."

Kip shook his head and took a long pull of his beer.

"So, what are you doing in this joint in the middle of the day? Shouldn't you be in Washington?" Bill Fletcher, the man Annie said had been complaining about the pipeline at the crab feast, asked as he looked at Kip over the rim of his beer mug.

"I've been in meetings this afternoon with Friends of the Bay and the county extension agent."

Bill grunted. "I bet they gave you an earful."

"Now, Bill, don't get started," Virgil said. "Can't you see the boy's had a bad day?"

"I don't give a shit what kind of day he's had. This pipeline has got to be stopped." Bill slammed his hand on the table. "Now, I'm sorry, Kip, but you need to know how I feel—how all of us feel. You push that bill through Congress and you can kiss the election goodbye. You won't be able to show your face in this district if that pipeline comes through. Might as well stay in Washington because you won't be welcome here."

"I gathered as much," Kip mumbled, taking another long drink from the cold mug.

"You want to return to Washington in January? You find a way to stop that bill. That's the only way you'll get my vote."

"Bill, I appreciate your candor and believe me I'm listening to you... to all of you. But it's more complicated than you think."

"Look, Kip, I understand that oil needs to get distributed efficiently, but can't that pipeline be laid somewhere else? Why here?" Virgil asked.

"It seemed like a good location with its proximity to several large East Coast cities. And there's the economic benefit…"

"Economic benefit?" Bill bellowed. "What about the environmental impact?"

"Bill, I know." Kip laid his hand on Bill's shoulder. "I agree. It's probably not the best location after all. I have a lot of work to do if I want to get the pipeline moved."

"Can you do that, Kip?" Virgil asked.

"I'm going to do my best, but it has to be done with as little fallout as possible."

"Well, son, as long as you're trying, we'll stand behind you." This time it was Bill who placed his hand on Kip's shoulder. "But if you can't get it done, you can forget another term. Sorry."

Kip drained his mug and stood up, straightened his tie, and buttoned his jacket. "Thanks, guys. Have another round on me." He tossed forty dollars on the table and walked out of the bar.

"…And then this afternoon, he finally texted me saying he was meeting with some people on the Eastern shore. Not a word about dinner or seeing me tonight," Annie was complaining to Kate as her feet soaked in a hot bubbly tub. Since she and Kip hadn't made plans for the evening, Annie decided to call Kate to have dinner and a pedi. Luckily, she caught Kate at a stopping point in her work load and she readily agreed to an evening with Annie away from the office.

"You said he was dealing with the bill. Maybe he's busy still meeting with people," Kate said.

"Too busy to even send a text letting me know something about tonight? Please!" Annie took a sip of wine and furrowed her brows at Kate, who was sitting in the pedicure chair beside her. "I haven't heard from him since ten o'clock." She lifted her right foot out of the bath and directed her gripes to the nail technician. "Do you think I'm being unreasonable? How hard is it to send a quick text to let me know about tonight?"

The woman agreed with Annie in broken English and then said something in her native language to the tech working on Kate's nails. Both women burst out laughing. Annie's technician walked to the back room and came out with a wine bottle, refilling her client's glass to the rim.

Annie turned her attention back to Kate, who was reclining in the chair and slowly sipping her wine. "He couldn't get enough of me over the weekend and now it's like the weekend never happened. Oh, and I haven't told you about the way he dismissed me in a meeting yesterday."

"What do you mean?"

"We were meeting with Tom, who acted like I wasn't there, and then suddenly Kip rushes me out of the room. Totally brushed me aside, didn't acknowledge the research I've done, and whisked me out of the room."

"Did he ever explain why?"

"Sure. He gave some lame excuse. *Me and Tom have things to discuss,*" she said in a bad imitation of Kip. "Sometimes he acts like I don't know anything about politics." Kate leaned across the arm of her chair and pierced Annie with a stern look. "This is your first job in politics. Just because your dad is a Senator and you watched every episode of *The West Wing* in high school doesn't mean you're a political expert."

"Gee...thanks."

"I'm just saying, they've been working together for years and they're used to doing things a certain way. That's all."

"It just pisses me off."

"Then dump him," Kate muttered, her body rocking and rolling from the massage chair.

"Dump him? You think I should dump him?"

"Obviously he's a lemon. Throw him back. There're other fish."

"But I don't want to throw him back. He told me last night that he thinks I'm smart and he really does listen to me." Annie leaned her elbow on the arm of her chair and looked at Kate. "He's not a lemon, he's... wonderful and smart and hot and...he's dealing with a stressful situation."

Kate sat up and leaned across to Annie's chair. "Exactly, so quit bitching. Be patient and understanding. You said yourself he's under a lot of pressure. Give him a break." She settled back into her massage and closed her eyes.

"Fine," Annie huffed. She pushed a few buttons on her own chair and tried to relax, resolving not to niggle over the past few days.

Annie slid the key into the lock of her apartment door and entered the dark room. She flipped on a lamp and felt her phone vibrate in her hand. Nine-thirty and she was getting a call from Kip.

"Hello?"

"Hi, sweetheart, sorry I'm only just calling. I ended up having dinner with my mom and Rob."

"Oh? How are they?" Annie flopped on the sofa and pulled off her sandals. The pedicure and talk with Kate had calmed her, and she was determined to be a patient, understanding girlfriend, no matter what.

"They're okay. They say hi. What did you do tonight?"

"Well…since I got stood up by my boyfriend…" she said with a chuckle. "Kate and I went out to dinner and had pedicures."

"I'm sorry." Kip sounded exhausted, defeated, and Annie felt instantly terrible that her quip had fallen flat.

"It's okay. I'm glad you got to have time with your family." Annie waited for a response, but none came. A moment later she realized the silence she was hearing was the sound of a dropped call. Had her comment put him over the edge? The loud ding of the doorbell brought her out of her reflection and she rushed over to peek through the peephole. Kip stood on the other side of the door, looking down at the floor.

Annie slowly turned the knob and peeked around the edge of the door to find Kip's hand braced against the doorframe and his head tilted down. "Hmm…what have we here?" she said with a lilt in her voice. He sure looked like he needed cheering up.

"Hi," was all he said as he continued leaning against the doorframe. He had dark circles under his eyes and his usually perfect hair was disheveled.

"Porter…it's kind of late…you're not making a booty call, are you?"

"Would you mind if I did?"

Annie laughed and grabbed both his hands, pulling him into the apartment and into her arms. "You look like you could use a little TLC."

"Exactly what I was hoping you'd say."

TWENTY-THREE

"Okay, next question: Which *American Idol* winner sang 'A Moment Like This' in 2002?" Kate looked from the screen on the wall to her two teammates. "Who do you think? Was it Kelly Clarkson?"

"That sounds right," Derek said.

Annie wasn't listening. She pushed her half-eaten hamburger from one side of the plate to the other, knocking some of the remaining cheese fries onto the table. With her elbow propped on the table and her cheek resting on her hand, she was lost in her own world, oblivious to those around her. She popped a gooey fry into her mouth and thought about what had happened last night and this morning at Starbucks.

Last night had been so perfect. After Kip arrived, she had opened a bottle of wine and he told her about his trip across the bay. He talked about his meetings with Friends of the Bay and the extension agent, and running into Virgil and his friends.

"I don't see how I can go forward with this bill, knowing how they feel," he said as she rested her head on his shoulder. "Oh, and I never thanked you for the information you put in my box. It just confirmed everything I've been hearing."

"I'm glad I could be of some help."

"You're always a big help."

Annie sat up and looked into Kip's dark eyes. "I want to be. But sometimes I feel like you don't want my input. It's obvious you're under a lot of stress. Assign something to me. You don't have to do all this on your own."

Kip wrapped her tight in his arms and whispered in her ear, "You're the best, you know that? How did I get so lucky?"

He had indeed gotten lucky last night—and again this morning—and everything between them felt right, like it had over the weekend. They walked hand-in-hand two blocks to the coffee shop on the corner and talked about the day ahead. Kip asked her to get copies of the petitions and other correspondence about the pipeline and brief him later that day. He treated her not only like his girlfriend, but a valued member of his staff. That is, until Tom had walked in.

"Bro, glad I found you." Tom shot a quick glance at Annie and grumbled, "Good morning, Annie."

"Good morning, Tom."

Tom pulled up a chair to their table and turned it so Annie was sitting behind his shoulder. He directed his words to Kip alone. "Listen, we have a meeting with the Energy Committee this morning to salvage this pipeline. I called it for ten."

"Considering I'm the chairman of the committee, don't you think I should have been the one to call it?"

"What's the big deal? I've done it before."

Annie was sure when Kip looked at her he could see her anger toward Tom. She stared at Kip, waiting for him to stand up to him for once. "It would have been nice to be informed earlier, that's all," Kip said.

Annie slumped back in her chair.

"I asked Annie to gather the petitions and correspondence we've received about the pipeline. Can you get them for her?"

"Really, bro? Are we back to that?"

"Yeah, we're back to that." Annie couldn't stay silent any longer. "I'm going to contact some of the names on the petitions to get their feedback."

Tom acted as if she hadn't spoken at all and said to Kip, "Those petitions aren't what we need to focus on right now. We need to get to the

Hill and meet with the committee to talk about next steps." Tom stood, keeping Annie behind him. "Come on, I'll give you a ride."

Kip stood and tilted his coffee cup, taking his last sip.

"What about your car?" Annie asked.

"Just leave it, I'll get it later. I'll call you." Kip tapped a quick kiss to her forehead and turned to leave, but Annie gripped the sleeve of his jacket.

"What about the petitions?"

"Leave it for now."

"But, Kip—"

"Let me handle this." He lifted her hand from his sleeve, planted a light kiss on her palm and followed Tom out of the café.

Kate had to repeat herself over the noise in the pub to get Annie's attention.

"Hey, are you playing or what? We're already down one person since Gail bailed."

"Annie," Derek said with a nudge to her elbow.

"What?" Her head popped up and she looked startled at the intrusion.

"I said, are you playing or what? Do you know the answer? Which decade saw names first appear on the backs of NFL jerseys?" Kate asked.

Annie shrugged as Derek replied, "You know who we should've called tonight to sub? Kip. He'd know the answer."

"Ha…if he's too busy for me why would you think he would have time for trivia?"

"Thanks, Derek," Kate muttered with an angry glare.

"Wait, I thought you said he's called you three times today. Am I missing something?" Derek looked back and forth between his teammates, confusion etched across his face.

"She's trying to prove a point," Kate said.

"And what point is that?" Kip appeared out of nowhere and towered over their table with his eyes riveted on Annie. "You're a hard one to track down. Mind if I sit?"

Simultaneously Kate and Derek said, "Not at all," while Annie replied, "Yes."

Kip lowered himself to the bench seat beside Kate and reached his hand across the table to Annie's drink, taking a long sip of her beer. "So, how's trivia going?"

"Actually, you came at just the right time. The question is—" Derek was cut off when Annie grabbed his arm and glared at him.

"We don't need his help." Annie snatched her beer out of Kip's hand and then pressed herself against the back of the booth. She folded her arms over her chest and glared at Kip.

"Oh, my God, are you kidding me? Come on, Annie," Kate said.

"No? I'd be glad to help answer the question," Kip said.

"Nope. Don't need you. Just like you don't need or appreciate my help."

Kip flagged down a waiter and ordered a shot of Jack Daniel's. He turned toward Kate and Derek and said, "I've had a hell of a week and for some reason my girlfriend refuses to answer my calls. And it's obvious she's pissed at me for some reason."

"I had my phone turned off," she mumbled.

Kip looked over his shoulder at her and sighed, returning his attention to Kate and Derek. "It's funny she says that because I talked to Pam at the campaign office twice today and both times she said she'd just gotten off the phone with Annie."

"Cell phones just aren't as reliable as they used to be." Derek tipped his mug toward Kip and took a sip, hiding his smile behind the rim.

"It's my prerogative whose call I answer and whose I don't." Annie sat up and directed her response to Kate and Derek. "Besides, he lets Tom run things, so why should he even call me?"

"That's strange…I thought it goes without saying a person should always answer a call from her boss." Kip tipped back his whiskey and it disappeared in a flash.

"Oh, we're playing the boss card, are we?" Annie leaned across the table at Kip, pushing her mug aside.

"The last I checked, you're still on the payroll." Kip drew himself within inches of Annie.

"Oh, shit, here we go again," Derek said.

"Maybe we should ask for some popcorn," Kate said. She and Derek laughed and settled in their seats, ready to watch the action.

"Forgive me, Congressman Porter. I didn't mean to break protocol by not answering your calls. Sometimes I'm not sure why exactly I'm even on the payroll. Am I your campaign manager and a member of your staff? Or am I just the woman you sleep with from time to time?"

"Yes to the first question and you're more than that on the second question. One would think you'd want to answer regardless of the nature of the call." Kip grabbed Annie's mug and drank the last of her beer, slamming the glass onto the table.

"I wasn't looking forward to being rebuffed again."

"Rebuffed?" His brows pulled together and he looked to Kate and Derek for an explanation.

Determined to remain a spectator, Kate looked up at the screen. "Next question. What famous spiritual leader said, 'I never see what has been done; I only see what remains to be done'?"

"Sounds like something I should have said." Annie looked sideways at Kate and then glared back at Kip.

"Man, it's going to be a long night," Derek mumbled against the rim of his beer mug.

"Look, I guess I'm clueless because I don't know what you're talking about." Kip threw

out his hands and cast a glance around the table as if seeking some kind of help. "All I know is I've been calling you and you refuse to answer." Their waiter was collecting plates at an adjacent table and then turned toward them. "Bring me a bottle of Jack, please," Kip said.

"And an extra shot glass," Annie added.

"Getting drunk with me, Coach?"

"I think I deserve it."

"Well, that makes two of us."

"Annnnd I think that's our cue to leave." Kate stood up and bumped her hip into Kip, forcing her way out of the booth. "Come on, Derek, let's split a cab."

Annie and Kip sat in silence, each looking somewhere else in the pub while occasionally catching a covert glimpse of the other. When the waiter set the bottle on the table, Kip poured the dark liquid to the brim of their glasses.

"Cheers," Kip snarled, tapping his glass against Annie's and swallowing in one gulp. She squeezed her eyes shut and threw back her head, pouring the burning liquid down her throat. She shivered violently. "Ugh, that's awful," she said.

"Gets better," Kip said as he refilled their glasses.

"So…what's your excuse?" Annie asked as she took another shot. This time she only quivered when the whiskey hit the back of her throat.

"Excuse? Hmm…I don't have one. And, frankly, I don't think I should need one."

"Were you not at Starbucks with me this morning? I guess not, since you acted like I wasn't even there. When you told Tom I needed those petitions, he shot you down and you didn't even say anything. Why do you let him treat you that way? Why do you let him treat *me* that way?" This time it was Annie who reached for the bottle.

Kip held up his finger while he took a shot of Jack. "First of all, I'm sorry."

"So you say, but nothing's changed." Annie took another shot.

"There's a lot going on with Tom and me." Kip refilled his glass and then pushed the bottle toward Annie. "I can't talk about it right now."

"Why?" After filling her glass, she let the bottle drop with a thump on the table. "Does it have anything to do with the Wentworths? What exactly is going on with them?"

"It's complicated." Kip threw back the whiskey and blew out the fumes. "Listen, please." He reached across the table and took her hand in his. "Tom and I have been working on this bill for a long time and there's a lot involved. When it's all over, I'll explain everything to you, but I just can't right now."

"I don't understand." Annie took another shot, but this time her body didn't react with a shiver.

"I'm doing what I can to shut it down. You just have to trust me." Kip gathered her other hand in his. "I meant it when I said you're smart. And you're more valuable to me than you realize."

That was all Annie needed to hear to knock the steam out of her fight. She could see the anguish on his face and the sincerity in his eyes. He was going through a tough time and she needed to do as he asked. She needed to trust him.

"I don't like fighting with you," Kip murmured against her hands, which he'd gathered to his lips.

"I don't like fighting with you either. I'm sorry. I should have answered your calls today." She leaned across the table and gave him a quick kiss.

Kip kissed her hands once more and then laid them on the table. He reached for the bottle and refilled their shot glasses. "This damn pipeline… I'll be glad when it's over." He threw back a shot and said, "Maybe then I can be a better boss—and boyfriend."

"Oh." Annie took a shot and refilled Kip's. She felt her cheeks growing hot and flushed. "Most of the time you're a great boyfriend."

"One out of two…not bad, I guess." Kip shoved the shot glass away and laced his fingers with Annie's. "So, we're good?"

"We're good."

"Come here." Kip wrapped his hand around the back of her head and pulled her in close for a kiss. "I'm sorry. I'll try to do better," he mumbled against her lips.

"I'm sorry, too. From now on I'll always answer your calls and be a cooperative employee." Annie cupped his face in her hands and plied him with kisses on his cheeks, forehead, and nose, before finally settling a long kiss on his lips, not caring who was watching. "I missed you today."

"Ah, babe, I missed you, too. That's why I came tonight."

"I'm glad you did." Annie refilled their glasses and held hers up in a toast. "To us."

"To us," Kip said, tinging his glass against hers. They took their shots together and went back to holding hands across the table.

"This bill...shit...I don't know what I'm going to do." Kip dropped his chin to his chest. "I should've never sponsored it. I'm screwed no matter what I do."

"How?" Annie refilled their glasses and then resumed holding Kip's hand. She knew she was getting drunk—or was already drunk. She felt her head swimming and her tongue getting thick. Her watery eyes were set on Kip and she sighed contentedly. His lips were moving, but she didn't know what he was saying. She was too busy looking at his gorgeous face and thinking how much in love she was with him.

"...screwed no matter what. Don't you think?"

"Hmm? Oh...yes...seems like it." Annie had no idea what she had just agreed to, but continued to admire Kip with dreamy eyes.

"You weren't listening," he said.

"No, I was." It came out as wasth. Annie started to laugh. What began as a snicker broke into raucous laughter, though she had no idea what was so funny. Kip joined in and soon everyone around them was staring.

"I think I better take you home," Kip said as he rose from the booth, a bit unsteady.

"Please do." Annie plastered herself against him, wrapping her arms tight around his waist. As they walked between the tables, she reached up and tugged his head down, planting loud smacking kisses on his cheek as they stumbled out of the tavern. "I'm so glad you showed up tonight."

"Me, too, sweetheart."

"I love it when you call me sweetheart and babe and angel and honey," she said between kisses. "I don't think I've ever called you angel or honey," Kip said, holding her face in his large hand.

"Oh, fine. Potato, potahto. Whatever you call me—I love it." He smothered her laughter with a kiss and flagged a cab without releasing his lips from hers.

They made out in the back of the cab, catching angry looks from the driver, but Annie didn't care. I'm in Kip's arms and everything is rosy. Another giggle escaped her lips when she thought of the word "rosy." It was something her grandmother would have said. For some reason she couldn't stop laughing.

"I think you're drunk." Kip's hot breath brushed her ear and his hand slipped under her blouse.

"Are you going to take advantage of me, Porter?"

"May I?"

"Please do," she said.

Kip pushed her down on the seat and locked his mouth on hers, plunging his tongue deep. The cab came to an abrupt halt, nearly throwing them to the floorboard. He handed the driver several bills and told him to keep the change as Annie tugged him out of the cab. They stumbled through the door, across the foyer, and into the elevator, where Kip pushed her against the wall and kissed her voraciously on her neck. She held his head with one hand and snaked the other inside the waistband of his trousers, pulling him tight against her. He unfastened the first few buttons on her blouse and trailed his kisses to her breast, nibbling through her lacy bra. The elevator stopped with a ding and they broke their embrace, hurrying through the doors. The hallway was deserted as Annie fumbled with the key to her door. Kip kept up a steady onslaught of kisses on the back of Annie's neck while cupping her breasts in both hands, rubbing her nipples with his thumbs through the lace.

"If you don't stop, I'll never get this door open." It came out as a whine. She couldn't wait to get him inside and his touch was making it hard to concentrate.

"Let me." Kip spun Annie around, once more pressing her to the wall. He grabbed the key from her hand and plowed his tongue into her mouth, holding her hostage while he inserted the key in the lock. As soon as the door was open, he slid both arms under her rear-end and lifted her up, bringing her to his full height. She wrapped her blue-jeaned legs around his waist and locked her arms around his neck, kissing him with equal fervor. They collapsed on her bed and tore away their clothes, desperate to make up for the past few hours.

A bulldozer slowly churned toward Annie as she lay helpless on the red clay shrouded in mist. She heard the clanging of metal and pressed her hands against the raw dirt, pushing herself to her knees. The clanging got louder and she felt herself lifting out of the fog. Her eyelids were heavy and she used all her force to open them, the grittiness making it hard for her to focus. After blinking a few times, she realized she'd been dreaming and the clanging was actually the obnoxious bell tower alarm she'd set on her phone. She reached over and turned it off, then rolled to the other side of her empty bed. Sitting up quickly, she felt a wave of nausea. *Last night. Whiskey. So much whiskey.* She dropped her head in her hands and waited for the spinning to stop when the alluring aroma of coffee touched her senses.

"Thought you might need this." Kip handed a steaming mug to Annie, fully dressed in the clothes he'd worn last night. She looked up at him smiling down on her and took a grateful sip of what might as well have been nectar from heaven.

"Why are you leaving so soon?" she croaked.

Kip sat beside her on the bed and brushed her hair away from her face. "I've got to go. I wish I could stay, but there's so much going on."

"Tell me what I can do."

"Cancel all my campaign appearances until further notice."

"What?" Annie sat erect, her eyes growing large as she stared at Kip. "What's going on?"

"Just through next week. I need to concentrate all my energy on shutting down this pipeline bill."

"You're not going through with it?"

Kip chuckled and nuzzled the base of her neck. "I knew you weren't listening to me last night."

"I was too busy keeping up with you." Annie's head throbbed. "Not a good idea after all."

"No, it wasn't. As your boss, I order you to stay home today. You're in no condition to drive an hour to the campaign office."

"Thanks, boss. I'll take you up on that." Annie tucked herself under the covers and laid her head on the pillow, draping her arm across Kip's thigh. "Will I see you tonight?"

"I can't make any promises. With it being Friday, I'm trying to do all I can before the end of the week—see all the folks I can to stop the vote on Tuesday. It might go late into the night." Kip bent down and kissed Annie's closed eyes and then touched her lips tenderly. "I will call you—that's a promise—and let you know what's going on. But tomorrow? Tomorrow I'm all yours."

"Mmm," she whispered. "I like the sound of that." Within seconds, she'd dropped into a deep sleep. Kip kissed her once more and walked out of the apartment.

TWENTY-FOUR

Kip flicked the turn signal and continued rolling past estates with pillared entryways and iron gates. His palms were beginning to sweat; he rubbed them against his chinos and glanced over at Annie, who was checking her make-up in the visor mirror. He drew his SUV to a stop and looked up at the Cooper home, perched on a knoll in an exclusive neighborhood—a wealthy Washington suburb. There was a shiny textured driveway that circled to the front of the stone and white-brick mansion, complete with perfectly trimmed shrubs and stone retaining walls. The house even had a turret, which added to its imposing grandeur. He had known the Coopers were wealthy—the Senator was a partner in a Raleigh law firm and Mrs. Cooper was heir to a large tobacco company—but he hadn't counted on such opulence.

"Now, listen, just be prepared. My mother can be over the top. She has no filter but she's harmless. My dad, well, he can be a bit gruff and not so nice to my mom. My sisters can be snobs, but I like their husbands. I wish my brother was here. You'd like him."

Kip looked over and noticed Annie wringing her hands and chewing her bottom lip.

Why did she look so nervous? He was the one meeting her parents for the first time—and in a freaking mansion! He pulled in front of the wide stone porch and cut the engine.

"If you get uncomfortable or want to leave, just squeeze my leg. That will be our signal. If either of us wants to get the hell out of there, we'll squeeze the other's knee. Okay?" Annie's eyes were practically bulging and her cheeks were pale.

"Annie, what's wrong?" Kip picked up her quivering hand and pressed it against his lips. "I'm the one who should be nervous. Are you worried they won't like me? I mean, look at this." He pointed up at the house and swallowed hard.

"Don't let the house scare you. It's the people inside you should worry about." Annie tittered and then said, "Look, my mother already loves you and she hasn't even met you yet. You're not the problem…they are."

"So it's going to be fine?"

"For you? Yes." Annie wrinkled her brows and grimaced. "Probably."

"Come on. Let's do this." Kip climbed out of the car and smoothed his polo into his waistband as he walked around to Annie's door. He held out his hand and kissed hers as she got out of the car.

"Remember, one squeeze and we're out of there."

Just as they stepped onto the stone porch, the door flew open and a tiny woman with red bobbed hair greeted them with wide open arms. "You're here! I'm so glad you came, darling. We've missed you." She drew Annie into a tight hug, pushed her aside just as quickly, and extended her hand to Kip. "Hello, I'm Marjorie Cooper and you must be Kip."

"Yes, ma'am."

"It's so nice to meet you. Please come in."

"Thank you, Mrs. Cooper." Kip and Annie entered the massive marble foyer with its sweeping curved staircase and all of Kip's trepidations returned. The house looked more like a movie set than a home.

"Please, call me Marjorie." She linked her arm through Kip's and led him down the marble hallway, leaving Annie to trail behind. "You know I had hoped to meet you at the Women's Club event you attended, but Ann wouldn't introduce us." She stopped and looked at Annie, wide-eyed and worried. "Oops."

"It's okay, Mom. He knows everything. It's fine."

"Yes, it's too bad she didn't introduce us then," Kip said, taking in the plush furnishings. Everything in the house was gold or cream, including the wallpaper, columns, and woodwork. They passed double doors that opened to an enormous living room and across from it was a formal dining room with a gleaming wood table surrounded by twelve chairs. They entered a sunroom flooded with light from floor-to-ceiling windows, furnished with upholstered rattan. When Kip looked outside he saw a huge infinity pool surrounded by a stone patio. In all his years in politics, he'd never been in a private home so lavish.

"Did you bring your suits? Maybe you'd like a swim after brunch," Marjorie said with a huge smile on her face.

"No, Mom. Maybe next time."

"Well, have a seat. George is supposed to be fixing mimosas for everyone, but I don't know where he is." As Annie and Kip sat on the loveseat, Marjorie flitted across the room and looked through the French doors to a side yard. Her quick movements reminded Kip of Annie when she'd rushed around the campaign office that afternoon. "He was showing your sisters his new putting green out back…"

They all turned when they heard voices coming down the hallway. "Here we go," Annie whispered, just loud enough for Kip to hear.

Senator Cooper, wearing plaid pants and a Carolina blue golf shirt, walked into the sunroom followed by Annie's two sisters, who each wore floral sundresses. Their husbands were dressed like junior versions of the senator. The whole lot could have modeled for the cover of *Town and Country* magazine.

"Annie bug, so glad you could make it today." George pulled Annie to her feet and engulfed her in a bear hug. She looked over her shoulder at Kip with an expression that said, "What the hell?"

"Senator Cooper, so nice to finally meet you." Kip gripped her father's hand with a huge smile across his face. He was finally meeting Senator George Cooper, the man who could make this pipeline bill go through as planned, and it was the last thing Kip wanted to think about. He was so happy to meet Annie's family and anxious for them to like him. Annie had already experienced Kip's world and he was hoping to fit into hers.

"This is my sister Rachel and her husband Jim." Kip shook hands with the attractive couple and then turned to greet Annie's other sister and her husband. "And this is Sarah and her husband Brian."

"What in the world are you wearing?" Sarah asked, running her eyes up and down Annie's outfit.

"It's called a romper. Or a jumpsu—whatever," Annie replied.

"But it's gray…in the middle of summer," Sarah said.

"Not everyone can pull off Lily Pulitzer floral," Rachel added.

"Or afford it," Annie said. Under her breath, Kip heard her mutter, "And who would want to?"

Kip chuckled. "I think you look gorgeous," he said as everyone settled into their seats. The group quickly fell into comfortable conversation while sipping mimosas in the warm sunlight. Annie's family made him feel at ease and he noticed she no longer looked scared. He picked up her hand and held it in his, deciding there was no way he'd bring up the pipeline today.

After everyone had finished eating, they went out to the poolside patio, where Senator Cooper opened a bottle of white wine. There was a light breeze and the hot August sun was kept at bay under a canvas awning.

"Thank you for brunch today, Mrs. Coo—Marjorie. It was delicious," Kip said, as he accepted a glass of wine from the senator.

"It was my pleasure."

"I see now where Annie gets her cooking and decorating talents."

Annie's mother beamed while pressing her open hand against her chest. "Why, thank you, Kip. You're too kind."

"Good one, Porter," Annie mumbled. He gave her a gentle nudge in reply.

"He's right, sweetheart. You outdid yourself," Senator Cooper said, giving Marjorie a kiss and a quick hug. Annie's mouth dropped open. She had warned Kip that her father could be cruel to her mother, but all Kip had seen that day were two happy people appearing very much in love. They weren't at all what he'd expected.

"So, Kip, tell me about this pipeline bill you've introduced. How's it going?" Senator Cooper asked as he emptied the bottle of wine into the last glass.

"Daddy!" Sarah whined.

"Now, George, you promised no political talk," Marjorie said.

"Really, Dad, do we have to talk politics?" Rachel said.

"They're right, Senator Cooper. No need to bore everyone. Annie for one has heard enough about it." Kip winked at Annie and she replied with a wry grin. Just then the conversation was interrupted by her cell phone.

"Oh, it's Emberly. Do you mind if I take it? I won't be long."

"You go ahead, dear. I'll get the desserts," her mother said, following Annie into the house.

"Kip, I understand you played football at Maryland. How about I show you some photos from my Carolina football days?" George held out his hand, directing Kip back into the house.

"Thank you, sir, I'd like that."

Kip and her father stepped through another door off the patio and entered the senator's home office. There was a massive mahogany desk flanked by leather upholstered chairs and a bookcase that ran the length of an entire wall.

"Have a seat." George directed Kip to a green velvet sofa and the senator sat across from him in a Queen Anne upholstered chair. Her father leaned his elbows on his knees and said, "Look, I brought you in here to talk about this pipeline. The football pictures can wait until another time."

"Sir, it's not necessary that we talk about this today." Kip sat up straighter on the sofa.

"I think we should. Your chief of staff has apparently been calling mine trying to set up a meeting between us."

Kip slumped against the back of the couch and squeezed his temples between his long fingers. He shook his head, frustrated Tom had gone behind his back to contact the senator's office. "Look...I'm sorry. I had no idea he did that. I apologize. Lately, he's been going a bit rogue on me, especially about this bill. It's been..." Kip's sigh echoed off the walls.

"It's more than I can handle." He felt his stomach tumble and his hands begin to shake. Kip would've given anything for the floor to open up and swallow him.

"I've been hearing rumors about the driving force behind the bill. People like that can be demanding."

"It's not that, sir. I'm in a jam and don't know how to get out of it."

George reached out and patted Kip on the knee. "Why don't you tell me what's going on. I've been in your shoes. Maybe I can be of some help."

"I'd appreciate that. So much has happened and I don't know—"

"How about you start from the beginning?"

TWENTY-FIVE

"I'm so excited you're coming to see us, Em. I can't wait to tell Kate. I'll call you later." Annie tapped her cell phone's screen and bounced up the steps. She had been sitting on the front porch talking to Emberly and was excited to tell Kip she'd be here in two weeks. She walked into the foyer and was just turning toward the sunroom when she heard Kip and her father's voices coming from his study. She slipped off her sandals and tiptoed down the short hallway to the office door and pressed her ear against the wood. A huge grin spread across her face when she heard Kip talking to her dad.

"I went into politics because—and I know this sounds cliché—because I wanted to make a difference. We had the same congressman for twenty-four years from my district, and he didn't do anything. He had no influence, no clout—he was just a lame duck. I knew I could represent my constituents better than he could."

"I think it's the reason we all go into politics. We want to make a difference. Sometimes that can be tough to do. I've heard nothing but great things about you and your work. You've represented your district well. You might want to consider running for senate someday."

Kip chuckled. "Believe me, sir, I've considered it."

Annie stepped away from the door and gave herself a mental hug as adrenaline tingled through her body. Even though her relationship with her father had been strained over the years, she couldn't help but be thrilled that he and Kip were getting along so well. It meant more to her than she realized.

Walking as delicately as she could, Annie turned to rejoin the rest of her family on the patio. As she passed the antique table along the wall, she was struck by one of the dozen or so pictures hanging above it. Most depicted her father posing with various political leaders; there was a photo of him with Ronald Reagan, another with George H.W. Bush on the capitol steps, and one of her parents with George and Laura Bush at a fundraiser. The collage had hung on the wall for so long, Annie rarely gave it a glance. But today she noticed, to the left of the grouping, a small framed photo of her father with her and her friends at a golf outing a few years back. He was smiling and his arms were extended around a group of people that included Annie, Kate, Emberly, her brother and…Tom Garrett. Annie leaned in closer to be sure she wasn't imagining it. A tall, strawberry-blonde, shaggy-haired guy resembling Tom stood behind three other people from the tournament. She lifted the picture off the wall and tilted it in the light. Annie drew in a sharp breath. It was Tom Garrett; she was sure of it. His hair was longer and he was about fifteen pounds thinner, but she was sure it was him. As she thought about that day, she now remembered a guy named Tom whose foursome played ahead of hers. All day he had been flirting with Kate. Actually, the things he said to her that day were so crude, it couldn't really be classified as flirting. She remembered they all thought he was a jerk and were happy when the tournament was over.

As quietly as possible, she replaced the photo on the wall and did a quick calculation of when the tournament had taken place. It must have been four years ago because she, Kate and Emberly were in graduate school at the time. She tiptoed back to the study door and heard Kip say, "I was eager for Annie to introduce us so we could talk about this bill. We have all the votes we need in Congress, but I was hoping you'd get on board and the Senate would fall in behind you. Plus, your influence on the Appropriations Committee would guarantee Wentworth Global would get the bid. If that happened, I would be in line for several key congressional positions, as well as enormous financial gain."

"Interesting," her father said.

Annie took an unsteady step backward, her heart pounding against her ribs. He said he didn't want to talk about the pipeline, was doing all he could to stop the bill, but there they were in her father's study, strategizing. She stormed away from the door, fury and hurt surging through her body. Tom Garrett had to have known all along who she was…which meant Kip knew all along, too. That day at the Independent, she remembered Tom mentioning he thought they'd met before. Why didn't she remember him or ask him where he thought he knew her from? She looked at the golf photo again then walked back toward the office door with her hand raised, ready to pound on it. She should storm in there and confront Kip, but her eyes filled with tears and her throat clogged with emotion. The shock sent her reeling; all she could think to do was rush out of the house, letting the front door slam behind her. She plopped down on the porch and dropped her head in her hands.

The only reason she had been hired was to position Kip closer to her father. This whole relationship was a sham. All the sweet words, the loving touches, everything was part of the plot to pass the bill. And like an idiot, Annie had fallen for it.

Senator Cooper handed a tumbler of scotch to Kip and resumed his seat across from him. "Go on…you were telling me about meeting the Wentworths."

"Yes. Tom and I were at a political fundraiser in Dallas about two years ago. It was during the convention. Anyway, they took us to dinner and talked about the work they were doing on a pipeline in Canada, and how beneficial an expansion could be to the east coast. Energy independence is one of my goals and it just sounded like a great opportunity. By the time we were done having dinner, we were excited about the prospects."

"They can be convincing." George emptied his glass of scotch and set it on an end table.

"They can. So as soon as we got back to Washington, I asked Tom to do some research on the pipeline, its benefits, costs, environmental impact, everything. All the data showed it would be safe. Wentworth would upgrade and expand the existing pipeline, provide jobs. It was a win-win all around. The Wentworths promised my campaign enormous financial support and introductions to a lot of important people. They took us to dinners, flew us to Dallas for lavish weekends, even bought me a Rolex. I just got caught up in all of it and didn't think about the consequences. Anyway, we knew the only way for this whole plan to fall into place was to get the Senate Appropriations Committee on board. Tom ran into Annie one day at lunch and he remembered her from a golf tournament, but she didn't remember him. He encouraged her to come work for me."

"That was the day she quit working for John Wolfe, right?"

"Right," Kip said, taking a small sip of the scotch.

"Best thing she could have done was to get away from that asshole." Senator Cooper picked up his glass and walked to the small bar cart behind his desk. He refilled his glass and returned to his seat.

"So, the idea in hiring Annie was..." Kip looked at her father and felt his heart drop to his feet. If he was going to get help from the senator, he had to be completely honest with him, no matter the consequences. "I was eager for Annie to introduce us so we could talk about this bill. We have all the votes we need in Congress, but I was hoping you'd get on board and the Senate would fall in behind you. Plus, your influence on the Appropriations Committee would guarantee Wentworth Global would get the bid. If that happened, I would be in line for several key congressional positions, as well as financial gain."

"Interesting."

"Yeah, we had it all figured out."

"Sounds like a pretty underhanded plan," George grumbled.

"It was...it is. But, sir, believe me, I had no intention of talking to you about this bill today. No intention of carrying out the plan."

Kip and her dad jumped when they heard the front door slam.

"Damn door. When the wind catches it just right, it rips right out of your hand. Gotta have someone look at that," her father said. "Go on, son."

"Well, to be honest, I want out from under this thing. Since meeting Annie…everything has changed. In the process of getting close to her, so that I could get close to you, I've…well, sir, I've fallen in love with you daughter."

"I thought that might be the case." George chuckled and took another sip.

"She's made me see this bill is a bad idea—that my constituents don't want a pipeline running through their backyards. My constituents—the people I grew up with—are more important than any political clout I might gain. She's done all kinds of research and polled the folks in my area. It if weren't for her, I'd still be wrapped up in this mess with no regard for the people I care most about."

"Isn't the vote on Tuesday?"

"It is. I met with the Speaker last week and he told me it was too late to do anything about it. I've tried to talk to Tom, but he won't listen, probably because he's been promised God knows what by the Wentworths. I've met with the Energy Committee and several key legislators. They all tell me the same thing. It will probably be political suicide, but I'm going to do all I can to stop it. If I could, I'd stop the Wentworths, too."

"Why don't you let me help you? I've been down similar roads before. And I can tell you the first thing we're going to do is call a friend of mine—a lawyer. Because I think you're going to need one."

"A lawyer?" Kip felt his eyes bulging, a streak of fear surging through his veins.

"If you want to really make a difference…you need to stop people like the Wentworths. They are a poison that runs unchecked in Washington. John Wolfe was another one. I'll stand beside you all the way."

"Thank you, sir. I appreciate this…more than you know." For the first time in weeks, Kip felt a glimmer of hope that the pipeline could be stopped and he could get out from under the crushing scheme.

The men stood and shook hands. Senator Cooper's piercing eyes bore into Kip. "I'm glad you and Annie found each other. You're a good man, Kip. Lord knows Annie hasn't exactly grown up seeing what a good man looks like. I'm doing my best to change that. Now, we better get back out there before we're in hot water with our women."

Kip and George walked back onto the patio, where Marjorie was serving warm bowls of her homemade peach cobbler with whipped cream.

"Marjorie, my love, I believe you're trying to fatten me up." Annie's father took a big bite and dropped into a cushioned lounge chair.

"Where's Annie?" Marjorie asked.

"That's what I was just wondering." Kip looked through the French doors into the sunroom. "Maybe she's still on the phone with Emberly. I'll find her."

Kip strolled through the sunroom, retracing the route back to the foyer. When he opened the front door he found Annie sitting on the steps with her head in her hands. Her hair fell around her like a curtain and he couldn't see her face.

"Hey, babe, still on the phone?" he asked.

Annie shook her head.

"Your mom is serving dessert. Do you want some?"

Once again Annie shook her head and said, her voice strained, "Take me home please."

Kip sat down beside her on the steps and reached out to brush her hair out of her face. Annie pulled away as if a jolt of electricity had run through her.

"Are you okay?"

Annie shook her head. "Just take me home."

"Why don't you get in the car and I'll tell your parents we're leaving," Kip said.

He stepped through the patio doors and said to the Coopers, "I'm sorry everyone, but Annie isn't feeling well. I'm going to take her home."

"Oh, Kip, such a shame. We were enjoying the two of you so much. Tell Annie to feel better and I'll call her later. Maybe we could have dinner sometime next week." Annie's mother reached up on her toes and gave him a hug.

"Kip, let's talk again tomorrow morning. In fact, I might give you a call this evening if that's okay with you," George said, gripping Kip's hand.

"Absolutely. I need all the help you're offering, sir. Thank you." Kip said goodbye to Annie's sisters and their husbands and then walked out of the house, being careful not to let the front door slam.

He climbed into the SUV, turned the key, then turned to Annie. "Babe, are you feeling sick?"

Annie replied with a quick nod.

"Oh, man, I'm sorry. I'll drive slowly. If you need me to pull over, just tell me, okay?" Kip lifted her hand and kissed the back of it just before Annie pulled it away.

On the ride back to the district, Annie stayed silent, all the while staring straight ahead through the windshield. Kip kept up a monologue about meeting her parents.

"Your parents are just great, babe. I thought it went well, didn't you?" When Annie didn't answer, he went on. "I liked your brothers-in-law, too. In fact, Jim asked me to play golf with him next weekend. I told him I'd check with you…didn't know if we had any plans." Annie continued to stare through the window, her gaze unfocused. Kip reached over and pressed the back of his hand against her cheek. "Do you have a fever?" Annie turned her face away and slumped into the seat.

"Okay, I'll let you be. I know when I'm sick it's better to just leave me alone. I understand. How about I turn on some music and you can rest until we get back?" Kip turned on the radio to a classical station but kept the volume low. The thirty-minute trip continued with only the strains of violin music and the sounds of passing cars.

TWENTY-SIX

"How long have you known?" Annie felt numb, shell-shocked as she looked through the windshield; the parked car ahead of them was a mere blur. Kip had pulled the SUV to the curb a half-block from her apartment and cut the engine.

"What do you mean?" he said.

"How long have you known?" Annie rotated her head toward Kip as if someone were turning a crank, making it move mechanically. She took a deep breath while closing her eyes. When she opened them, she exhaled and nearly screamed, "How long have you known I was Senator Cooper's daughter?"

"Annie."

"Damn it, answer the question."

"Let me explain."

"Answer me! When?" The numbness drained from her body and she felt her whole being fill with rage. How dare he act like he didn't know what she was talking about? His avoidance of the question proved his guilt.

Kip reached out to take her hand, but she pulled away. "Okay, okay." He threw his hands back in surrender and glanced out the window as if looking for answers. "Tom called me right after he met you in the bar. He told me who you were that day."

"Oh, my God."

"Please just listen and I'll explain everything."

"I don't need an explanation. I know about the whole plot."

"What?"

"I heard you telling my father that you needed his vote. The only reason you hired me was to get to him." Annie turned away from Kip and dropped her head in her hands. "Everything makes sense now. I'm such an idiot."

"Babe, listen to me, please." Kip draped his arm around her shoulder, but Annie shrugged it off. "If you'll give me a chance, I'll tell you everything."

As if in a trance, Annie recounted the past few weeks in a dull, lifeless monotone. "How did I miss it? You came on so strong and I was flattered. I let you screw me on your sofa. Fell for your stressed-out *I need you, Annie*." She released a strangled laugh. "How could I be so stupid? I fell for your bullshit. Romancing me at your cabin...oh, my God. You never took me seriously from day one. You brushed me aside when I wanted to help. You ignored the research and the things I overheard. Of course, you had no intention of dropping the bill. I should have known you were just using me." With tears streaming down her face, she turned to Kip and said, "You're no better than John Wolfe or my professors or any other creep that wants something from me because of my father."

"But I am dropping the bill."

"I heard you. I heard you asking my father for his vote and support in Appropriations. Your secret is out." Annie reached for the door handle, but Kip reached across and locked her hand under his.

"Wait, Annie, you have to hear me out. I promise you it's not like that."

"I'm tired of your promises." She elbowed his arm away and pushed the door open, rushing away from the car without shutting the door. Kip climbed out and ran after her. He reached out his hand and pulled her around by the arm to face him. He gripped her shoulders and leaned down to her eye level.

"Annie, please don't walk away without hearing my side of the story. You've jumped to conclusions before and they were wrong. Don't make the same mistake."

"I'm the one making a mistake? I don't think so, Kip. I think I'm done. I'm just...done," she mumbled and then hiccupped a sob.

"We're not done. Don't say that. Do you hear me? I love you, Annie."

"Oh, great. Nice time to throw out the L-word, Congressman. A cornered animal will do anything in times of desperation." She tried to pull away but he had her locked tight in his hands.

"I'm not saying it out of desperation...well, maybe I am. But it's true. I love you. Don't you get that?" Annie felt his hot breath against her face; his nose was nearly touching hers and his eyes seared into her own. For a split second, she considered throwing herself against him, kissing him with all her strength, hoping what he had just said was true. But she gave herself a mental shake, reminding herself once more that she had been duped.

"You know what I get?" she seethed. "I get that I got a liar *manhandling* me. Maybe I should scream for help."

Kip dropped his hands and stepped back from her. He turned in a full circle and then stepped to within inches of her face again. "A liar, huh? Is that what I am? Well, let's not forget who spewed out the first lie in this scenario."

"That was different."

"How so? You lied about your identity from the very beginning. What if I didn't know who you were? I would have hired someone using an alias. Sounds pretty unethical, if not illegal, to me."

"I told you who I am. You could have confessed that day."

"How could I? You told me you'd be crushed if you thought you were hired because of your father."

"So you admit that was why I was hired?"

"Yes, damn it, yes—that was why you were hired. But if you'd listen, I can tell you that I aborted that plan weeks ago."

"I've had enough of your lies." Annie rushed toward her apartment building.

"Congratulations," he called after her. "Since the day you met me you've been trying to find me guilty of something. Well, now you have. Good for you."

"It was only a matter of time," she yelled back.

"Fine. Stay up on that high horse of yours. Ignore the fact you started this whole thing." Kip closed the gap between them in a few long strides, blocking her entrance to her building. "Have you ever considered maybe you put yourself in these situations? Big deal—you're a senator's daughter. Stop acting like a child. At least your dad's still here, and he's a better man than you give him credit for."

"You don't know anything." She stepped left and then right, trying to get around Kip's blockade.

"I know that you're being stubborn, unforgiving, and self-righteous. Maybe when you fall off that high horse, you'll come to your senses." Annie felt a clenching ache in her chest as she watched Kip storm away, taking long, fast strides toward his car. She took a timid step forward, considering going after him, but just as quickly that familiar rage surged through her body. She jerked open the door and ran to the elevator.

Tuesday morning Annie sank chin-deep in a tub of scalding hot water full of iridescent white bubbles. She hadn't slept well the past two nights, perhaps because she'd spent Sunday evening and all day Monday lying on her couch watching old chick flicks, eating more ice cream than she would have consumed in a typical month, and crying—more accurately, sobbing—over Kip. She couldn't believe it was over. She couldn't believe he had lied to her—that he'd known her true identity all along—and that he had used her. She chastised herself again for being such a sucker, a target for plots and schemes. What was the matter with her? Couldn't she be loved and respected just for her? Why couldn't people just be honest? She thought Kip was different. She trusted him. She loved him.

She missed him.

Annie began crying again, but this time the tears fell silently down her wet cheeks. Maybe he had been right. Was she stubborn and self-righteous? Her father certainly thought so.

Monday morning Senator Cooper had called to ask how she was feeling and she blurted out, "What do you care?"

"Well, now, Annie bug, of course I care about you."

"Really, Dad? What I seem to remember is being ignored most of my life and you never being home. The only time you showed any concern for any of us was when the press was around."

"Annie, that's not fair."

"Not fair? I'll tell you what's not fair: getting dressed up in our finest for the annual Christmas picture so you could send out cards to your constituents and supporters showing you and your perfect, happy family. But come Christmas morning, you weren't even there. Or how about being paraded around at campaign appearances every six years when you didn't have the decency to come to my dance recitals or school plays? Was that fair? And, what about the scandals—"

"I'll admit I've made mistakes in my life, but believe me—I've paid for them."

"Oh, really? Like when?"

"Like now. You're furious with me. We can't even have a level-headed conversation."

"I don't see the point. We never have, so why start now?"

"You know, Annie, I'm not the only one who makes mistakes."

"Oh?"

"You're not immune to the occasional error in judgment."

"What are you talking about?"

"I'm talking about Kip."

"Don't stick your nose in my personal life...not now."

"Honey, now is the best time for me to stick my nose in. You need to hear Kip out."

"Oh, great...first he gets you on board with this pipeline and now he has you intervening on his behalf with me. Save it for someone who cares." Annie tapped off the call and threw her phone across the carpeted floor. She had spent the rest of the day intermittently crying, fuming, eating, and crying some more.

When she had woken up Tuesday morning and saw her frightening reflection in the mirror with her puffy eyes and dark circles, she decided she would no longer play the victim and get on with her life. She drew a hot bath and tried to relax for a few minutes before once again starting a new job search and putting the past behind her.

After her bath, Anne donned her favorite sleeveless dress, applied her make-up to perfection, straightened her hair with a flat iron, and slipped on her strappy sandals. She picked up her laptop and shoved it into her messenger bag, and opened the door, planning to head to the Starbucks on the corner for a latte while she scoured job sites. Standing in the hallway with his fist in the air, ready to knock, was her father.

"Dad, what are you doing here?"

"I've come to pick you up," he said, stepping into her apartment.

"Pick me up for what?" Annie shut the door and lowered her bag to the floor.

"We're going to the Hill. There's something important you need to see."

Annie crossed her arms over her chest and glared at her father. "There's nothing important on Capitol Hill that I need to see. I've seen and heard enough."

"There you go again with that stubborn way of yours. Or mine, I guess. You had to have gotten it from somewhere."

It was the second time in three days someone had called her stubborn and she didn't like it. Speaking her mind, doing what she wanted to do, and standing up for herself wasn't what she'd call stubborn.

Senator Cooper sat on her sofa and laced his finger together, resting his elbows on his knees. He looked up at Annie, who was still rooted to the same spot beside the door.

"You know, Annie, I've learned a lot in my sixty years; some things took longer to understand than others. When I was your age, I was probably as stubborn and determined to be right as you are."

Annie puffed out a breath. "What are you talking about?"

"Come sit beside me. I want to talk to you."

Annie inched toward the couch, looking at the floor. She could feel her temperature rising and she wanted to scream. He was messing up what had begun as a potentially productive day and the last thing she wanted to do was listen to her father's rhetoric. She gingerly sat on the opposite end of the sofa.

"Have I ever told you about the time I met your mother?"

Annie shook her head and wrung her hands in her lap, not looking up at her father. Did she really want to take a stroll down memory lane?

"I met your mother at a cotillion. She was nineteen and being presented that summer and I was asked by a fraternity buddy of mine to escort his sister to the ball. When they called out the name Marjorie Mae Merriman, I remember laughing with my buddies, but when I looked up and saw her, well, I fell instantly in love. She had dark hair and dark eyes—a lot like yours—and she floated down the staircase like an angel. I couldn't get over to talk to her fast enough. Here I was this big oaf, country boy from Boone, North Carolina, hoping to charm this sophisticated, elegant beauty from Raleigh and well, I fumbled all over myself. Thankfully, I could dance—otherwise, I don't think she would have given me the time of day." Her father laughed and had a gleam in his eye the likes of which Annie had never seen before.

"I've never heard this story," she said, turning to look at him.

"Oh, and she was smart. When she told me she was going to Wellesley, I had to ask her where it was. I didn't know about any college outside of North Carolina. In fact, I probably wouldn't have gone to college if it weren't for football. She intimidated me from day one, but I was mesmerized by her. Then, when I found out her granddaddy had started the biggest tobacco company in the U.S., well, you can imagine I was really intimidated."

"So, how did you two get together?"

"Like I said, we danced all night at the cotillion. I asked her if I could call on her and she said, 'First you have to ask my daddy.' You know how scary your Pop could be."

"I remember him as a big, gruff teddy bear." Annie laughed and scooted an inch closer to her father.

"Gruff was right. I introduced myself to him that evening and told him I'd like to date his daughter. He started asking me all about my family, my home, what I was majoring in at college. Of course, I didn't have any answers. I was only there for football. But then he said, 'Son, I'm impressed that you'd come to ask my permission, but I'm afraid unless you plan to be a doctor or lawyer or senator, you won't be good enough for my little girl.'"

"Oh, that's harsh." Annie leaned her head against the sofa back.

"As soon as the semester started, I changed my major to pre-law and sent her father a letter telling him of my plans to become an attorney and eventually run for office. That December when she was home on winter break, he allowed me to take her on a date. We've been together ever since."

"That's a great story. It's not at all what I had expected. I've sometimes wondered why she's stayed with you, to be honest, Dad."

"I have, too. I've spent my whole life trying to live up to her father's expectations, to be worthy of a woman as wonderful as your mother. Along the way, I've made a lot of mistakes. But, you know what?"

"What?"

"With everything we've been through, we still love each other and your mother has an amazing ability to forgive. And I thank God every day she does, because I don't know where I'd be without her."

Annie chewed on her bottom lip and looked down at her lap. This was the first time she and her father had ever had a heart-to-heart talk. He'd always seemed too busy or distracted to share his feeling with her, or ask about her own. She felt tears welling in her eyes as she thought about all the times she would have liked to have had conversations just like this.

"I'm sure your mother hasn't said anything, but we've been in counseling for six months and it's made all the difference in our marriage. We've never been happier. In fact, I plan to retire at the end of this term. We want to travel and spend as much time together as possible."

"Oh, Dad, I had no idea. That's...that's wonderful." Annie pressed a finger to the corner of her eye, catching a wayward tear.

"The point is, Annie bug, none of us is perfect, including you. We all screw up from time to time. If you truly love someone, you need to forgive them when they make a mistake. Same way you'd like to be forgiven when you mess up. If you run at the first sign of trouble, you might miss out on the greatest happiness you've ever known."

"Who are we talking about right now? You and Mom?"

"Yes, but I'm also talking about you and Kip. I saw the way you looked at each other on Sunday. I've never seen you like that with anyone. He got lured into what he thought was a good situation, but along the way he lost sight of himself and what's most important—until he met you. It was because of you he decided against the bill, even at the risk of losing respect from his colleagues."

"Did he tell you that?"

"He did. Meeting you changed everything. He couldn't go through with the original plan because he fell in love with you."

"He said that?" Annie sat erect as a tingle of hope surged through her body.

"He did. Now, don't take my word for it. If we hurry up, you can hear it for yourself."

TWENTY-SEVEN

"I'd like to thank my colleague from Delaware, Congressman McVey, and my colleague from Pennsylvania, Congresswoman Blake, for their work on this bill. Mister Speaker, this bill would expand the already over-burdened East Coast oil pipeline by getting much needed resources to consumers more efficiently and at a lower cost. Until two months ago, I was proud to sponsor the pipeline expansion bill and was enthusiastic about the economic benefits it would yield both nationally and in my small Maryland district along the shores of the Chesapeake Bay. All the research I'd received proved this would be an essential piece of America's energy independence." Kip took a deep breath as he gripped either side of the podium and let his eyes scan the House chamber. He looked back down at the crisp white pages of his prepared speech and released an audible sigh before he flipped the sheets face down. He cleared his throat and slid his hands deep into his trouser pockets.

"The truth is, ladies and gentlemen, this pipeline may very well help our oil distribution, but at what cost? In recent days, several wise, insightful people brought to my attention the potential risks of building the pipeline in such a delicate ecosystem. The truth is the risks far outweigh the benefits. Did you know the Chesapeake Bay supports over twenty-five hundred species of fish and animals and produces over five hundred million pounds of seafood each year? The approximate three hundred thousand acres of tidal wetlands provide critical habitat for fish, birds, and other species. We could never measure the enormity of damage a pipeline break could cause. And what about the economic risk? For generations men and women have been making their living from the Bay's bounty. Recreational fishing, hunting, and boating attract millions of visitors each year. Even a small spill could devastate the economy in several states." Once again Kip let his eyes search the members sitting with rapt attention. He noticed confusion on some faces and anger on others. He leaned an elbow on the podium and continued.

"I see the confusion on some of your faces. I'd be confused, too, if I were you. Many of you have listened to my plea for this bill's passage, sat with me in committee meetings, or had private discussions about the importance of this bill. In actuality, the only thing I've been focused on was money and furthering my own career." A murmur spread through the crowd. Kip could feel his audience's attention focus on him like a laser.

"I was approached by a very influential, convincing donor who stood to make millions from this project. I foolishly entered into an agreement with an international construction firm to make this pipeline happen and did it with no regard for the people I love and respect in my own district. I allowed the flash of money and the desire to rise within the ranks of Congress to cloud my better judgment. I was sucked into the behind-the-scenes political maneuverings we in Congress are so often criticized for. Did I recognize this as nothing more than a shady business deal that could damage the delicate environment along the Bay? No. All I could see was how this pipeline would benefit me. But now I'm announcing my withdrawal of support for the pipeline bill. I'm sure I'm not the only one in this hall who's been approached with opportunities for financial gain, but I hope to be the last."

Kip looked up into the visitor's viewing gallery and surveyed the faces of each representative present. "I implore you to vote against this bill. Tomorrow morning, I will be meeting with state party officials to remove my name from the ballot in November, and I plan to fully cooperate with the Department of Justice's investigation into campaign corruption. Thank you."

Kip gathered his stack of papers and walked up the aisle while members talked in hushed whispers among themselves, staring in shock as he passed. He kept his head down, not wanting to make direct eye contact with his soon-to-be former colleagues, many of whom he admired and respected. When he pushed through the double doors, he was assailed by a swarm of press members shoving microphones in his face.

"Congressman Porter, what's the name of the international construction firm you referred to?"

"Does this mean you'll be resigning right away or fulfilling your term?"

"How much money were you offered to sponsor this bill?"

Kip pushed through the crowd and walked briskly down the hall to the nearest elevator. Once the doors closed, he found himself alone and he collapsed in the corner as a sheen of sweat formed on his brow. His solitude quickly ended when the doors opened into the hallway that led to his office. Thankfully, the corridors were mostly empty and those who passed him only nodded hello. Word of his speech hadn't yet reached the upper floors of the capitol building.

"Contact the major news outlets and let them know I'll be holding a press conference in an hour here in the conference room," Kip barked as he rushed past his assistant's desk and into the quiet sanctuary of his office. The room was dark; all the blinds were flipped closed. When Kip hit the light switch, he jumped in surprise. Annie was sitting behind his desk with her feet propped up on the corner.

"What are you doing here?" he asked. Her shapely legs were perched on the desk and he couldn't help but follow them from her ankles to her thighs, dreaming of what lay above and between.

"I was just reading an interesting article about sporting injuries," Anne said as she tapped her toe in mid-air. She kept her eyes on a magazine in her lap, but Kip noticed her steal a quick glance in his direction.

"In *People*?"

"They have all kinds of articles in here. It says here that one of the world's most dangerous sports is horseback riding."

"Horseback riding?" Kip took a tentative step forward and slid into a leather chair across from Annie.

"Yep, it says the higher the horse, the bigger the risks. When you fall," she said as she dragged her finger across the page, "injuries range in severity from simple bruises to serious concussions and broken bones. Though the most common injury is having the wind knocked out of you."

"Interesting."

"Right? I thought so too. Then just this morning, that very same thing happened to me." She dropped her legs to the floor and pulled open the bottom drawer, extracting the bottle of Jack Daniel's. She carried the bottle to the credenza and poured some whiskey into a coffee cup.

"You fell off a horse?" Kip asked.

"Yep, a really high one." She took a quick sip and then turned to look at Kip. "You look like hell, Porter. You need a drink." She carried another coffee mug over and handed it to him.

"Thanks, Coach." Kip reached for the mug and drank it in one shot. "So, you were telling me about this fall."

"Oh, yeah, so this morning my dad came over and we had a very enlightening talk." She leaned her hip against the credenza and held the coffee mug close to her lips. "And then I rode into the viewing gallery. That's when it happened."

"Didn't know they allowed horses in the House chamber."

"New rule: if you are firmly perched on said high horse, you may both enter."

"Good to know." Kip walked slowly toward the credenza and sat on the edge, looking deeply into the coffee cup.

"I heard a very brave man give a speech where he admitted his lack of judgment and asked Congress to vote against a bill he sponsored, even though he knew it would cost him his career. He made the right decision to abandon a bill he knew wasn't good for anyone. It was really inspiring."

"Inspiring?"

"Yup. So inspiring I fell flat on my ass. And, Porter, it was a long way down."

Kip took Annie's cup out of her hand and placed both mugs on the credenza. Then he took her right hand into both of his and studied her delicate fingers and creamy skin. "Did you get hurt?"

"No, but it did jolt me into realizing I've been an intolerant, childish bitch who doesn't deserve for you to even be listening to me right now."

"Shh, hey now, don't call yourself that."

"It's true." Annie's voice clogged with emotion and her eyes were brimming with tears. "I should have listened to your side of the story—your whole side of the story—on Sunday. I said some terrible things to you."

"Come here; it's okay." Kip pulled her against his chest and pressed his lips to her forehead.

"I'm so sorry. From now on I promise I'll be patient, let you explain yourself, not jump to conclusions. Be more forgiving. I mean it this time." She wrapped her arms around his waist and buried her face against his chest, letting her tears fall. "I love you, Kip," she mumbled into his necktie.

"What was that?" He leaned back and took her face in his hands, using his thumbs to swipe away the tears.

"I said I love you. Did you mean it when you told me you loved me?" Annie sniffled a few times and focused her watery eyes on Kip.

"Yes, I meant it. I love you, Annie…so much." He locked his lips against hers. She wrapped her arms around his neck and pressed herself into him as his hands raked through the ponytail hanging down her back.

After several minutes of breathless kissing, Kip released her mouth and pulled her ponytail over the front of her shoulder. "What's this? What did you do to your hair?"

"Oh, I straightened it. You like it?"

"Why?"

"It's part of the new me—the understanding, flexible, open-minded me."

"But I liked the old you," he said, stroking the long, sleek ponytail.

"Really? The old stubborn, unforgiving, self-righteous me?"

"Who called you that?" Kip laughed and covered her face with kisses. "I love the old you, the new you, all of you." He picked up her hand and led her over to the leather couch where they'd made love for the first time. Annie sat with her back against the arm and draped her legs across Kip's lap.

"So I would assume if you're no longer running for office then I'm out of a job," Annie said.

"Your job as campaign manager will come to an end as soon as you can shut down the office. But as it turns out I have an opening which will run until January."

"Oh? What kind of position?" "Chief of staff. I asked Tom to resign yesterday morning. Most of the interns will be leaving soon, so I'll need help in the remaining months as I finish out my term. There's no one I trust more to help me bring it to a close."

"I don't know if that's a good idea." Annie grazed her nails up and down Kip's jacket sleeve.

"Why? I think it's a great idea."

"If my memory serves correctly, it seems like whenever we work together, we end up arguing."

"Nah, not anymore. I think we've worked through every potential problem, don't you?" He removed her hand from his sleeve and kissed each fingertip. "Besides, if my memory serves me correctly, we have great make-up sex after our fights."

Annie swung her legs to the floor and then repositioned herself across Kip's lap, straddling her knees on either side of his legs. She slowly loosened his tie and opened the top button of his shirt. "Hmm, I'm not sure about this. We might not get much done around this office…you know, being in such close proximity all the time."

"Come on, what are you afraid of? Be my chief of staff."

"Is that all?"

"My right-hand, my confidante."

"And," she whispered against his ear.

"My girlfriend, my love."

"That's what I was hoping to hear." Annie ran her tongue around the rim of his ear.

"My best friend, my sweetheart."

"Mm, that's nice." She pecked kisses from his temple to his lips, where she hesitated a moment and said, "Whatever you call me is okay with me, as long as I can call you mine."

"Deal."

EPILOGUE

The warm sunshine and cloudless sky made the March afternoon feel more like May. Kip pulled his hoodie over his head and draped it over the wood piling, smiling with satisfaction at his latest purchase. Bobbing lightly in the water was a mint condition twenty-foot white cabin cruiser—something he'd been saving for most of his life. Since leaving office he'd promised himself he would spend more time out on the water—no more weekends holed up in an office studying pending legislation. These days he worked long hours Monday through Friday, but his weekends were reserved for time with Annie. In February he had become the new executive director of the Friends of the Bay Foundation and had moved permanently into his riverside cabin. Annie seemed happy in her new job at an Annapolis non-profit firm. His life was nearly perfect, but there was one thing he knew would make it absolutely perfect.

He looked up when he heard the crunch of tires on the gravel driveway and took off running down the pier to meet the silver convertible. As soon as Annie stepped out of the car, he lifted her into a tight hug and spun her around, then pulled her in for a long, overdue kiss.

"You're never leaving me again. You got that?" Kip said.

"Oh, you big baby. Did you miss me?" Annie laughed as she brushed her fingertips over his stubbled face; her deep brown eyes making him melt all over again.

"You have no idea."

"I missed you, too. Now shut up and kiss me again." They kept their lips pressed together as he carried her, legs dangling in the air, toward the cabin. He lowered her to the floor inside the door and drew her tightly to him, her cheek pressed against his chest.

"Mm, so glad you're back." He kissed her once more and then said, "Okay, so tell me—how's Kate?"

Annie took his hands in hers and led him to the new sectional, which had replaced the hideous brown plaid couch. Slowly but surely, she was pulling this place into the twenty-first century and making it a real home. They sat facing one another on the sofa and held hands as she recounted her weekend in West Virginia.

"Kate's great—better than ever. She's like a new person. You never knew the old Kate; all you saw was the stressed-out, cynical, basically unhappy Kate. Next time, you're going with me. It's a cute little town and her grandmother's house is coming along beautifully."

"And the mountain man—did you meet him?"

"Oh, yeah, I met the mountain man. Very hot."

"Excuse me?" Kip feigned jealously and sat back against the sofa cushions.

"Don't worry, he's not my type, but for Kate he's perfect. Very earthy, laid back, but fun. I think he's been a good influence on her."

"And Emberly? How's married life treating her?"

"She's deliriously happy, of course. Those two are ridiculous. I don't think an hour went by when they weren't calling or texting each other. She always says Nico can't live without her, but I'm thinking it's the other way around."

"Sounds like us—minus the constant texting." Kip lifted her hands to his and planted several kisses across her knuckles. "I sure couldn't live without you."

"Luckily, you don't have to." Annie cupped his cheeks in her hands and gave him a quick kiss. "So what have you been doing all weekend?"

"Good segue because I have something to show you. Let's grab a beer and walk down to the dock."

While Annie changed into jeans and sneakers, Kip grabbed two bottles of beer from the refrigerator, pulled on a lightweight jacket, and patted one of his pockets. They walked hand-in-hand across the grass as the sun began its slow descent to the horizon, leaving an orange beam reflecting off the water.

"What's this?" Anne let go of Kip's hand and jogged the rest of the way to the pier, stopping by the gleaming white boat tied to the pilings. "You bought a boat while I was gone?"

Kip came up behind her and rested his hand on her shoulder. "Yep. You know I've been looking. Virgil called Friday morning and said he had a boat for sale. As soon as I looked at it, I knew it was the one. Check out the name."

Anne took a few steps backward and leaned down to read *What's in a Name?* painted across the stern.

"It was an omen, don't you think?"

She turned, laughing, and wrapped an arm around Kip's waist. "Of course you couldn't pass this up. The name is too perfect."

"That's what I thought. The best part of the deal is that it was about to be repossessed by the bank and the guy accepted my ridiculously low offer. He bought it new and only had it for six months. It needs absolutely nothing."

"That's awesome." Annie held out her bottle and tinged it against Kip's.

"Except a new name," he said.

Annie rotated her attention back to the boat and tilted her head to the side, examining the name painted in big black letters. "Do you think?"

"Yeah, since it's ours we need to give it a new name—one we've thought up. You know how a lot of boats are named after the captain's woman?" Kip tucked himself behind her, setting his beer bottle on top of the wooden piling, and gathered her in his arms.

"You want to name it *Annie*?" she asked.

"I was thinking we should call it *Mrs. Porter.*" Kip held his breath while he waited for Annie's reaction. He'd been planning that line all day and couldn't wait to see the look of surprise on her face.

"That's sweet. You want to name it after your mom?"

Kip dropped his arms from around her and took a step back, shaking his head as he stifled a laugh. How could she have missed his hint? He decided he would have to spell it out for her, so he dropped to one knee.

"I thought when you said 'the captain's woman' you meant me, but naming it after your mom is a nice gesture, too." Annie was standing with one hand on her hip and the beer in the other, oblivious to Kip kneeling behind her. He reached up and took the bottle from her hand.

"Annie, please turn around."

She glanced over her shoulder and then looked down at the dock. "Did you drop something?"

"Damn it, Annie, just turn around, please. You know I have a bad knee."

She finally turned around and Kip gathered her left hand in his. What he was about to ask finally seemed to hit her because she released a tiny squeak as her eyes brimmed with tears.

"I'm not naming the boat after my mother. I want to name it after the woman who changed my life, who gives me more happiness than I could've ever imagined, who I want to spend the rest of my days with. Annie..." Kip kissed her quivering hand. "Will you marry me?"

Annie nodded her head as a barrage of tears streamed down her face. She choked out her response—"Kip! Yes, I'll marry you"—as Kip reached into his pocket and opened the velvet box. His hands were shaking as much as hers and he feared he'd drop the ring before it made it onto her finger. He looked up at his future wife and couldn't hold back the huge grin from spreading across his face.

"I love you, Annie," he said, slipping the gleaming diamond on her left hand.

"It's beautiful," she muttered and then pulled him to his feet, wrapping her arms around his neck and kissing him with all her might. "I love you, Kip."

"I love you, too, babe." He lifted her off the dock and smothered her lips with his, savoring this incredible moment—something he never would have imagined less than a year ago. "So, what do you think?" He gave her a wry grin and nuzzled his lips against her neck.

"I think I couldn't be happier." Annie palmed the back of his head and brushed her lips beside his ear, whispering, "*Mrs. Porter* is exactly what we should call the boat...and me."

Read on for a special preview from the next
contemporary romance by Leigh Fleming

Whatever You Say

Coming Soon!

PREVIEW FROM WHATEVER YOU SAY

"Pretzels, yes." Kate grabbed a bag of fat Bavarian pretzels out of the pantry and handed them to Brody, who was hovering behind her. "Food of the gods." She pushed a few cans aside and picked up a jar of peanut butter. "Now we're talking."

"I thought you wanted chocolate." Brody set the peanut butter on the counter and walked to the opposite side of the kitchen, where he picked up a plastic cake plate.

"Haven't you heard of sweet and salty? Best combination when you have the munchies." Her fuzzy, drug-induced head was clear, but it was still a good excuse for indulging in forbidden junk food. She closed the pantry door and turned around to find Brody setting the cake plate on the kitchen table. "What's that?" She carried the pretzels and peanut butter to the table and plopped down in a wooden chair.

"I have just the thing for your chocolate craving." He removed the plastic lid with a flourish and presented her with an expertly frosted dark chocolate cake topped with chocolate curls and finely chopped nuts. Kate's mouth began to water.

"Where did you get that?"

"I have an admirer at the post office." Brody crossed the kitchen, pulled two plates out of the cabinet, and retrieved two forks out of a drawer. "At least once a month I'm guaranteed a cake or a pie from the lady who runs the counter."

"The talkative lady? The one who gives out fashion advice?"

"The very same." On his way back to the table, Brody grabbed a half-gallon of milk out the refrigerator and tucked it under his arm. He pinched two glasses between his thumb and fingers and placed everything on the table. "I thought about giving up my post office box, just get my mail delivered out here, but it's worth the trip."

"So, you've got a not-so-secret admirer."

"Jealous?" Brody carried two napkins to the table and laid them at each place as he sat in an adjacent chair.

"Terribly." Kate spread the napkin across her lap. "You're pretty good at that. Ever wait tables?" Kate ripped open the bag of pretzels and unscrewed the lid on the peanut butter jar.

"Plenty of them. I worked at a barbecue place in Nashville for a couple years during the day and played music at night." Brody jumped up and crossed the room again. "We need some knives." When he returned, he plunged one knife in the peanut butter and sliced the cake with the other. "As soon as I started making enough money to pay my bills, I gave up the serving job. We've talked about me enough. What about you?"

"The jobs I've had? Other than law?" Kate took a big bite of cake and dropped her fork on the table as if she'd been stung. "Oh, my God," she mumbled through her stuffed mouth. Brody started laughing and sprayed a fine milky mist on the table. Holding a napkin to his mouth, he swallowed and laughed out loud.

"You should've seen your face."

"Whaa—?" Kate said, her mouth too full and sticky to complete the word. She'd taken too big a bite and was having difficulty swallowing, but at the same time she was savoring every rich, decadent, chocolaty morsel.

"Do you always roll your eyes like that?" he asked.

"Like what?" Kate took one last swallow and finally emptied her mouth, able to speak clearly again.

"Like that. Like you're in ecstasy."

"I *was* in ecstasy. This is the best cake I've ever eaten." This time, Kate made sure to take a smaller bite of the cake, but noticed Brody wasn't eating. He was still watching her with a half smile on his face. "Why aren't you eating?"

"I like watching you." He shoved his plate and glass aside and propped his elbows on the table, easing closer to her. Kate slowed down, feeling self-conscious. His eyes were hooded, glassy, his expression soft, contemplative.

"You're making me uncomfortable." Using the side of her fork as a knife, she cut off a bite of her cake and extended it to Brody, feeding it to him without protest.

"Mm." He ate it slowly, sensuously, and Kate became mesmerized by the movement of his mouth, his chiseled jaw. She took another bite and tried to move her lips in sync with his.

"Delicious, right?"

"Delicious," he said in that silky, seductive tone Kate had come to know so well—the one that never failed to send her heart pounding. With his eyes locked on hers, he slid the fork inside his mouth, depositing another chocolaty piece. Now it was her turn to watch him eat. His lips were soft, full, kissable. They moved fluidly, pressed together, in a circular motion, sucking her in like a slow-moving whirlpool. Her eyes traveled to his jaw, tightening, releasing, with each bite.

"…better than sex," he murmured.

"What?"

"Were you listening?"

"Um, yeah, I was listening."

"She called it 'better than sex cake'." Brody chuckled and raised his eyebrows at her. "What do you think of that?" He swiped his finger across the top of the cake and plunged a dollop of icing in her mouth. Kate let the gooey confection melt off his finger onto her tongue, savoring the sensuous feelings coursing through her body.

"Hm. I don't know…" Returning the gesture, she offered him a fingertip full of icing and rather than take it in his mouth, he slowly licked it from her finger. Damn, he wasn't playing fair. Kate wasn't sure how much longer she could sit here without touching him, kissing him. "What do you think?"

"I think." This time, Brody took a swath of chocolate and dotted it on her lips, then proceeded to tenderly lick and kiss it from her mouth. "You need to tell me." He whispered against her lips.

"Well." Kate cleared her throat, feeling the need to pull off her sweater, she'd grown so warm. Scooting her chair back from the table to put a little distance between them, she tossed her cardigan on the chair beside her. Brody wasn't hiding the fact that he wanted more than just cake and now that the moment had arrived, her heart was pounding and her stomach twisted in knots. She picked up her plate and carried it to the sink. "This cake is incredible. It just might be better than sex."

In only a few long strides, Brody was across the room and scooping Kate in his arms, folding her over his shoulder. "You want to bet?"

"Brody." Kate giggled uncontrollably. "What are you doing?" She uselessly pounded on his back, feigning outrage while her head hung upside down. "Put me down."

"Nope." He bound up the staircase as easily as if he'd been empty-handed, and entered his bedroom. "There's only one way to find out." He tapped the door shut with his foot.

Thank you for reading *Whatever You Call Me.* I hope you enjoyed it. If you did, please help other readers find this book:

- Write a review on the site where you purchased the book.
- Share this copy with a friend.
- Keep up with news of upcoming releases by signing up for my newsletter at www.leighfleming.com.
- Like my Facebook page: www.facebook.com/leighhflemingauthor.
- Follow me on Twitter: www.twitter.com/leighhfleming1

About the Author

After several years of saying she would write a book someday, Leigh Fleming finally fulfilled her ultimate bucket list item by publishing a novel. In 2013, she completed her first work, *Precious Words*, a suspenseful romance set in the glittering world of men's professional tennis, taking the reader on a whirlwind trip full of love and danger.

Leigh continues to hone her craft and learn what it takes to create a page-turning story. *Whatever You Call Me* is the second novel in a five-book series. *Whatever You Say* will be released in 2017. She is also working on a women's fiction book and an historical novel based on real family events.

Leigh lives with her husband, Patrick, in Martinsburg, West Virginia, and is mom to adult children, Tom and Liza, and her two dogs, Lula Belle and Napoleon.

www.leighfleming.com
Contact: Leigh@leighfleming.com

Made in the USA
Lexington, KY
07 January 2017